The Strange Year of E.G. Rawlings

by Jane McCulloch

Published by JJ Moffs Independent Book Publisher 2019

JJ Moffs Independent Book Publisher Ltd
Grove House Farm, Grovewood Road,
Misterton, Nottinghamshire DN10 4EF

Typeset by Anna Richards
Cover by Jeremy Hopes

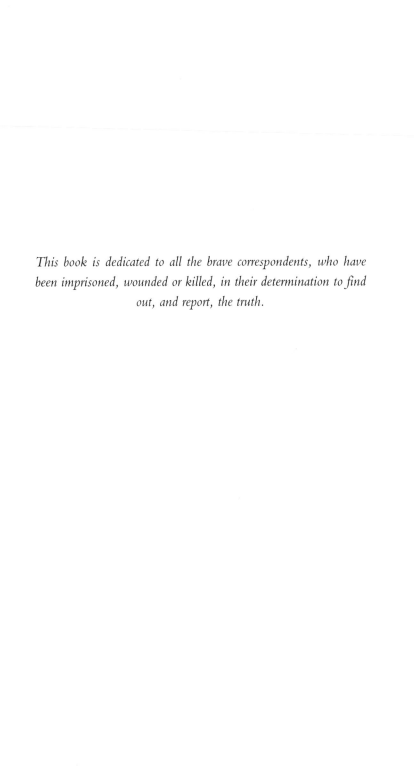

This book is dedicated to all the brave correspondents, who have been imprisoned, wounded or killed, in their determination to find out, and report, the truth.

Foreword

It is always a pleasure to read a novel by Jane McCulloch, who I have counted as a good friend since I worked as an editor on the second volume of her excellent *Three Lives Trilogy* and, subsequently, *The Brini Boy* and the novel you presently hold in your hands. *The Strange Year of E.G. Rawlings* is no exception, maintaining the standard of the previous novels and an absolute joy to read. As ever, Jane's crisp prose style manages to be light yet deep, which makes for a deceptively easy read. But once you put it down, you find you can't stop thinking about the issues it raises, both cultural and spiritual.

Archetypally, this is a 'rebirth' story, in which the protagonist is cast under some dark spell either instigated by themselves or an outside force. In modern fiction this is often the result of psychological trauma. They can sometimes even be a villainous or otherwise unlikable character who redeems themselves over the course of the story. Liberation can only be achieved through realisation of one's own inner demons and barriers or the actions of other good forces, often the redemptive power of love. The beautifully drawn Rawlings – Jane's knowledge of war reporting is impressive – is trapped within his PTSD at the start of the story, emotionally and literally adrift, in spiritual and physical pain, bereaved, unable to work and searching for a mooring. Through a year spent on the river as part of an eccentric but nurturing community, he finds his way again, but little does the jaded reporter realise that another event is just around the corner that will not only profoundly affect his life, but also the lives of all those around him.

Mirroring Rawlings' gruelling personal journey, those around him who are lost or in pain also find some sort of peace, hope and recovery, all through different kinds of love and letting go. This is a moving and positive story, and it is also always a pleasure to read about characters over the age of fifty in a modern novel! (Lord save me from the literature of millennial navel-gazing.)

At the same time, Jane doesn't shy away from the harsh truths, despite this idyllic little pastoral oasis, using current events as part of her background setting, conveying a sense of change and increasing menace, as if the magical estate on which the irascible Rawlings finds himself is a bastion of a more civilised England that is passing away to be replaced by something much smaller and crueller. And this is also implicitly cross-referenced with his vivid memories of Kosovo, Iraq and Afghanistan and how quickly a society can become brutalised. Jane is also starkly honest about her hero's many flaws.

What has stayed with me the most was the theme of 'turning points' in one's life, in which a chance meeting or event sends one off in a different and frequently completely unexpected direction. This is how Rawlings sees his life, good and bad, and it becomes a leitmotif throughout the book, made flesh in the turning points that take place for several characters during the course of the year, most notably Rawlings himself. It's a lovely literary device, in which this close-knit but oddball community and their lives interconnect and rebound in the same way that made the *Three Lives Trilogy* so memorable.

Dr. Stephen Carver
Author and Editor

One Year On

January 6th 2018

Marnie sat on her terrace, hunched and miserable, wrapped up in an old quilt. The intense cold was making her shiver, and she fervently hoped the sun would soon make an appearance to give some warmth to her aching bones. Meanwhile, her mind was filled with bitter thoughts. Today should have been like other birthdays, a day of happy celebration. But it wasn't, not now. How could it be? She thought angrily that because of *him*, all her future birthdays would be ruined. What the hell was there left for her to celebrate after what had happened? From now on, everything would be different. She would be different. And why? Because exactly one year ago, Rawlings had arrived. He'd loomed out of the early morning mist, resembling some ancient mariner or warrior and from then on took over her existence. Damn him, damn, damn, DAMN him!

The longer she sat, the more the memories flooded back, his arrival etched on her mind like a painting. Her artist's eye had quickly taken in his appearance; noting he was clad in an old fisherman's sweater and jeans, that he was tall, well over six foot, craggy in the face but thin in build, with a shock of grey hair. Somewhere between Charles Dance and a grizzled George Clooney. She also saw that he walked with a severe limp. Like today, it had been barely light, and she'd been up especially early, smitten with a childlike excitement because it was her birthday, despite the fact she was now well past fifty. She'd sat on her terrace waiting for the sun to appear above the willow trees on the other side of the river. But unlike today it hadn't been particularly cold. That winter had been unusually mild. She remembered how happy she'd been, sipping her coffee, watching the steam from it merging with the mist, and waiting for the usual procession of swans to make their stately way downstream. It was a moment she always enjoyed, especially when there was low mist and they glided past her like a scene from *"Swan Lake"*. There was something satisfactory in the fact they were such creatures of habit, returning upstream in the evening as the sun was setting. You could almost set your clock by them.

This then was the peaceful scene that exactly one year ago had been so suddenly interrupted. Now, as Marnie sat in the same place, she wondered if even then, she'd had some premonition of how her life would be turned completely upside down by this stranger walking towards her.

Chapter One

January 6th 2017

'Oh good, I'm glad to have found someone about. Do you by any chance own this mooring?' There was urgency in his voice, and he almost barked out the question. Marnie was so startled by this sudden appearance she took a moment to answer.

'No, I don't, I just rent this boathouse from Lady Mallinson who owns the big house up there,' and she pointed towards the gardens and a row of trees that rather obscured the building. He hesitated, obviously not sure what his next action should be, and then he looked at his watch.

'It's probably a bit early to call on her. I'll go back to the boat and wait for an hour or so.'

Marnie was suddenly curious. 'I didn't hear your boat come in, are you moored down below?'

He gave a curt nod. 'Yes, I came in about two hours ago, but thought I'd wait until it was light.' He turned to go.

'Wait', she said, on impulse, 'come in and have some coffee. Then I can ring Isobel a bit later and let her know you're here.'

He climbed the steps and followed her inside. She waved at a chair, but he remained standing as Marnie went into the galley kitchen.

'Did you say Isobel?' he called out. 'Is that Isobel Mallinson?' She came back, and he repeated, 'Is that Isobel Mallinson, married to Peter Mallinson, the diplomat?'

'Yes, it is. Do you know her?'

'How very strange.' He sat down and repeated, 'Very strange. I haven't seen them for five years. I stayed with them at the Embassy in Kabul for a few weeks back then. They were both very good to me.' He gave a laugh that was more like a bark. 'Of all the moorings in all the world, I have to arrive at this one.'

Marnie sat down opposite him. 'I'm sorry to have to tell you this, but I should warn you before you see Isobel, Peter died, just over two years ago.'

'He died?' He seemed genuinely shocked by this news. 'Peter can't have been very old. He was due to retire just after I left them, and he always appeared a fit man. What happened?'

'Pancreatic cancer. It was very quick, less than six months from the diagnosis.' She stood up and went back to the kitchen to fetch the coffee. Carrying the tray in she said, 'I'm Marnie by the way.'

'I'm Rawlings' he replied. She looked questioningly at him, and he smiled. 'E. G. Rawlings. I'm either known as E.G. or Rawlings.'

She also smiled. 'That's like the man in *MASH* who was always known just by his initials. Don't you like your name?' Privately she thought it a bit affected.

As if he could read her thoughts, he answered wryly, 'I'm afraid I had a strong aversion to my name from an early age. My mother had a passion for Dickens and insisted I was called Edwin. I think she must have been reading *"Edwin*

Drood" at the time. Where I grew up, in a working-class area, such names did not go down well. I could not rely on my second name either, as it was Garrioch, a family surname, so I had to find a solution, and that was it. Even my mother gave up calling me Edwin after a bit; I just didn't respond when she did. Actually, in my line of work, initials worked out rather well.'

'And what is your line of work?'

'A journalist. I was, until recently, a war correspondent.'

This was somehow impressive, implying an exciting life. She wanted to question him further, but his expression indicated this particular conversation was closed. Instead, she said 'I rather sympathise with you about your name. I was christened Marina, but it always sounded so severe. My mother's nickname for me was Marnie, and finally, it just stuck that way.'

For a few minutes, they sipped their coffee in silence, and then he put down his cup and examined her room.

'It would appear you are an artist.'

'Well, I only paint for my own pleasure.' She felt embarrassed by his scrutiny. It was early in the day, her room looked a terrible mess, and for that matter, so did she. 'I teach art at a nearby school and take evening classes as well, at the technical college.'

He asked her about the local area, and nearest shops and the idle chatter continued for a while, until he inquired if now might be a good time for him to see Isobel. She suggested that she rang to see if it were, and minutes later Rawlings was limping up the steep slope of the garden to where Isobel was waiting for him at the open French windows.

'Good heavens, Rawlings, this is a surprise,' she said. 'And where is it you have sprung from this time?'

She held out her hand and he took it, holding on to it for a moment as he studied her. She was little changed; still beautiful and elegant. Only maybe in the face, something in the eyes betrayed some of the strain she must have been through with Peter's illness. She led him into the living room, and he sat down on one of the two sofas either side of a marble fireplace where a fire was burning. He was grateful for that, and stretched out his hands, trying to thaw them, while he calculated the age of the house deciding it must be Edwardian, or thereabouts. The ceilings were high and the long windows looking down to the river let in plenty of light. The contrast between this graciously appointed room and Marnie's chaotic, small cave, caused him an inward smile. It somehow reflected the difference in appearance between the two women as well. He'd always had an eye for this sort of detail. Isobel, now sitting opposite him, was immaculately dressed in a grey cardigan – no doubt cashmere – over a crisp white blouse, with long matching grey skirt and a cameo brooch fastening the collar at the neck. Marnie had been in an oversized, green towelling dressing gown, not the cleanest, with fisherman's socks in sheepskin slippers, her red hair in an untidy mop. Isobel had not a hair out of place.

Isobel was now regarding him with the same careful scrutiny. 'How's the leg? I saw you were limping.'

Rawlings gave a grim laugh. 'I should have taken the surgeon's advice and had it removed. It's caused nothing but trouble. Four operations later and now they tell me there's nothing more they can do, I just have to live with the problems, and the bloody pain.'

Isobel could see he was suffering but knew enough about him to realise it wasn't all physical. Rawlings obviously still had many inner demons.

'You were adamant about keeping the leg at the time,' she remarked gently.

'Well yes, I thought, mistakenly, that once the leg had been put back together, I'd be able to return to work. My stupidity. Far from it. No paper would employ me now. Apart from anything else, I'd never get insurance to go abroad; there's just no knowing when further complications will arise. These, unfortunately, happen all too frequently, and then the blessed doctors do their best to patch me up again.' He paused and added with a hint of bitterness. 'At least Frank Gardner knows where he's at. They can deal with that, wheelchair and all.'

He broke off, and Isobel could hear the anger in his voice. She decided to leave it at that. 'Would you like coffee, or maybe some breakfast?'

He shook his head. 'I had two cups with Marnie, but thank you for the offer.'

There was an awkward silence. Rawlings glanced across to the silver framed photographs on the mahogany table behind the sofa where Isobel was sitting.

'Marnie told me about Peter. It was a shock. I am so sorry.' And he added gruffly, 'He was a good man and far too early for him to go.'

'Yes, it was, and a great shock to us too.' She sighed. 'We were only two years into his retirement and had so many plans. It was such a horrible illness. I hate the phrase "merciful release", but I suppose, in the end, it was a relief that it was quick…' Her voice trailed away and then she said briskly, 'So, here you are, moored at the bottom of my garden. Was this by accident or on purpose?'

Rawlings sounded contrite. 'Purely by accident I can assure you. When Marnie told me that you owned the mooring, it took me completely by surprise.' He paused. 'I think I should explain why I'm here. For the last six months, I've been paying extortionate mooring fees to a crook landlord a few miles up-river. Finally, I'd had enough of him, along with his terrible one-sided licence and all the other spurious costs he inflicted on his tenants. I'd had a row with him almost every month. None of the other six tenants dared complain for fear of being thrown off their moorings. His license meant he only had to give a month's notice and they would be forced to leave. The only alternative was to fight him legally, involving huge costs.' He gave a shrug. 'In any case, they would have been bound to lose. This landlord is a wealthy man and has connections with the great and good of the community, no doubt Masonic. It was the typical David and Goliath situation, unfortunately with Goliath holding all the cards. Until the law is changed, nobody stands a chance against him.' He gave a grim smile. 'I knew he was about to evict me, so I left before he could.'

Rawlings would dearly have loved a cigarette at this point, but given Peter's cancer, he knew that would be out of the question. He glanced across at Isobel, who was obviously listening, but saying nothing, so he continued, 'I was luckier than the other tenants. I had a boat with an engine and could easily transport it to another mooring.

However, this was not an ideal solution for me because it would mean I'd be in close proximity to other boats on a marina and not in such beautiful surroundings, but, in the end, I couldn't stand being exploited and robbed a day longer.' He was talking angrily now. 'The other poor bastards had static houseboats, large floating homes which would need to be towed away at huge expense – and then where would they go? There are no marinas for that kind of houseboat, and vacant private moorings are like gold dust, which is why private landlords have total control and are free to exploit the situation and charge whatever they like. It's a scandal, and the laws need to be changed, but I am sure the government will do nothing about it, not a Conservative government anyway.' His voice took on a note of exasperation. 'This country is full of rivers and waterways, and the creation of moorings would be one way of helping the housing shortage, but I don't see that happening…' He broke off and said with a rueful smile, 'I apologise for the rant, Isobel, it's a topic that is rather on my mind'.

'You and Marnie will have a lot in common.' Isobel said drily, 'She was thrown off the same moorings some years back and lost everything, which is when Peter and I offered her the boathouse.' She looked at him. 'So, I'm rather presuming you would like to use my mooring?'

Rawlings shifted in his seat. 'If that were possible, it would suit me perfectly. I was actually making my way, with some reluctance, to a marina where I knew there was a space. It filled me with dread. I didn't want to be part of a 'boat community', slotted in between boat neighbours. My object in buying the boat was for peace and solitude. Which is why, when I saw your mooring, I thought I'd investigate it. Of course, I had no idea it belonged to you until Marnie told me.' He waited while Isobel considered this.

'Well, it's vacant, and all set up with connections to the mains and ready to be used.' Pausing for a moment, she went on, 'When we returned here, Peter intended to use a boat on the mooring for some kind of office at the bottom of the garden. His great grandfather built this house and always used the mooring. I believe all the men in his family have, which is why there have always been connections to the mains. Peter had them modernised about ten years ago, along with the boathouse when Marnie moved in. Sadly, he never had time to get his boat before he became ill, and since he left us, well, I just haven't really thought about it.' She hesitated, 'Before giving you an answer, there are others I would have to consider. There is Lydia, Peter's carer, who just stayed on and has rooms upstairs and also Rose, someone Lydia wanted me to take in but who, between you and me, has become a bit of a problem ... which I don't need to go into now,' she added briskly. 'The mooring is well hidden and shouldn't pose a problem. I'm sure Marnie would have no objections, and she would be the nearest to you. There's a path that leads up from the mooring alongside the boathouse and which ends up in the road that takes you to the village, so you would be completely independent.' She looked at him. 'I'm intrigued, why are you on a boat? Is there some reason?'

Rawlings stood up and walked up and down. 'Sorry, if I stay sitting too long my leg gets locked, and it's difficult to get moving again.' After a moment he returned to the sofa. 'I had my last leg operation nearly two years ago, then spent some time recuperating at a friend's house in France before returning here. My personal life is complicated,' he gave a smile here, 'I won't bore you with that, suffice it to say, I returned to England with no fixed abode and, it soon became apparent, no job as a foreign correspondent either, let alone a journalist. My position isn't desperate, I am comfortably well off, so I don't need to work. The problem is, I'm used to having an occupation, can't really survive without one, so it was while I was considering what to do, my old editor summoned me to lunch and made a suggestion, which I found I couldn't refuse. It was to write a memoir of my time as a war correspondent. It sounded like an easy proposition. I'd written my way through six or seven major wars, there was plenty of material, so I agreed and suddenly found myself with an agent, a commissioned book and an advance. There was no going back. Another friend had this boat he wanted to sell, already on the mooring I told you about. At the time, it seemed like an ideal solution, until I came up against that crook landlord. Which is why I find myself here.'

Isobel again took time considering this. 'Well, Rawlings, I don't really see anything against it. You would certainly have peace and quiet for your writing. How long do you think the book is going to take you?'

He hastened to reassure her. 'About a year, it can't be more as I'm up against a deadline.'

Isobel stood up. 'I'll talk to Lydia and Marnie. I don't envisage any problems but will let you know this evening. Let me have your mobile number.' She held out her hand and smiled. 'It's good to see you again.'

He also stood, holding her hand for slightly longer than necessary, thinking again what a beautiful woman she was. Searching in his pocket, he took out a card, handing it to her.

'My mobile number,' and smiling, he added, 'I can't believe you have swum into my life for a second time and that you're about to rescue me again.' Then abruptly he turned, let himself out of the French windows and limped back down the garden.

'That man is a dangerous charmer,' Isobel thought to herself.

Later that day Marnie had a summons to the house.

'It seems we are to have a lodger.' Isobel said as she handed her a glass of wine. 'That is unless you have any objection?'

'Why should I object?' She sounded surprised by the question. 'It's your house and your mooring.'

Isobel smiled at this. 'I know Marnie, but you will be the closest in proximity, it might change things for you. Rawlings will have to pass by the boathouse to go out to the road, so you'll no longer be completely private.'

Marnie shook her head. 'I honestly can't see that worrying me at all. Anyway, he seems very agreeable and perfectly charming.'

That produced a laugh. 'My dear Marnie, that is another of the things that worries me. Rawlings has been bowling women over for years with his charm, and the worst thing is, he seems oblivious of the fact. I wouldn't want to add a further complication to your life.'

'I am sure I can manage to resist him,' she said stiffly, 'After all, I turned fifty-six today, far too old for another attachment.'

'Is it your birthday?' Isobel sounded contrite. 'Why didn't you tell me? I would have taken you out to supper.' And as if to make up for the oversight, she poured Marnie another glass of wine.

'I am getting too old for birthdays, as well as for men. Having a drink with you is celebration enough.' She paused. 'Tell me about Rawlings.'

Isobel thought for a moment. 'I don't know a great deal. He's a very private man and can be positively hostile at times. Peter really liked him and knew him far better than I did. Rawlings came to stay with us when they released him from hospital, which must be five years ago now. He was in a bad way. Although physically well enough to leave the care of the doctors, he was in no fit state to return to England. It was the reason we took him in.'

Marnie leant forward. 'Was that when he'd damaged his leg?'

'Yes. He'd been on an assignment in Helmand Province, working with the Major in charge of the Task Force there. I gather Rawlings was out with some troops on a routine patrol when there was one of those wretched roadside explosions. He sustained terrible injuries, but his leg was the worst. It was a miracle he kept it. The surgeon wanted to amputate, but Rawlings kicked up such a fuss, they did what they could to put it back together. From what he tells me, there have been complications since, and he is in constant pain. I think he said he'd had four operations and now they can do no more.'

Marnie murmured, 'No wonder his manner is a little taciturn.'

'I'm afraid there was more. His girlfriend of many years,

a very gifted photographer, was with him at the time. From what I can gather, she was the only woman with whom he'd ever had a long relationship. Unlike Rawlings, she sadly didn't make it and was literally blown away. It was dreadful. On hearing the news, he went to pieces and had a complete breakdown. The army surgeons had done all they could for him but were worried about returning him in such a bad mental state, so we suggested he stay with us for a while. Peter was wonderful with him. To be fair, he was also good for Peter. Kabul wasn't exactly our most comfortable posting, there had been recent explosions in the diplomatic quarter, and Peter was under enormous strain. He and Rawlings would have long conversations or play games of chess. I think it helped them both…'

She broke off, and neither of them spoke for a moment. Then Isobel added, 'Don't try and probe Rawlings about his life, Marnie. He'll talk to you if he wants to. In any case, he has a book to write, his memoir of being a war correspondent, so he'll probably keep to himself.'

Marnie smiled as she stood up. 'Advice duly noted. She turned to go, 'By the way, how did Lydia and Rose take the news?'

'I'm afraid Lydia didn't look too pleased at all. I have the feeling that if Rawlings had been a woman, she wouldn't have minded at all.' She gave a laugh. 'Lydia sometimes has this way of looking at you, as if you'd made an enormous faux pas. But she merely said, rather huffily, that it was none of her business and entirely my decision and we left it at that. It shouldn't affect her anyway. She is out doing her caring work most of the time.'

'And Rose?'

Isobel frowned. 'It really has nothing to do with Rose. She's only here as a favour to Lydia, and quite frankly I'm beginning to regret it. I need to have a long talk with Lydia about finding somewhere else for her.' She stood up and kissed Marnie on the cheek. 'Happy birthday again, Marnie. I insist on taking you out to supper soon.'

And that was how that year began. A year that was to change them all.

Chapter Two

January 2017

Rawlings lay back on the sofa bed in his living room; his injured leg raised up on a pile of cushions. He was not convinced this helped in the slightest, but the last nurse he'd seen had insisted on it, so he was giving her the benefit of the doubt. As he listened to the gentle lap of the river against his boat, he reflected on all that had happened in the last two weeks. It was still an amazement to him that he felt so comfortable here, even settled. All that was required now was for him to sit at his desk and start the bloody book. He'd run out of excuses. He stared with hostility at the papers piled up beside his laptop, the articles and notebooks assembled from the many wars he'd covered, all neatly stacked, ready for him to take the plunge. There remained within him, however, a deep reluctance to get started. Memories would be unlocked, which he had carefully tried to obliterate. It had come as no surprise when, after his return to England, he had been diagnosed not just with PTSD, but with 'complex' PTSD, which was obviously a worse condition. Why should he be surprised? It usually only took one traumatic event to trigger it off. His entire life had been filled with endless horrifying images and events, ending up with the most significant trauma of all, and one that had nearly finished him off. It had certainly done for Mia...

He pulled himself up and limped over to the table to fetch his cigarettes. Thoughts of Mia had to be banished; it did him no good. He lit up and lowered himself carefully back on the bed, returning to the subject of PTSD. It was something in which nobody seemed to have taken a great interest. Here he corrected himself. More notice was indeed now being given to the army, but certainly not to war correspondents. He'd once inquired, from a fellow correspondent, the best way of dealing with it. His laconic reply had been an abrupt, 'Drink yourself into oblivion'. Rawlings had indeed tried turning to an excessive intake of alcohol but found that the reprieve was only momentary and the side effects extremely unpleasant.

His mind wandered to more recent events and thoughts of Marnie. He was intrigued, finding her something of a mystery. Instinctively he felt she was somehow damaged and was curious to find out why. She had an elusive quality he hadn't yet pinned down. Maybe it arose from a strange mixture of the artistic and the practical. Thankfully it was the latter that had been so valuable to him. Without ever being intrusive, she had dealt efficiently with all the difficult questions he'd thrown at her, always tactfully withdrawing to her boathouse afterwards. It was thanks to her that Paul had arrived. He turned out to be the Polish husband of Isobel's cleaner Maria. The man had worked miracles. Although referred to as a plumber, there seemed to be no problem Paul couldn't turn his hand to and solve. While working on the broken washing machine, he told Rawlings that he'd had a similar boat back in Poland and was only too happy to help with any difficulties that might arise on the *Esme Jane*. The *Esme Jane*! Why on earth had the boat been given that terrible name? Was it a wife, a mistress, a daughter? Rawlings had no idea, and his friend had never divulged the reason.

Taking over the boat had been an impulsive gesture. He knew nothing about boats, and until arriving on this mooring, he'd been content to endure the many problems he'd inherited, never bothering to deal with them. It was, therefore, a relief to hand them over to someone who had all the solutions. Rawlings told Paul that as long as everything more or less worked, he could live with it. Paul didn't seem shocked by this cavalier attitude but set about explaining a few things. The discovery that Rawlings had no bilge pump installed had worried him, and he quickly remedied this. Apart from the plumbing, he'd also sorted out all the electrics and put up a new aerial for the television.

A shooting pain went up his leg, and Rawlings rubbed it vigorously. Thank the Lord he was at least keeping warm. With some extravagance, he'd indulged in buying several electric radiators, quickly making the decision to abandon the old wood-burner which had stood in one corner of the living area. It would have been aesthetically pleasing, but too much trouble to maintain. It seemed sensible to let Paul take it away and replace it with an electric stove that burned artificial logs, with an added flame effect. One had been found with gothic shaped front windows which opened out and gave off a good heat. Paul had even managed to add a tall funnel for authenticity. Rawlings showed it to Marnie, anticipating she'd declare it vulgar, but she assured him she liked it and that it actually did look real. Was she being tactful? He was just relieved to be warm. The temperature had plunged and was set to drop still further.

He'd seen Isobel only once since their initial conversation. With predictable efficiency, she had instructed her lawyer to draw up an agreement, allowing him to rent the mooring for a year. This he'd willingly signed, especially as financially it was extremely reasonable and included all the 'utilities', as Isobel so delicately put it. He'd protested he could pay more, but she had been adamant her demands were perfectly adequate, and they'd left it at that. Isobel wasn't someone with whom you argued.

The hideous ringtone from his mobile had him leaping up, screaming 'ouch' and hobbling to his desk. He made a mental note to change it and take down the volume.

'Yes?' he almost barked.

It was Marnie, sounding nervous. 'I'm sorry to bother you, but some post has arrived. Isobel had it brought down to me from the house. I just wondered when would be a good time for me to bring it across?'

Rawlings thought for a moment. 'Well, I think I owe you a drink to repay you for all your many kindnesses. What about tonight? You can bring the post over then. It can't be anything important. I've only given Isobel's address to a couple of people. Shall we say about six?'

'Yes, I'd like that.' Marnie hesitated before adding, 'I've made a beef casserole which I could bring over and heat up in your oven…' she hesitated again, 'I wouldn't stay long. I have an early start with teaching tomorrow.'

'Sounds a great idea. I look forward to it.'

Rawlings rang off and smiled to himself. Marnie was

obviously worried about imposing on his time. Had Isobel spoken to her about him? Isobel had certainly talked to him about Marnie, telling him severely he should refrain from getting involved, as a past relationship had left her damaged. He wanted to know more, but on this occasion, his hackles went up, and he replied, somewhat huffily, that he had no intention of involving himself in any further relationships in his life. Which was true. That had all ended with Mia, and no, he wasn't going to think about her now – or ever.

Marnie arrived punctually at six. He heard her footsteps, opened the door and watched with some amusement as she manoeuvred herself with difficulty up the narrow gangplank, a casserole in one hand and a large carpet bag in the other. Alarmed she might topple into the river, he quickly relieved her of the bag, and she carefully carried the casserole in and placed it on the table.

'It's lovely and warm in here. You've made it look...' she searched for a word and finally came up with 'charming.'

Rawlings waved her to sit in one of the two armchairs and flung himself into the other. 'Not really down to me, I've had countless helpers. Plumber Paul has almost lived here over the past week, and Isobel sent Maria over to me for the day, and she worked a miracle. Everything has been dusted and polished to within an inch of its life, and she has vowed to return once a month to make sure it stays that way.' He looked at her, 'and you have been sending over food parcels, for which I am eternally grateful.'

Marnie laughed at this. 'What nonsense, a few cups of coffee and some shortbread doesn't quite add up to food parcels.' She stood up, fetched her carpet bag and foraged inside, at last producing a tin which she opened and handed over to Rawlings. 'I made some cheese straws which I thought would go well with the wine.'

'Wine!' Rawlings leapt to his feet and then gave a loud yelp as he put his foot on the ground.

'Are you all right? That sounded painful.'

He rubbed his leg. 'Yes, I'm fine; it suddenly catches me if I put the leg down too suddenly. Would red be all right? I do have some white if you prefer, but I thought with beef casserole…'

'Red would be fine' she assured him, and they both sipped in silence for a while.

Marnie was the first to speak, 'I'm surprised how spacious the boat feels. I always thought a boat like this would be claustrophobic.'

Rawlings nodded. 'I think a narrowboat would have been. This is a wide-beam canal boat, and I was reliably informed it was eleven feet wide and fifty-seven feet long, which seemed plenty of room for a single occupant. I'm over six foot, so my main worry was the height, but I find I don't have to duck, except with the main room front door.' He stood up. 'I'll take you on the grand tour if you like. It won't take long.'

She followed him to the back, where there was a well-equipped galley kitchen. Marnie was relieved to see what looked like a new and efficient oven.

'Everything's electric,' he told her, 'makes for easy living. It's a luxury for me, after living like a nomad for most of my life., sometimes in very primitive conditions.' He led her back through the living room, past a cupboard, containing the now working washing machine, and then into the bathroom with a shower, basin and loo. 'Another luxury' he said, 'to have plumbing that works. The loo is fitted with a macerator, which seems to work perfectly efficiently if a little on the noisy side.' He opened a central door, and they entered a bedroom large enough for a double bed, with a chest of drawers and cupboards either side of the centre door, leading to the outside. He now threw it open, revealing a good-sized deck. A blast of chill air hit them. 'When the weather improves, I'll purchase some garden furniture. Nice to be able to eat outside. There's also a stern deck which I'm sure will come in useful.'

Returning to the living room, Marnie said, 'It's a great space,' and added, 'surprising, from the outside it looks smaller.' She picked up the casserole. 'I'll just warm this up. It shouldn't take long.' and bustled off to the kitchen.

When finally seated again she remarked, 'I do like the way the round windows go all the way down the river side of the boat. We're lucky that the opposite side of the river is so unspoiled, just willow trees and not a building in sight. It is a perfect spot.' She smiled. 'I'm rather envious of your boat, it's so tidy and ordered. My place is a complete mess in comparison.'

'Have no fear, this won't stay organised for long. I'm not known for being a tidy person. You've just seen the results of Maria being here for the day.' He looked at her. 'I've been meaning to ask you, why is your boathouse built so high? I like the way you have to walk up steps to your front deck. Is it in order to have a better view of the river?'

'It was Peter who organised that,' Marnie told him, 'when the place was re-built. It's actually to allow for any flooding. It's good to have an elevated view of course, but I was really thankful for being high up a few years back when we had the terrible floods. The river ran so high it was up to my front door, which is three feet up from the bank. I went to stay with Isobel until the floods subsided because the water went over the top of my wellington boots. In spite of the steep slope in her garden, the floods reached the top, and were a couple of inches in the carpark.'

'I suppose I'd have been all right on my boat', Rawlings commented, 'it would have just risen with the water.'

'Yes, but you would have needed high waders to get ashore.'

Rawlings laughed as well and said, 'That's true.'

After a moment Marnie ventured, 'You must have had a very interesting life.'

He shrugged. 'I don't know about that. I've certainly seen many places and witnessed certain events…' He reached for a packet of cigarettes, 'Do you mind if I smoke?' She shook her head, and he paused to light up before going on, 'I suppose some might call it interesting. Up until now, I've been continually active. If I stopped, I became restless. Now I have to accept my life will be more static and just hope I don't go mad with cabin fever.' He seemed disinclined to say more, but then suddenly mused, almost to himself, 'If I think about my life at all, I realise that a few major incidents, which have happened at various intervals, have set me off in completely different directions. I suppose you'd call them turning points.' He gave a laugh. 'My arrival here seems to be the latest of these.'

Marnie was immediately curious. 'That sounds interesting. When did these incidents start? I mean, what was the earliest one?'

Rawlings frowned and cursed himself for embarking on

the subject, but then, seeing her earnest expression, he said, 'Why don't we have your casserole first and then, if you still insist, I'll tell you.'

An hour later, the supper had been tidied away, and they were sitting back with their glasses of wine. Marnie looked at Rawlings expectantly.

'You were going to tell me about the first incident?'

He'd hoped she'd forgotten. He wasn't used to talking about himself. Indeed, he'd always carefully resisted it. Deciding on evasive action, he asked, 'Why don't you tell me a little about yourself first? Were you ever married?'

She shrugged and said abruptly. 'Yes, I was, to a controlling bully, from whom I finally escaped after eleven horrible years, only to find another controlling bully in the form of a landlord, who forced me and my boat off the mooring. It wasn't until I came here that I managed to find some happiness and settle down.'

'You were lucky to have your art', he said, 'that must have provided you with some escape.'

She smiled. 'If only it were that simple. I do have plans for 'my art', as you refer to it. But these plans are continually thwarted, for financial and bureaucratic reasons. Not very interesting, I can assure you.'

Rawlings observed her. There was sadness in her expression, and he wanted to know the real reason, but before he could probe any further, she burst out,

'You've had a far more interesting life. I want to hear about the incidents that you said made you change direction. I mean, how early did these incidents start?'

Rawlings gave a weary sigh and was about to protest when he suddenly decided to relent. To tell her a bit about his early life could do no harm. He hadn't thought about it in a long while, so it would mean dredging up stuff he'd forgotten about, but at least it would take his mind off the bloody wars.

'You're a glutton for punishment,' he told her with a smile, 'but if you absolutely insist.' A cigarette was lit. 'I'll skim over the background details, otherwise you'll be here all night.' He blew the smoke out slowly as if considering where to begin. 'The first incident to have an effect on my life must have been about 1961. I was ten and had just passed my eleven plus into the local grammar school. We lived in a small terraced house on the outskirts of Dagenham. My father worked in Ford's as a car fitter, and my mother in the local library. From that you can see my parents were rather different and I think, looking back, totally incompatible. My father was a rough diamond. He'd been through an extremely tough war on the Russian convoys. Knowing what I do now about PTSD, it was pretty obvious he was suffering, but in those days, they did nothing about it. He was given to violent moods and was a heavy drinker, which didn't help their relationship. My mother was different; refined, academic and obsessed with romantic literature. They'd met in Scotland and were both in their early thirties. He was a handsome man, and after a whirlwind courtship, against all the wishes of her family, they married and came down south. I knew nothing of my father's family; he never mentioned them at all. My mother's parents at once distanced themselves from us, so we never knew any of our grandparents, but two old maiden aunts in Scotland would send us money at Christmas.'

Marnie leant forward. 'Us? she queried.

'Yes, I had a sister, two years older, named Estelle.' He smiled, 'I told you my mother liked Dickens, she was named after the character in *"Great Expectations"*. It turned out she didn't care much for her name either, and she quickly became Stella.' He stubbed out his cigarette. 'So, to the incident.' He paused, searching his memory. 'It came about after something quite trivial. I'd clumsily knocked over my father's beer, a criminal offence as far as he was concerned. He'd been drinking already, so his temper quickly flared, and he yelled at me, 'Get out of my sight you little **shit**.' I took his advice and fled two doors down, to see my best friend, Billy. Billy was a year older than me, but we spent a good deal of our time together. He was streetwise, and I'd continually look to him for advice. I described what had happened and after some hesitation asked him why my father had called me a shit, and what on earth was shit?' Marnie looked amused and Rawlings, noticing this, explained. 'You have to understand that in spite of my father's rough ways and often foul language, my mother was very protective, and her refinement had rubbed off on us. Billy was as amused by my question as you. He didn't answer at once but told me to follow him, and we went out beyond the street, over the fields to the sewage works. We ran up the slope to the round cylinders with the rotating rods spraying water, climbed the wall and peered down at the foul-smelling brown mess below. Billy pointed to it and declared triumphantly 'That's it, that's shit.' The penny dropped, and I started to laugh, then Billy laughed, and we rolled back down the slope and laughed all the way home, chanting shit, shit, shit.'

Rawlings stood up and poured the remains of the wine

into Marnie's glass. 'I think this is going to require another bottle.' He went out to the kitchen and on returning replenished his own glass. Curiously he found that once he'd started, it was easier than he'd thought it would be. In a strange way, he was almost enjoying it. Settling back in his chair, he continued.

'We now get to the actual incident. Billy and I parted company and hoping it was now safe I let myself in through the front door. At once I could hear an almighty row coming from the sitting room. My mother, who hardly ever raised her voice was shrieking with alarm. My father, by now nine sheets to the wind, was yelling obscenities and Stella was sobbing loudly.' He paused to drink his wine. Marnie wondered if this memory was painful for him, but she said nothing, and after a moment he started talking again. 'There are some moments in life, however brief, that you remember with great clarity. This was one of them. As I entered the room, my father lunged at my mother, as if to hit her. Now, this was odd, because although he was often verbally violent, I'd never seen him physically threatening before. In that one disastrous moment, Stella moved in front of my mother trying to protect her, and my father caught her on the side of the head, sending her flying towards the fireplace where she lay in a crumpled heap. I remained rooted to the spot unable to move. I could see blood coming from Stella's head where she'd hit her head on the hearth. My father sank into a chair, and to give him his due I think he was shocked by what had happened. I remember he had a dazed, almost puzzled expression on his face. My mother knelt down beside Stella and screamed out for me to fetch Billy's father Jim, which I did with all speed.

It didn't take Jim long to assess the situation; the police and an ambulance were called, and that was more or less that.' He looked at Marnie. 'There you have it, incident one.'

Marnie felt stunned and stared at him. 'What happened afterwards?''

Rawlings shrugged. 'Our lives completely changed. My father was taken away and sent to prison for GBH. We never saw him again. After he came out, he disappeared. I often wondered where he went, but my best guess is that he returned to the sea in some capacity. It made me realise at a young age that it doesn't take much to turn a normal life into a tragedy.' His expression changed. 'I wish I'd known him better. I can see now that he was obviously damaged by his war experiences and then became an alcoholic, but I also remember some good times when he would tell me stories about the war and the destroyer he'd been on. He was proud of that. I later found some war medals in the drawer and have always kept them. Strangely I had a far more remote relationship with my mother in those early years. After the incident, she started to work full time as a receptionist at the local surgery, but she became bitter and withdrawn. The divorce came through eventually. I think the old aunts sent her money because we seemed to manage, although it was all pretty frugal and obviously a struggle. I went to the grammar school as planned. It was poor Stella who suffered the most. We thought she'd recovered from the head wound, but then she started having epileptic fits. It took a few years to get these under some sort of control. She became nervous and reserved, very changed from the way she'd been before.'

There was a long silence between them after that.

Marnie put down her glass and stood up. She felt at a loss, not knowing quite what to say, but finally blurted out, 'I'm so sorry, I didn't realise how late it was. Thank you for telling me all that. It was sad but very interesting. Don't worry about the casserole, I'll collect it tomorrow.' Picking up her bag she added, 'I'm so hopeless, I forgot to give you your letter...' Once more she delved inside and then produced the envelope, handing it to Rawlings.

'I'll watch you safely down the gangplank,' he said. 'I must get a rail put up on either side. It's a bit hazardous at the moment. Another job for poor Paul.'

'Or maybe Jake the young gardener. He's done a lot of carpentry work for Isobel.'

Rawlings nodded, then gave her a peck on the cheek. 'Your stew was delicious. We must do it again some time.'

She was tempted to say she couldn't wait to hear about the next incident, but some instinct told her that wouldn't be a good idea, so she just thanked him for the evening and tottered off towards the boathouse. As she reached the towpath she called out, 'it's a beautiful clear night, but definitely getting colder.'

Rawlings went inside and poured himself the last of the wine. The envelope was on the table beside him and looked very formal. He decided it was a tomorrow problem. He'd had quite enough for one day.

Chapter Three

Early February 2017

Rawlings soon found he'd fallen into a routine. Some progress had already been made with his war memoir project, and he was reluctant to let social events interrupt the work. He also knew instinctively that another supper with Marnie would automatically lead to further probing into his past. For this reason, he rarely left the boat and then it was only to replenish his cigarette supply and buy a newspaper. These were purchased from the local newsagent, which was run by a charming, and talkative, Indian man by the name of Patel, with whom he'd struck up an instant friendship. Why were newsagents always called Patel? Did they have the franchise? This Mr Patel was a fascinating source of local information and even provided the odd piece of gossip.

It was on one of these daily visits that Rawlings happened to overhear Rose and Lydia in an argument by the dustbin area. He presumed it was Rose and Lydia. It was undoubtedly two women. One had a deep, commanding voice, the other spoke in a high whine, and was sounding on the defensive. He couldn't resist listening and tucked himself out of sight by the hedge. It struck him as a rather Shakespearian scene. Shades of

"Twelfth Night" or was it *"Much Ado."*?

The deep voice spoke first. 'I'm telling you again; this has to stop Rose. Isobel only invited you for a couple of weeks. She won't let you stay on here if you continue to abuse her very kind hospitality.'

'Abuse her hospitality? I have absolutely no idea what you mean.'

The reply was weary. 'Rose, I have explained at length what I mean. You're just not listening to me. If you don't correct these problems, Isobel will ask you to leave.'

Rose's voice became sharp. 'Lady Mallinson can't throw me out onto the streets. It would ruin her reputation. Isn't she a JP? It wouldn't look very good, would it? Throwing a penniless invalid onto the streets. She knows I have no money. Where would I go?'

'I have no idea, Rose. Which is why we have to address these problems…'

The whine became more of a shriek. 'Problems? What problems? You talk of problems and of my abusing her hospitality, but I have no idea what you mean. Lady Mallinson has said nothing to me of any of this.'

Lydia began to sound exasperated. 'Of course, she hasn't, but she has expressed her concerns to me. After all, I was the person responsible for asking Isobel to take you in.' Nothing was said for a moment, then Lydia continued more calmly, almost as if she were talking to a wayward child.

'I am sure we can sort things out, Rose. You just have to listen to me and make some adjustments to the way you're living. For a start, stop using her washing machine all the time. I can't believe you have that much to wash. It's a waste of electricity.'

The whine turned into a hysterical wail. 'You're just like everyone else, getting at me all the time when you know perfectly well what a difficult time I'm having. I'm not in good health. If you must know, the doctors say I am very ill. So why are you being so unkind...?'

Rawlings decided he'd heard enough. He walked on, disturbed by this exchange, but not wishing in any way to get involved.

★

If Marnie had hoped for a quick follow up to incident one, she was to be disappointed. Three weeks passed, and it was as if Rawlings had more or less gone into hibernation. Occasionally he walked past the boathouse deep in thought, and it was obviously not the moment to disturb him. She decided to leave the next invitation up to him and just hoped it wouldn't be too long. Meanwhile, Isobel kept her promise and took her out for a birthday meal.

As soon as they were seated, her opening words were about Rawlings. 'And how are you finding our new neighbour?' Isobel was looking at her searchingly, and to Marnie's annoyance, she found her cheeks were reddening. There was absolutely no reason for this, so her answer was somewhat sharper than perhaps it needed to be.

'Apart from taking over his post one evening, I haven't seen him. I think he's shut himself away to write his book.' She added with a smile, 'He's made himself very warm and comfortable on that boat, I think he has more radiators than rooms.'

Isobel seemed content with this, and the conversation

moved on to other topics, the problem of Rose being utmost in her mind.

'I'm at my wit's end with the woman,' Isobel said with an unusual flash of annoyance. 'It is really becoming quite a problem for me.'

Marnie looked across at her and was rather alarmed to see Isobel looking pale, with dark rings under her eyes. 'I've only met Rose a few times,' she said, choosing her words carefully. 'She appeared rather affected to me, with a kind of Mary Poppin's voice.' Here she gave a laugh. 'She insisted on telling me about all the high-powered careers she'd had, which unfortunately she'd had to forgo because of ill health. It is obvious she resents having to live on charity and was altogether irritatingly grand, and I personally thought, ungrateful to you.'

'The woman lives a life of complete fantasy,' Isobel said with some exasperation, 'even down to having a double-barrelled name. For some reason, she calls herself Rose Penton Jones. Her family name is just Jones, so I've no idea when the Penton crept in.'

'Can't Lydia tell you about her? After all, it was Lydia who landed Rose on you.'

'I have asked her about it, but she was annoyingly vague.' Isobel gave a sigh. 'From the little I have been told, I gather Rose's mother is still alive and living in a home in Sussex. I only know that, because given Rose's precarious health, I insisted on the name of a next of kin.'

'Well, can't her mother help?'

Isobel shook her head. 'Apparently, her mother has some form of dementia.' She added with a wry smile, 'This means she wouldn't actually be much help in an emergency.

The only other snippets of information that Lydia has given me are that unfortunately for Rose, the rest of her family, which I think consists of two married brothers, are no help at all. Her father died a few years ago.'

'What about Social Services, can't they do something?'

'Lydia said they'd tried talking to the brothers, but they refuse to have anything more to do with their sister. This makes me realise Rose has been a problem for a long time and tested everyone's patience. The result is she is now on her own and basically destitute.'

'I still feel annoyed with Lydia for landing her on you,' Marnie sounded cross.

'Well I do too if I am honest,' Isobel admitted, 'but at the beginning, it was only meant to be a few days. Now it has been over six weeks. The Social Services are so over-stretched they're just relieved Rose has a roof over her head and are disinclined to find her anywhere else. It seems inevitable she will be with us for a long time and if I'm honest, I'm not sure I can bear the thought of that.'

It was unlike Isobel to complain, let alone sound so stressed. Their food arrived and Marnie, hungry as always, dived in. Isobel didn't but continued on the subject of Rose. 'I know I shouldn't mind helping out; after all, I do have a large house with plenty of spare rooms. It's just that Rose has multiple problems that are becoming increasingly difficult for me to live with.'

Marnie put down her fork and looked at Isobel. 'What sort of multiple problems? I mean I can see she must have some sort of eating disorder. She is painfully thin, even in all her bulky winter clothes. Is there something else that's wrong with her?'

Isobel took time in replying. 'It's as if something has gone wrong with her body clock. She never gets up before midday and then never goes to bed until the small hours…'

'How do you know that?' Marnie was so bewildered by this latest information she had stopped eating.

'Well, my room is directly below Rose's, and her nocturnal activity keeps me awake. Lord knows what she is doing. I think she must have a food blender of some kind and is making herself soups or fruit shakes well into the small hours. That is noisy enough, but she bangs about as well as if she is knocking things over. I know it sounds odd, but she has crammed the room full of stuff, so it would be easy to bump into things.'

'What sort of stuff?'

Isobel sighed. 'It seems that hoarding may be another of her problems. I only know this because Maria went to take a message to her the other day and had a terrible shock. She told me that Rose's room was full of boxes, with stacks of papers everywhere and hardly any room to move. And more is added every day. When Rose finally does get up, she takes herself off to the charity shops, of which there are so many now, and always seems to come back with something and she never throws anything out.'

'How can she afford that if she is penniless?' Marnie sounded indignant.

Isobel shrugged. 'I suppose she must be getting some government income support or pension.'

Marnie frowned, 'I don't mean to pry, but are you charging her rent?'

'Not really. After about two weeks, I asked Lydia to arrange for her to make a small contribution to gas and electricity. I thought this only fair because, for some reason, she likes to monopolise the washing machine and drier every day in the afternoon. What she is washing, I can't imagine, but there is a terrible smell of bleach that pervades the whole house. It's just another example of her obsessive behaviour.' She sighed. 'The real problem is, either she is an official tenant, which means I have to put it on a legal footing, or, she's a guest, who I'm afraid has become an extremely unwelcome one. I really don't want it to become an unpleasant legal wrangle, but it may come to that.'

Marnie studied her and felt concerned. She had no idea the situation had become so bad. Isobel looked exhausted and had hardly touched her food. Something needed to be done, and quickly, but she wasn't at all sure what. Maybe she should tackle Lydia about it. It wouldn't be easy, but action was needed. Lydia somehow had to be forced to take responsibility for the Rose problem and give some relief to poor Isobel.

*

Rawlings managed ten days of concentrated research and had now reached the point of putting some of it down. He was quite pleased with his progress, although so far, he'd only tackled the Falklands war, which wasn't a difficult one to do, as he'd remained in London for the duration. Not having witnessed it first-hand meant he remained detached. The Gulf War would be next and then the Balkans. They were going to be a far more draining and difficult exercise.

He'd just decided on a coffee and fag break when he was interrupted by a loud knock on his door. Limping to open it he was astonished to find Dennis Jackson, the previous and greatly disliked mooring landlord, standing in front of him. In fact, he was so shocked he allowed the man to follow him in.

'Is there something you wanted, Mr Jackson' he asked coldly, 'because you are interrupting my work.'

'Yes, indeed, there is.' The man spoke with compressed anger. 'There is the matter of money outstanding from when you left my mooring in such a hurry, Mr Rawlings,' and he slammed an envelope down on the table.

Rawlings opened the envelope and looked astonished. 'Do you mean to say you have made a special journey here to demand from me the sum of £11.20, for,' he peered at the letter again, 'outstanding service charges? This is ludicrous. Why didn't you send it through the post?'

Mr Jackson sneered, 'You left me with no forwarding address, Mr Rawlings.'

Rawlings was silent for a moment, then spoke slowly and deliberately. 'Firstly, Mr Jackson, I have no intention of paying this spurious charge, so you can sue me for the amount if you wish. Even with your connections, it would be laughed out of court.' He paused to let this sink in. 'Secondly, I would remind you that at this moment you are trespassing on private land…

'I believe the towpath is still a public right of way?' This interruption was said with a great deal of sarcasm.

'The towpath yes, but you came through a gate in order to reach my boat, and that is marked 'Private Property'. You are on private land belonging to Lady Mallinson…' he emphasised the title as he knew that would make some impression on the man. 'There is a way of reaching me without trespassing on Lady Mallinson's land, and that is by the lane that leads down to this mooring from the road. I suggest you use that on your way out.'

He opened the door. Jackson stood speechless. Rawlings gave his Parthian shot, 'On your way up the lane you will pass the boathouse, which is now occupied by Marnie Peters, who you threw off your moorings some years back. Lady Mallinson, being a friend, took her in. I would only add that Lady Mallinson is also a J.P., so if you take me to court, we may well appear before her.'

Jackson, rendered utterly speechless by this, left, and in his hurry slipped at the bottom of the gangplank, only just managing to maintain some dignity and not land on his backside in the mud.

Rawlings closed the door and smiled. It had been a minor victory of sorts. He screwed up the invoice and dropped it in the wastepaper basket and made a mental note to get rails put up on the gangplank before the freezing weather arrived in full force. The forecast was for next week, so there was little time to get it organised.

Marnie had watched in shock as she caught sight of Jackson arriving at the mooring. She lingered by the window and saw Rawlings let him in. She also witnessed his angry departure past her boathouse. Finding herself shaking, she sat down for a while, and then unable to endure it a moment longer, she decided to tackle Rawlings and ask what the visit been about. Feeling nervous about bothering him, she knocked on his door. He flung it open, trying not to look cross at being disturbed again.

'I'm really sorry,' she burst out, 'but I just had to know what Jackson wanted.' Rawlings noting her anxious state, told her to come in and decided to give up on any more work that day. In any case, it had been difficult to settle back to it after Jackson's visit.

'You're looking a bit pale, Marnie. Does that bloody man affect you that much?' She just nodded, not trusting herself to speak. Rawlings gave her a look. 'I think tea is called for, or would you prefer something stronger?'

'Tea would be fine. Thank you.'

He returned with a mug of tea and then told her of his brief encounter with their mooring landlord. His account revived her, and she burst out laughing.

'I wish I could have seen his face when you told him he was trespassing. What a cheek that man has, to demand such a paltry sum. Why didn't he send one of his employees? Why come himself?' She thought about it for a second. 'Do you know, I think he is being driven mad by the fact that you found another mooring so quickly, and one that's far nicer than his. Somebody probably told him about it, and it drove him into a fury. He's a control freak and wouldn't like the fact that he lost control over you.'

Rawlings took a cigarette from the packet and lit it. 'The man's a bully Marnie, and like all bullies, when finally confronted, they crumble. But bullies are dangerous. Alas, I've been around too many of them. With their power, they destroy people's lives...'

'Jackson destroyed mine,' Marnie said angrily, adding, 'I did try to stand up to him, but I was powerless. He was always complaining about something. He finally gave me a month's notice because I'd painted my boat with a white colour wash. That was all. Apparently, there was a small clause in his licence that said boats had to be either natural wood or painted green, to fit in with the surroundings.' Rawlings reflected that the *Esme Jane* was black and there had never been any complaint, but he let her go on. 'I tried to argue with him, even consulted a lawyer, but there was no way around that stupid clause. Eventually, I had to pay a large sum to have my boat towed away, and because I couldn't find a mooring that was free, it was taken to the local boatyard. It turned out my boat was too large for the marinas, and after a year, I gave up looking for a suitable mooring. During this time, I had to rent somewhere to live and was also paying the boatyard for housing the boat. I couldn't let it, and anyway, it was starting to rot from neglect. In the end, the man at the boatyard paid me a paltry sum and gave it to his son to do up. It meant I lost all my savings. I later learned Jackson had wanted my mooring for a family member and just used my painting the boat white as an excuse. And do you know what the colour of the replacement boat was? White!'

She looked close to tears, and apart from agreeing the man was a monster, Rawlings decided to pursue the subject no further. Instead, he changed tack and asked cheerfully,

'What's new on the home front? I'm afraid I've been rather unsociable for the past three weeks.'

Marnie, glad to be talking about something else, told him the saga of Rose and how she was worried about Isobel. Given the conversation he'd overheard between Lydia and Rose, Rawlings wasn't altogether surprised.

'Can't she just tell the bloody woman to leave?'

Marnie shook her head. 'I think it's become more complicated than that. Rose has no money and nowhere to go. Isobel knows this, and it puts her in a difficult position.

I also believe Rose is an utterly devious character and knows exactly how to play the situation for all it's worth. It makes me furious,' she said with some vehemence, adding, 'but my anger is also directed at Lydia. She's taking no responsibility for the situation, and it's all her fault that Rose is even here.'

Rawlings made no comment. He sympathised a little with Lydia and reflected that Marnie's observation that Rose was devious had a definite ring of truth.

A few days later, Rawlings had his first encounter with the lady in question. They met in the dustbin area, arriving with their rubbish at the same moment. She held out a gloved hand.

'Rose Penton Jones,' she said. Gone was the high whine, now she spoke in perfect Mary Poppins tones. 'And you must be the famous E. G. Rawlings.' He frowned at this but didn't comment. Instead, he shook her hand and then went back to putting his rubbish in the appropriate bins. Rose continued, 'We really must have a chat one day. I worked as a journalist too you know, a long time ago,' she gave a tinkling laugh, 'in a minor role of course and not successful like you, but I was sad to have to give it up, through my ill health.'

Rawlings was just about to make a polite enquiry about which paper or magazine she had worked for, when she gave him an airy wave.

'Must go, things to do,' and with that, she walked briskly back into the house.

He watched her go. She was wearing many layers of clothes on the top half, but her legs were clad in what would have been tight trousers on any other person, but on her had a distinctly baggy look. She was very thin, alarmingly so. It was obvious she had some sort of eating disorder.

Rawlings sighed. He didn't want to be involved in this kind of problem, but like Marnie, he was worried for Isobel.

Chapter Four

Mid-February 2017

It only took two days for Paul and Jake, the young man who worked in the garden, to complete the task of putting up the gangplank railings. It was just in time. The river was running high, causing the gangplank to be at a steep angle and this, combined with a sharp frost, resulted in an icy slope, which made negotiating the walk down to the bank a treacherous business. Now at least there were rails to cling on to. The other hazard Paul warned him about, was the likelihood of the pipes freezing up. He'd lagged them as best he could, but the fact that they ran over ground to the connections meant they were exposed. He cheerfully assured Rawlings the pipes usually thawed out quickly and he'd only be without water for a day or two at the most. This was mildly encouraging. Somewhere, at the back of his mind, Rawlings remembered one of the tenants from the old moorings telling him that a good trick was to leave a tap dripping through the night, which helped save the pipes from freezing up. As the thermometer dropped even lower, Rawlings decided this might be a sensible action to take, even though the whirring sound of the macerator through the night would be rather disturbing.

In the middle of the night, Rawlings awoke and realised the macerator was no longer making a noise. He stepped out of bed to investigate, and his feet landed in water. There was an inch of icy water across the floor. He padded into the bathroom and turned off the dripping tap. Putting the seat down on the over-flowing loo, he sat down, watching the water drip from the basin. He quickly worked out what had happened. The macerator was obviously no longer working, due to the fact the pipes had already frozen, so the water had no way out, and thus the boat had become flooded. Wearily he started to clean up. Having mopped up the worst of the water, tipping the bucket over the side, he laid towels across the floor and padded back to bed, chiding himself for his stupidity in not checking with Paul first.

As soon as it was a decent hour, he rang the man. Ominously it took him a while to get through, the line being permanently engaged. When at last he'd explained the problem, Paul assured him he would visit as soon as he could, but there were several people with burst pipes ahead of him. Thankfully there was enough water in the kettle to make a cup of coffee and Rawlings put all the radiators up to full. By the time Paul arrived, Rawlings was sitting in something that resembled a steam cabin. A quick instruction was given to turn the radiators down and open the windows. After that, it didn't take long for Paul to ascertain what was wrong.

'You were given bad advice Mr Rawlings. The dripping tap has caused the macerator to burn out. I'm afraid you will need a new one.' Paul gave a grin and said in his impeccable English, 'It is a good thing we installed the bilge pump. That will take out any water that has gone through the floorboards.' He walked over to the door and opened it a little. 'I know it is cold, but we need to let this steam out. It is not good for the wood. You will need a new macerator, and my advice would be to buy a de-humidifier as well. They are a good thing to have on the boat, takes out any dampness.'

Rawlings, relieved there was at least a solution, agreed to all the suggestions and asked how long it would take? Paul considered this. 'It might take a couple of days. Just depends on how quickly I can find the right size macerator. You only have room for a small one, which is why it burnt out so quickly. For the same reason, you should not take a shower at the same time as putting on the washing machine.'

Rawlings made a mental note of this and then assured Paul expense was no problem. The man then departed, giving his parting advice to get large containers of drinking water at the garage just up the road.

By mid-afternoon, Rawlings was feeling distinctly chilled and fairly miserable. Although he had enough water for his immediate needs, it was a rather cheerless existence. By six o'clock, he'd had enough, and he rang Marnie to explain his dire situation. Her immediate response was to invite him over. He needed no persuasion, grabbed a bottle of wine and minutes later arrived at the boathouse.

It was a relief to feel warm again. He now understood the phrase "being chilled to the bone". Settling into the chair nearest to the log burner he began to thaw out and once he'd been fed and watered, was positively cheerful. Taking advantage of his mellow mood, Marnie felt emboldened enough to inquire whether this might be a good moment for him to tell her about the second incident in his life.

'I can't believe you're interested in this.' Rawlings said with some irritation, regretting he'd ever mentioned the damned incidents. Marnie assured him that she was, and almost as a bribe filled up his glass. Rawlings sighed. The woman had come to his rescue in his hour of need; it would seem a little churlish to refuse her request. He took a large gulp of wine. 'I'll need to smoke,' he told her. Marnie nodded, fetching him an ashtray. He was silent for a moment gathering his thoughts.

Marnie prompted, 'Your father had left, and you'd gone to grammar school'.

'You're right. Well, to continue. The years that followed my father's departure were uneventful. The second incident didn't happen until a few years later. My friend Billy hadn't managed the grammar school entrance and had gone to a comprehensive. I missed him making me laugh. He'd been the joker in the pack. I remember once in a religious education class; we had been asked what the Holy Paraclete was. Quick as a flash, Billy's hand had shot up, 'A kind of parrot Sir,'. Marnie smiled but made no comment. 'Yes, I missed Billy. He still lived two doors down, but our lives now moved in separate directions. I did well at school, in fact well enough to go to university, but I knew my mother was struggling and felt I should get a job and start earning a living. I also knew, rightly as it happens, that if I became independent, she would move with Stella back to Scotland and the old aunts.'

Rawlings took time out to light a cigarette and Marnie didn't want to stop the flow, so again said nothing but waited for him to continue.

'My English master, who had always taken a kindly

interest in me, suggested I should try a career in journalism. He happened to have a friend who was editor of the local newspaper and made the introduction. The editor was a journalist of the old school and thankfully decided to take me on. From him, I learned the necessities for being a decent journalist, which for him were to work fast, be meticulous with language, and always check the facts before going to print. He added that the main asset of any good journalist was to have a nose for a story, a sort of instinct, some angle that others might have missed, and this was something, he told me cheerfully, that you were born with and couldn't be taught. He obviously thought I might have this asset, and I did my best to prove him right. His advice was good, and under his guidance, I progressed quickly. By the age of twenty-one, I'd advanced from tea boy to reporter, covering everything from local events such as school concerts, amateur dramatics and church fetes, to more lurid stories of burglary and even a rape case. I had acquired small, but decent digs, a small, but rather clapped out sports car and managed to indulge in quite a racy lifestyle.' He gave a rueful laugh. 'We were now into the seventies where the results of the swinging sixties had made it easy to have casual relationships with no permanent involvement, as long as you were careful.'

Marnie thought that it didn't take a great deal to imagine the sort of life he had led and probably needed no further description. Instead, she asked, 'Did you ever take night classes for your journalism?'

Rawlings shook his head. 'It never seemed necessary, as I say, I learned far more from old Sam, the editor than I ever could have done taking a course.' He stubbed out his cigarette. 'So here goes, the second incident that radically changed my life.'

Before continuing, he held out his glass and Marnie dutifully filled it and then, with a slightly weary sigh, he began.

'One of my duties, as a general reporter, was to cover major social events in the area. One of these was the retirement party of Sir Gerald Sykes of Sykes Industries. I did the usual round of checks and found out that Sir Gerald had made his name in the war, manufacturing instruments for planes. He continued with this line after the war and expanded the business with further factories, not only becoming extremely wealthy but also having importance as a major employer in the region. He was generally known as a good and popular boss, and his large contributions to charity had earned him a knighthood. He was therefore considered a good egg and his retirement was news and an event that needed to be reported.'

Marnie leant forward. 'Did this all happen in Dagenham?'

Rawlings shook his head. 'It was nearer to Romford. That is where I had settled.' He gave a wry smile. 'Romford now seems to be part of Greater London, but back in 1970, there were areas that were not built up and still quite rural. Gerald had a large place, Loden Manor, just outside the village of Great Warley. On the evening in question, I bowled over to this bash and introduced myself, telling him I was covering the party for the paper. He couldn't have been more welcoming and told me to hang around. Apparently, there was to be an interesting announcement later on in the evening.' Rawlings took out a cigarette, pausing while he lit it. 'I was then introduced to his daughter, Gillian.' Marnie smiled; she thought she could see where this was leading. 'We were the only two young people there, so we spent most of the evening together. Looking back, I find it rather hard to describe my first impression of her. She was on the plump side but pretty, in a conventional way.' He smiled. 'Rather how I imagine Miss Joan Hunter Dunn in the John Betjeman poem must have looked. At the start of the evening, she was incredibly shy, but after a couple of drinks she opened up, telling me that her mother had died when she was ten, and since then it had just been her and her father. Her great passion was horses, and the Manor had a large stable block, and she owned two horses of her own. This was all Greek to me. I knew nothing about horses, but I let her babble on. I gained the impression she'd been spoiled, being the only child, and probably over-protected by her father. She'd gone to the best schools and a finishing establishment, but now was at a loose end and trying to persuade her father to let her expand the stables into a business. At this point the speeches began, and with them came the announcement that Sykes Industries had been sold out to Aerospace. This was the major news story, and I left quickly after this to write it up. And that would have been that...' He put out his cigarette and became infuriatingly silent.

'I think I can guess what happened next,' Marnie ventured.

'Well, of course you can,' Rawlings said irritably. 'It's all extremely predictable and rather dull.

'No, it's not. I find it fascinating. I'm presuming Gillian fell for you.'

'That's about the gist of it. We went out a few times, and I was very careful to behave myself. It was a whole different way of life, and I have to admit, it fascinated me. I started going to lunch parties at the weekends and joined in with the tennis and croquet.' Here he gave a laugh, 'but she never got me on a horse. Sometimes it was just the three of us for dinner, and I grew to like Gerald and to admire him. He was a man who spoke his mind and had made it up the ladder from humble beginnings, somewhere in the North, I believe.'

Rawlings broke off and looked across at Marnie. 'I think I need another glass of wine and then I will finish off this turgid tale as fast as possible.'

'It isn't turgid at all' she said as she emptied the bottle into his glass.

He shrugged and then said thoughtfully, 'It may seem odd looking back, but at the time I didn't see it coming. As I say, I was always extremely careful, having given Gillian no more than the occasional peck on the cheek. She was certainly not like my other girlfriends. It was like taking out the vicar's daughter; you had to be on your best behaviour. But I liked her, she was easy to be with and had a quirky sense of humour, once you got to know her.' He stared into his glass. 'It must have been 1974. I was twenty-three, and Gillian was having a big party for her twenty-first birthday. We'd both had far too much to drink that I do remember, which I like to think accounts for the fact that on this occasion I was stupidly careless. To give me my due, at the time I didn't realise how drunk Gillian was. At some point, we went over to the stables, and she threw herself at me and stupidly I didn't resist.' He paused, then said grimly. 'You can imagine the rest. Six or seven weeks later, I was summoned over to Gerald to be told that Gillian was pregnant. It was a terrible shock, as I have to admit I'd completely forgotten the incident. I was mortified and managed to stammer out profuse apologies, saying that of course, I would do whatever was necessary. To my surprise, Gerald didn't reproach me or even fly into a rage. He sat me down, poured me a drink and laid his cards on the table, almost as if he were making a contract with a supplier. He told me Gillian was adamant about keeping the baby, so that left me with a choice. I could walk away from the situation, or I could marry the girl, simple as that. If I chose the former, there would be no reproaches, but I would not see her again, or the baby. He said he would talk to me plainly, man to man. By this time, I was on my third brandy and probably would have agreed to anything. He explained his daughter was besotted with me. She was a naïve girl, and she'd had only a few boyfriends in the past but had decided I was the only one she wanted. He explained that since her mother died, he realised he'd spoiled her, added to which she'd missed the maternal guidance he hadn't been able to give her. He then came to the point. He apparently liked me. If I took on his daughter and married her, he'd trust me to do right by her, and in return, he'd do right by me, simple as that. I wasn't quite sure what that meant at the time. He put it all down in a document which I later duly signed.'

'You went through with it?' Marnie looked astonished. 'Whatever made you do that? You were so young, your whole life ahead of you.'

Rawlings gave a grim smile. 'I was also extremely ambitious. I admit my motives were not entirely honourable, but I knew if I went through with the marriage, I would get huge help with my career as a journalist. Not very admirable, but I was right. Gerald had a great many connections in the newspaper world, and after we were married, I soon found myself in Fleet Street. He also gave me a handsome allowance and organised a flat in London, where I spent the working week, only returning to the Manor at weekends. It was all very agreeable. At the time, I was convinced I'd made a clever decision.'

Marnie was frowning, her feminist hackles rising. 'He must have known you weren't in love with her. Wasn't he at all worried about his daughter? It was such a risk.'

Rawlings shook his head. 'He was a shrewd man. I think he knew what would make her happy and recognised she'd make very few demands on me, which would suit me as well. In the settlement that was made, there were no real curbs on my freedom. The main understanding was that I should never cause her unhappiness, or a scandal, or ask for a divorce. If that happened, all financial support would immediately cease. I was always very careful to keep to his instructions to the letter. Of course, if Gillian had wanted a divorce that would have been different, but Gerald rightly surmised she never would.'

'It's all so bizarre,' Marnie said, 'almost Victorian.'

Rawlings looked at her and smiled. 'I know it must seem so to you, but it worked in a weird way. Gillian and I became good friends, and unlike many married couples, we never quarrelled. I was away all week, and very soon became a foreign correspondent and spent long periods abroad. This didn't seem to worry her in the least, the reason for this only becoming apparent later on. Nor did she pry into my private life. She was content with her home life, her horsey friends, and of course, the child. As for Gerald, he saw that his daughter was happily settled and he had a grandson, to whom he became devoted.'

Marnie thought for a moment. 'How did your mother and Stella take the news?'

'It came as something of a shock. They travelled down from Scotland for the wedding, which was a lavish affair in the Great Warley church – which by the way is worth a visit, a fine example of Art Nouveau and you'd like it. At the wedding reception, Gerald went out of his way to look after my mother and Stella, for which I was grateful. Afterwards, they returned to Scotland again, bemused by the whole affair. Billy also came to the wedding. He got very drunk at the reception as I remember.'

He stood up and said abruptly, 'That's quite enough for one night. I must return to my freezing cabin. It was good of you to rescue me, Marnie.'

'When do you get your new macerator?'

'It may take a couple of days.' He smiled. 'Don't worry. I've been in far worse situations.'

She handed him a key. 'I'm out every day for the rest of the week. Take my spare key and let yourself in if conditions get unbearable over there.'

'Has anyone ever told you you're a saint?' She smiled and gave him a friendly shove. He kissed her on the cheek and left.

Marnie started clearing up, and as she put the two empty bottles in the bin, she reflected that her wine intake had somewhat increased since the arrival of Rawlings.

Chapter Five

Late February, early March 2017

At the end of February, the snow arrived, giving the place a strange beauty. It was also eerily quiet, no birdsong or the noise of boats going up and down the river. The willow tree, on the opposite side, took on the appearance of fine white lace and the river ran grey and cold between the two snowy banks. A solitary heron took up position under the willow, standing without moving for hours. Occasionally Rawlings would look up from his work, and the heron would still be there. He marvelled at its patience and missed the bird once it had finally flown away. Otherwise, there were no distractions. His new macerator was fitted, and all was back to normal in the plumbing department. He hardly moved from his desk chair, except for the occasional trip to Mr Patel at the newspaper shop. Isobel had given him instructions on how to arrange a food delivery. This marvel of modern living meant he rang in his food order on a Monday and it duly arrived the next day. It was a great relief, as carrying back food, particularly heavy bottles of wine, would have ended up with his leg giving him grief. He considered getting a car, but for the moment it wasn't necessary, something for when the weather improved.

It only took two months for him to admit he was not enjoying writing the book. The fact that it hadn't proved much of a challenge was its only advantage. The task was straightforward enough: to refer back to his coverage of each war, make a selection, and then bind it together into some sort of personal memoir. Selection proved to be the main problem. There was certainly no shortage of material, both archive and his own, but in the end, would anyone be interested in all this regurgitated stuff? He doubted it. The country was deluged by present news, twenty-four hours a day. Why would anyone want to remember the horrific events of the recent past? In any case, a few pages in, he had concluded he was writing the wrong book. It would've been far more interesting to investigate the lasting effects that witnessing these horrific events had on the war correspondents who wrote about them. A couple of his friends weren't coping with their lives at all well, and one, last year, had committed suicide. There were, of course, those who managed to return to stable jobs in the UK, some as newsreaders on television, or even chat show hosts, work that was far removed from the grim reality of what they'd witnessed. Personally, he'd never wanted the television work, even as a correspondent in war zones, preferring to set down his reports in print. He disliked talking to cameras. It left him wondering if the correspondents, who now reported from the safety of the studio back home, were still plagued by their war experiences. Their seeming complacency, as they delivered the news, left him bewildered. Shocking images of war and its inevitable aftermath were crammed between news on Brexit, a fresh Trump scandal, some royal announcement, or the latest sporting event.

He stood up and gave his leg a shake. Was it his imagination or was his other leg starting to give him pain we well? It might be a different sort of gip, but definitely there, and he'd noticed the ankle had begun to swell up after walking. Once this damned memoir was written, he'd take himself back to the last specialist, a good man and he liked him, although his warning of impending arthritis had filled Rawlings with gloom. He just had to get the bloody book done. Christ! He still had to tackle Kosovo, Iraq, and Afghanistan and that could well bring his nightmares back.

He sighed, walked over to the window and noted his heron was back.

★

Marnie was also occupied with her thoughts. Since Rawlings had revealed the story of his early life, she'd felt perplexed. The facts had been skimmed over so glibly. Had it really been that easy? How could a marriage, based on such shallow foundations, possibly work? It was like those arranged marriages you heard about in India and Pakistan. But they worked out, didn't they? Then there was the child. Now there was no sign of him or mention of a present family or home. What had become of them? Rawlings seemed isolated and alone, and from the little she'd already gleaned, there was bitterness and anger that lay just below the surface. And what about that girlfriend Isobel had mentioned? Maybe she figured in the next incident.

She looked again at the sketch she'd made of him and was disturbed by what she saw. Unintentionally she had drawn a face that appeared ravaged by suffering, but it wasn't a true picture. He was attractive, amusing and charming. Marnie put her sketchbook down and chided herself for this pre-occupation. The main part of the Rawlings' story was surely yet to come and maybe would provide some of the answers. Meanwhile, she just had to curb her impatience and live with the enigma.

She was about to set off for the school when her telephone rang. It was Isobel, sounding so distressed and agitated Marnie found it difficult to make out what she was saying. Finally, she gathered that the problem was Rose, who was in a locked room and refusing to answer. Isobel thought they should break down the door and could Marnie fetch Rawlings, as this might be a man's job?

With some trepidation, Marnie went over to the boat. Her knock was answered by a surly,' Who is it?' She explained the little she knew and with not very good grace, he threw on a jacket, and they set off for the house.

Outside Rose's door, Isobel and Maria were waiting for them. Isobel thanked Rawlings for coming and explained that she'd received a call earlier, from the nursing home of Rose's mother. The woman had suffered a minor stroke, and they thought Rose should be told. Maria was sent upstairs with the news but could get no answer from Rose's room. Isobel then tried, but there was not a sound from inside.

'I am fearful about what might have happened to her,' she said.

'You presumably don't have another key for this door?' Rawlings inquired, and Isobel shook her head.

'Where the hell is Lydia?' Marnie sounded angry.

'She's away doing a caring job, I've called her, and she's driving back, but it will take her about an hour, and I do feel we should take some action now.' Isobel turned to Rawlings. 'Would it be possible to put your shoulder to the door and try and force it open?'

That, Rawlings thought grimly, would do his leg no good at all, let alone his shoulder, but he did give it a couple of tries. To no avail; the door was solid oak.

'We could try and find Jake,' Rawlings suggested, 'he is a good deal stronger than I am. But frankly, it seems to me this is a job for the ambulance men. If something has happened to her, the best place for Rose is in the hospital as soon as possible.'

Isobel nodded. 'You are right, of course. I probably should have done this earlier.'

She left to make the call downstairs, and Maria went back to the kitchen. Marnie and Rawlings remained on the landing either side of Rose's door. Marnie put her ear to the door but reported she could hear nothing.

'Not quite the peaceful existence I imagined when I arrived on this mooring,' Rawlings remarked laconically. Marnie started pacing up and down.

'I could murder Lydia. How could she land Isobel with this problem and then ignore it? It was obvious to all of us that Rose was an accident waiting to happen.' She looked at Rawlings. 'Do you think she's dead? Or maybe it's suicide. How absolutely ghastly. We don't need another death in this house…'

Rawlings put a stop to her speculations. 'Wait for the ambulance men to sort it out, Marnie. It won't help Isobel if you work yourself up into a lather.'

Marnie leant against the door, and he could see she was distressed. Was this partly out of guilt? He was feeling the same; she was right; all the signs of a crisis had been there.

'I don't think we should put all the blame on Lydia,' he said, and Marnie looked at him in surprise. He went on, 'I overheard her talking to Rose, trying to explain that she had to change her ways if she was to continue to stay with Isobel. Rose absolutely refused to listen or take any advice. In fact, she became hysterical. It was obvious Lydia was trying to deal with a mentally unstable woman. Rose should have been in care. Maybe now…'

His observations were cut short as Isobel came back up the stairs and told them the ambulance was on its way, 'I won't forgive myself if it would have helped to call them earlier.'

Thankfully it didn't take long for the ambulance to arrive. Maria let them in, and Rawlings was relieved to see two burly men coming towards them. Isobel briefly explained the situation to them, adding that Rose, who was temporarily staying in the house, had an eating disorder. It didn't take long for the two men to get the door open.

Marnie, recalling it later, thought it resembled a scene from a horror movie. The room had a terrible smell of vomit which made her gag. There were boxes, shopping bags and piles of paper everywhere, with hardly room to move around. In one corner there was a table with some sort of food machine or liquidiser on it — bowls of unappetising liquid lay half-eaten. But their eyes were all drawn to the middle of the floor where Rose lay, in a foetal position, on some old rags. She was scantily clad, only in a shirt and pants, like a skeleton in clothes.

They watched in shock as one of the men searched for a pulse.

'She's alive, Lady Mallinson, but her pulse is very faint. We'll have to get her to hospital as quickly as possible.' Isobel nodded and then followed the stretcher down to the ambulance. Rawlings shut the damaged door as best he could.

'I don't know about you, but I could do with a coffee, or maybe something stronger.'

Marnie, still in shock, led the way to the kitchen. Maria was given a brief account of what had happened, tactfully leaving out the more lurid details, and instructed to make coffee. The two of them then sat at the kitchen table in silence. After a while, Isobel returned and joined them. She looked pale and shaken.

'I think you need a brandy,' Rawlings said. 'And I could do with one too.' She nodded and pointed to the next room. He returned with two filled glasses. 'Drink this Isobel; it's purely medicinal. Do you want some Marnie?' She shook her head.

Maria tactfully took herself off to do her chores, leaving the three of them sitting at the table. Isobel was the first to speak.

'I had no idea things were so bad. If Rose's mother hadn't had a stroke, we wouldn't have discovered her until it was too late.' She sipped her brandy and after a moment added, 'What a terrible thing to have happened. I just had no idea,' she repeated and then her voice faced away. Marnie thought grimly that whatever Rawlings said, it was still mainly Lydia's fault. It was she who'd dumped Rose on them in the first place, but there was no point in saying this to Isobel now, who was obviously in shock.

'What will happen to her?' she asked.

Isobel thought for a moment and then spoke slowly as

if trying to gather her thoughts. 'I think Rose must now be taken into care once she leaves hospital.' She gave a sigh. 'It fills me with guilt to say this, but it will be a relief. As soon as Lydia gets back, she'll have to go to the hospital and fill in all the details I was unable to give.'

Marnie said hotly, 'It's absolutely out of the question for Rose to return here. You've been through enough.'

Isobel gave a wan smile. 'Well, I'm sure they wouldn't allow her to, Marnie. My feeling is she'll need treatment, and then supervision for her condition and that will take a good while.' She thought for a moment and added, 'I think that room will need to be completely cleared out and then I will have it re-decorated.' Marnie nodded grimly in agreement. It seemed the only solution, in view of the terrible scene they'd just witnessed.

'I'm sure Lydia can organise the clearing out,' she said severely, 'and I would be happy to help with the decorating.'

'That's a kind thought, but I will get in a firm of decorators.' Isobel was firm on this. 'I have been thinking about modernising that bedroom for some time. It might also be a good moment to put in a bathroom...' her voice trailed away once more. She looked utterly exhausted.

Rawlings stood up, and Marnie joined him. 'Get some rest Isobel; this has been a horrible shock for you. He kissed her on the cheek. 'Let me know if I can do anything.'

As they walked back down the garden, Marnie commented grimly, 'That was awful. I truly thought we'd find her dead.' Rawlings nodded. He'd thought the same. Marnie now looked at her watch. 'Oh God, I must ring the school. I am hopelessly late.' She looked at him, 'Sorry to have interrupted your work.'

He gave a short laugh, 'Don't worry. Emergencies are justified.' He started to limp back to the boat and called out, 'We must do another supper soon Marnie. My turn.'

Once returned to his desk, Rawlings found he was unable to settle and felt discombobulated. There was no other word for it. The morning's events had thrown him into a turmoil, and he didn't understand why. Over the years he'd witnessed endless terrible scenes; dead bodies and parts of bodies, women and children horribly burned, mutilations, torture. Why should the sight of Rose's curled up skeletal body upset him so much? It wasn't as if he even knew her. Where was his usual air of detachment which had always served him so well? He was also a little shocked by Marnie's reaction. She had maintained her fury and criticism of Lydia, even though he'd tried to explain that Rose had been impossible to deal with. Was she jealous of Lydia's relationship with Isobel? Surely not. Marnie had been a friend for far longer. No, his instinct told him that Marnie was unforgiving to those she thought had done wrong. And this would appear to stem from the past in some way – a past he'd like to know more about. It had obviously left her with a great deal of anger and bitterness, although in the main she kept this hidden. He reached for a cigarette only to find the packet empty. Damn and blast. He stood up. Maybe a trip to the paper shop in the cold air might do him good.

Never quite sure if there was ice just below the surface of the melting snow, he made his way carefully, his progress slow. As he neared the shop, he had the second shock of the morning. The window and glass door had been badly smashed, and cardboard and black tape were evidence of a recent repair. Mr Patel stood up at he entered.

'Whatever happened to your window and door?' Rawlings inquired.

'We had unwelcome visitors yesterday, Mr Rawlings sir,' Mr Patel answered with a certain irony. 'Some young men decided to smash up our shop. They brought bats and were shouting, "Pakis go home", which is a very inaccurate statement as we come from India. It was a most unpleasant incident.'

Rawlings felt concern, along with mounting anger. 'My dear fellow, I'm so sorry. Were you or your family hurt?'

Mr Patel shook his head. 'No, no, although my poor wife Beata is most upset. My family have been here for over sixty years Mr Rawlings sir, so we are puzzled as to why should they say all this now?'

Rawlings thought he knew the answer, it was bloody Brexit, but all he said was, 'Mr Patel, I am shocked that this should happen to you and so very sorry. Have the police been?' 'Yes, they have been,' the man shrugged, 'but there is little they can do, we know that. They tell me I must install cameras.' He sighed. 'I have insurance and all will be put to rights.' Then added, 'The most sad thing is that they took my son Sunil's new bicycle. It was outside while he had his tea in the back. He'd only had it for one week. It was a birthday present and was not insured, which is very bad. He is most unhappy.'

Someone entered the shop, and Rawlings called out, 'I'll be back.' He walked, as briskly as he could, up to the cashpoint at the garage and took out £100. He asked the man at the till for an envelope which was kindly provided. Rawlings walked back to the shop. He purchased his cigarettes and then handed over the envelope.

'Mr Patel, you are not to refuse this. I can well afford it. I am ashamed of the way you have been treated, and this is small recompense. I hope it will go some way towards getting your son a new bicycle. Tell him to buy a padlock for it as well.' With that, he left the shop, leaving Mr Patel too stunned to speak.

As he passed the boathouse, he noticed the light was on, so he knocked and went in. Marnie was sitting on the floor, in front of the log-burner, wrapped in a brightly coloured shawl over an even brighter long robe.

'I gave up on school and am now drinking hot chocolate as comfort food' she said. 'Would you like one?' He shook his head, sat down and relayed what had happened, his anger spilling over.

'What a horrible country we've become. Bloody Brexit. I don't want to live in bloody Britain anymore. We've become mean-spirited and insular…' He sat hunched miserably in the chair. Marnie watched him, alarmed. It wasn't that she didn't agree with him, but his reaction seemed so extreme. It was apparent he needed something to calm him down. It was only early afternoon, but what the hell. She got up and poured him a glass of the brandy left over from Christmas. He took it and gave her a rueful smile.

'I'm sorry. I didn't mean to come in here and vent my anger.'

Marnie resumed her place in front of the fire. 'As it happens, I agree with you. Brexit has had a terrible effect on the whole country. It's split families, communities, young and old. And worst of all this terrible xenophobia has crept in. Poor Maria and Paul have been on the receiving end of that, shouted at by complete strangers and told to go back to their own country. At first, they were so upset they considered leaving. It was Isobel who persuaded them to stay, assuring them it was only a few right-wing bigots who thought like that, adding quite truthfully, she couldn't do without them.' This was said with a smile, and the tension in the room began to ease.

Rawlings finished his drink and left soon after that. Turning up all his radiators, he sat at his desk, determined to get some work done. He opened up his laptop and started a new page, even managing to type in 'Kosovo'. But there his good intentions ended. After staring at it for a while, he decided it was not the day to start in on that particular ordeal, the nightmare that was Sarajevo. He thought again of the attack on the Patel's shop. Good God, if things went on like this in Brexit Britain, who knows where it would end up. Maybe not civil war, but a split country all the same and that was always a dangerous situation. It was all very depressing.

He opened a bottle of wine, put on the Bach' cello suites and lay on his daybed, watching the sun slowly sink in the sky. The white landscape was soon bathed in a rosy glow, and Rawlings closed his eyes and gradually dozed off.

Chapter Six

April 2017

Three weeks passed without further interruptions. March had slipped into April, and there were signs of spring everywhere. The willow tree had become a vibrant lime green and daffodils were out under the chestnut trees. Rawlings progressed with his work and made only brief forays outside his boat. During one of these, he finally made the acquaintance of Lydia. His first thought was that she looked like a female version of Wellington, with her hook nose and stern expression. Marnie had complained she always talked to people as if she were addressing a public meeting. Her voice was certainly loud, deep and precise. He couldn't make out her age, probably late forties or early fifties? He met her by the dustbins, which seemed to be the general meeting place for the residents of the house. After making the introductions, he inquired about Rose.

'She's making as much progress as can be expected at this stage,' came the clipped reply. 'Eating disorders such as hers are notoriously difficult to deal with. It's a relief that the Social Services are now, at last, taking her plight seriously. I am only sorry that Lady Mallinson should have been put through such an unpleasant ordeal. I didn't realise the gravity of Rose's multiple problems until it was too late. I blame myself for the terrible shock you all endured.' She looked at him. 'I believe I have to thank you as well, Mr Rawlings, for your help that morning.'

Rawlings shrugged. 'Unfortunately, there was very little I could do. The door of that room was solid. It took two hefty ambulance men to break it down.'

Lydia became defensive. 'I shall, of course, be reimbursing Lady Mallinson for the damage.'

Rawlings said tactfully, 'I think Isobel was quite pleased to have an excuse to re-decorate. I see the builders are there already.'

With a terse nod, Lydia departed. Rawlings sighed, thinking that could have gone better. Reflecting on this encounter later, he was not entirely sure he would want Lydia as his carer during the dying moments of his existence. Rather like Oscar Wilde's wallpaper. It was evident she was very efficient at her job, but to die with Lydia ministering to him? He would prefer to rely on morphine and whisky when his time came.

A few days later, he set out, with some reluctance, for London. As he passed the boathouse, Marnie was coming out.

'Good heavens Rawlings, you're looking very smart. Where are you off to?'

He explained he was off to the station and then to London. Marnie had noticed his limp was getting worse and been waiting for a tactful moment to suggest he used a stick. Now all she said was, 'I'll give you a lift. I pass the station on my way to school.'

He thanked her, and they walked to where her small Citroen was parked. Climbing in was difficult; he barely had room for his legs. When they reached the station, she said briskly, giving him no time to argue, 'Text me when you are on your way back, and I'll come and collect you.' Before he could reply, she slammed the car door and drove off. He sighed and tried to get some feeling back into his legs, making a vow to buy a car of his own.

It was early evening by the time he returned, exhausted and actually relieved to take up Marnie's offer. She noted with some amusement he'd bought a stick and commented on it.

'It cost a small fortune, from a shop in Jermyn Street,' Rawlings grumbled. 'I'm sure I could have found a cheaper one, but my leg was giving out, and I required an immediate remedy.'

They reached the house, and Marnie suggested he come in for a drink. He hesitated, then found he had no reason to refuse.

'How was London?' she asked once they were settled.

Rawlings sighed. 'I used to love London, but today I could only see its faults. It appeared noisy and dirty. My overall impression was a city in stress. Everyone looked downright miserable. My first journey on the tube was bloody awful. It was packed, and nobody seemed to notice I was struggling. On the return journey, it was equally full, but now, with the acquisition of a stick, I was immediately offered a seat. I should have purchased one sooner. Vanity, I suppose. I couldn't face up to the fact that I am old and crippled.'

'What nonsense,' Marnie said reprovingly. 'Stop feeling sorry for yourself.' She quickly changed the subject. 'What were you doing in London?'

'I had to see my agent first, rather a grand fellow, an old Etonian and doesn't let you forget it, goes by the name of Jolyon Jordan-Smith.' He paused, 'That's a bit unfair, he's a good agent as agents go, and he also treated me to an excellent lunch at the Wolseley in Piccadilly. Although an expensive joint, it was heaving, not a table to be had. Jolyon informs me that a table has to be booked well in advance.' He gave a hollow laugh. 'So much for austerity Britain.'

'Oh, there are still plenty of the rich about; it's just the poor that have got poorer.' Marnie said grimly and then asked, 'Was he pleased with your book?'

'I only gave him the outline and first two chapters. He thinks he's found someone interested in making it into a documentary and seemed very overexcited by this.' He shrugged. 'These offers come and go. I'll believe it when the contract is signed.'

'What did you do after lunch?'

'I went to the Royal Academy. Even that had changed,' he grumbled. 'It was packed. You couldn't get near the pictures for damned tourists. I gave up pretty soon and went to my last meeting of the day, which was with the family solicitor. By family I mean it was the firm Gerald used. The son has now taken over and has dealt with all the family legal stuff since.' He added grimly, 'He knows all the skeletons in all the cupboards. Today he had an extraordinary matter to put before me. I am to be my grandson, Felix's guardian in the unlikely event of the demise of his parents before me. It was a total surprise and a most unlikely request.'

'Why so unlikely?' Marnie asked. It seemed fairly logical to her.

'Because my dear woman, my son Hugo and I don't

speak to each other, unless absolutely necessary. I pointed this out to Graham, who told me rather bluntly there was nobody else to ask, which was not very flattering. It seems Hugo has no other relations still alive, apart from my sister who is old, decrepit and who he's never met. His wife has only one sister, and she's emigrated to Australia. So, I'm the only option they have. Graham tells me that Hugo and Susanna are a power couple, whatever that may mean, who travel abroad a great deal, so the appointment of a guardian is apparently necessary. Given that information, it seemed stupid to quibble, and I duly signed all the papers, giving Isobel's address and telephone as the contact and left as soon as was politely possible.' He tapped his forehead. 'I must let her know this tomorrow.'

Marnie had a great many questions she wanted to ask, but realised now was not the time. Rawlings was in a thoroughly grouchy mood, tired and probably in pain from all that walking. She removed his empty glass and taking the hint, he stood up and hobbled to the door.

'I believe next week is Easter, come to supper and I will cook you a shoulder of lamb.'

★

Easter turned out to be a beautiful, sunny weekend. Rawlings took over a bunch of lilies to Isobel in the morning. She was delighted with this gesture and invited him in for a glass of sherry.

'I was meaning to let you know Rawlings, an old friend of mine is coming to stay next week. She's an actress, Fanny Markham, and I'm only warning you because she is given to delivering the odd soliloquy or sonnet in loud tones at the bottom of the garden. It rather alarmed Marnie the first time she heard her.' Rawlings smiled at this, and Isobel added, 'She has just been on a long tour of *"Pygmalion"*, playing Mrs Higgins I believe. It has left her exhausted, so I invited her to stay with me for a few days' rest. You might warn Marnie about Fanny's arrival when you next see her.'

Rawlings nodded. 'I am seeing her tonight as a matter of fact. She's coming over for supper.' Isobel's eyebrows went up questioningly at this and Rawlings sensed a slight air of disapproval, but she made no comment. In view of this, he decided this was not the moment to ask Isobel for more information about Marnie's past.

At the appointed hour, Marnie arrived, carrying the usual carpet bag. She was looking resplendent in a dark blue kaftan with elaborate embroidery.

'You're looking VERY magnificent Marnie,' he said as she made her entrance, 'where on earth did that garment come from?'

She explained that a friend had brought it back from a trip to one of the more obscure parts of South America. 'I do like clothes that are both decorative and comfortable,' she said and delved into her bag, bringing out a box of painted eggs. 'These are hard-boiled eggs and edible,' she explained. 'Keep them in the fridge, and you can have them as a snack.'

Rawlings looked shocked. 'They look far too decorative to be destroyed and devoured.'

Marnie laughed. 'Nonsense. It's just a habit with me to paint eggs at Easter.'

It was something of a surprise to her that she now felt

relaxed in his company, even if it had taken three months. She'd quickly learned to take advantage of the sunny moods and make herself scarce when she could see the black clouds descending. She refused to admit that there was any more to this than the odd supper when his writing allowed him to take a break. But there had just been the odd moment when he had fixed her with those grey-blue eyes that she had felt something which she wasn't yet able to define. And of course, she was fascinated by his revelations.

'Wonderful smells coming from the kitchen,' she commented.

'It should be ready in half an hour, plenty of time for a drink first.' He sat down in the opposite chair and informed her of the imminent arrival of Fanny.

Marnie laughed. 'If you think I wear outlandish clothes, wait until you see Fanny. She adds in scarves and beads as well. She's also given to doing vocal exercises very loudly at the bottom of the garden.' Rawlings smiled and told her Isobel had warned him about this.

Later, when the meal was over, and they were once more settled back in their chairs, Marnie, desperate for a further instalment of his story, gently prompted him. Rawlings had anticipated this and once again felt tempted to refuse, but in all fairness to her, he'd been stupid enough to embark on the bloody thing in the first place, so he was really obliged to finish it. While he was considering the best way to continue, Marnie, unable to contain herself, burst out, 'Did your marriage continue to work out?'

He smiled. 'Yes, in some strange way I think it did, probably rather better than most marriages. After Hugo was born, I spent little time at the Manor. As I told you, I was ambitious and keen to climb up the journalistic ladder. Gerald had secured me a job on a reputable paper, and I certainly put in the hours. This meant I stayed in London all week, only occasionally returning on Sundays. Gillian didn't seem to mind at all. The one who probably did suffer was Hugo. I was an absent father for those early years.'

'Do you regret that,' Marnie interrupted.

This produced a sigh. 'In some ways, I do. Our relationship never really recovered. At the start, I like to think I tried to bond with the child, but quite honestly, he already had a doting mother and an even more doting grandfather and didn't need this outsider, whom he was informed was his father. He seemed to resent me from the start. I was superfluous. His every need was paid for by Gerald, and he was surrounded by people who gave him whatever he wanted. I tried to tell Gillian he was becoming spoiled, but she wouldn't have it. I did make an effort to be a good father to the boy initially, but after he hurled a rather expensive birthday present across the floor, I gave up. In all honesty, I didn't find him difficult to ignore, and it may sound shocking, but I was perfectly happy to get on with my life and not give him further thought. I knew he was well cared for, going to the best schools, his holidays filled with activities – skiing in winter, exotic places in summer. He didn't need me. It was always accepted that I had to be away, and frankly, it was a relief.'

'What about your relationship with Gillian?'

'That continued in the same way. I returned to the Manor less and less. Gerald once asked me if all was well with the two of us, and I answered him with an honest, 'yes.' As I say, we didn't argue; it was like having a very placid and pleasant friend. She made no demands on me physically. Almost from the beginning, we had separate rooms. I once asked her if she'd like more children and she was adamant that she wouldn't. I know she hadn't enjoyed her pregnancy or giving birth. It took some time for her to recover, but once she did, she happily divided her time between Hugo and her horses. Her horsey friends were always polite and charming, but I felt like an alien, our worlds were so different. It was easy for me to escape for long periods of time and pursue my career. I think in some strange way Gillian was proud of my work. She was always telling her father and friends about my latest exploits. Otherwise she never once asked me about my life, apart from what I was working on. She must have known I wasn't celibate, but this didn't seem to worry her in the least.' He stood up, filled their glasses, then went to the window and stared out.

'My heron's back,' he said. 'It is the most extraordinary bird. Just stands quite still for hours on end.'

Marnie joined him. 'I don't know if it's the same one, but there always seems to have been a heron on that bank, for as long as I can remember.'

They returned to their seats, and she wondered if that was the end of the disclosures for the evening, but he suddenly said, 'I think this situation would have continued forever had I not met Mia...' He stopped. 'But that was later.' Sipping his wine, he frowned as if searching his memory. 'I went through the Iraq war first, and that was the time I really learned my trade as a war correspondent.'

'Did you always work for the same paper?'

'No. After my first major article, on the Falklands war,

which had attracted some attention, I was offered a job on the foreign desk of another paper which was a definite step up.' He chuckled. 'I used to stare at the huge map of the world upon the wall, which was covered in pieces of paper where all the current conflicts were happening, wondering where I'd be sent. Soon after my arrival, I was offered my first job as a foreign correspondent in a war zone.' This produced a smile. 'I have been extremely lucky in both my editors. Where some would have seen me as trouble, they both allowed me the freedom to write the way I wanted, and cover aspects of wars that others didn't. My reports would cause mutterings from the establishment, and some of the bloody politicians got extremely hot under the collar, but on the whole, the paper stuck by me. I doubt I would have the same freedom now, and it did become increasingly difficult with each war…' he paused again.

'It's odd,' Marnie said, to break the silence, 'but it's easy to forget about these wars. The Iraqi conflicts seem to merge into one. When did the first one start?'

'1990.' Rawlings jerked himself back into action. 'George Bush Snr. and the blessed Margaret sent in coalition forces, in response to the Iraq invasion and annexation of Kuwait. Basically, it was about oil.' He looked at Marnie. 'More wine?' She shook her head, and he refilled his own glass, adding with a smile, 'If you want to know details of the war, you'll have to read my book. Suffice it to say I was actually in Kuwait when it was liberated. People forget, thinking the Allies did it all, but the Kuwait casualties far exceeded ours. After that, the Iraqis retreated along what became known as the 'highway of death' setting fire to 700 oil wells on the way.

'I remember that,' Marnie broke in, 'the pictures of the black smoke. The pollution alone must have been disastrous. The only other thing I remember is that American general, 'storming Norman' I think they called him.'

'Norman Schwarzkopf,' Rawlings gave an abrupt laugh, 'something of a character. I managed to interview him...' He looked at his watch. 'Marnie, if I am to tell you about the next important incident in my life, which you are so keen to hear, I'd better move on.'

Marnie noticed he was now gulping his wine rather than sipping. It was evident he wasn't finding these recollections easy, and she felt guilty for her persistence, but she had the distinct feeling that what he told her next, might be the piece of the story that would make some sense of what this man had become.

Rawlings, not for the first time, wondered why the hell he'd embarked on this. Marnie had made it difficult for him to refuse, of course, persisting like a bloody limpet, never letting go. He looked at her, waiting with expectation, urging him to peel back further layers of his life. Until now, it was something he'd steadfastly refused to do. The shrinks had tried but failed. Friends also had encouraged him to open up, but he hadn't. Yet Marnie, whom he hardly knew, had somehow managed to do this and he was at a loss to understand why he'd given in to it. Maybe it was the right time. Maybe it would help in some way.

'Sarajevo', he suddenly barked out. 'The Siege of Sarajevo was where the next incident happened. To quote Dickens, 'it was the best of times, it was the worst of times', and that was the great paradox of the situation. To anyone who didn't live through it, that might sound odd. I can only assure you that in the middle of the most horrific atrocities and suffering, there were great acts of bravery and sacrifice. Friendships were made that outlived those terrible years. And there was humour too. Admittedly it was pretty black, but I remember we laughed as well as cried. We wouldn't have survived without it.' He paused and lit a cigarette.

'I arrived in the spring of 1993, nearly a year after the siege had started. Before this, I'd had to return home. Gerald was suffering from a heart problem and his health was causing some concern. I remember thinking as I set out for Bosnia, that I wouldn't see him again. I'd had great affection for the man. He'd always been very straight and fair with me…' He broke off.

'How old were you when all this happened?' Marnie held out her glass, and Rawlings refilled it.

'I must have been in my early forties because while I was back at the Manor, Gillian had her fortieth birthday do…' He stubbed out his cigarette and took a deep breath as if willing himself to go on. 'I arrived in Sarajevo by road, in a jeep that somehow managed to dodge the sniper fire. The airport by then was closed and didn't re-open for another two years. I was bloody lucky not to be held up at the border, always heavily guarded by the Serb fighters and my God they were fierce. One journalist, with a female companion, had an extremely narrow escape. He overheard the guard saying, 'Shoot the man, but keep the girl; we can rape her.' Luckily, he understood enough of the language to realise the danger they were in. He put his foot down and managed to get away.'

Marnie looked shocked and Rawlings, noticing, gave a hollow laugh. 'The siege of Sarajevo must go down as one of the worst war crimes of the 20th century. It lasted three times longer than Stalingrad and was a far more complicated situation. Most of the West did their best to ignore it, maintaining it was just a civil war. But it was more than that; it was a blatant act of aggression. The Serbs wanted a new Bosnian state, and no atrocity seemed too great to achieve that aim. They encircled the city in May 1992 and then proceeded to cut off all electricity, oil, food and medicines. If it hadn't been for a tunnel, running from under the airport, bringing in a trickle of supplies, the people would have quickly surrendered. As it was, the hardships were terrible. The prison camps were full, with the inmates being raped, starved and tortured.' He was talking quickly now. 'We journalists stayed in the Holiday Inn, which supposedly was protected by being clad in yellow.' He gave a hollow laugh. 'In spite of this, we were often hit by mortar fire. Several of the upper floor walls were blown away and exposed to the sky. We were always in danger from the snipers who kept up their continual bombardment. They even targeted the cemetery where people were burying their dead. On one occasion, they killed two small children who were at their mother's funeral. Many journalists were killed or injured. At the suggestion of the BBC's Martin Bell, we pooled our resources, so only a few of us risked our lives each day.

We existed on one meal a day, usually a disgusting watery soup and we didn't have baths for weeks on end.' His voice became angry. 'The journalists risked their lives every bloody day to get their stories out, and the West did nothing. Nothing! It wasn't until 1994 that NATO finally organised air strikes and that was mainly because of the untiring efforts of one politician, Paddy Ashdown.' He shrugged. 'On many occasions, my more visual descriptions of the horrors were edited out, as being too upsetting for the public. It was frustrating. We were risking everything to get to the truth and then the public was shielded from it...'

He stopped for a moment and shook his leg as if it were cramped. When he spoke again, his voice was calmer, although Marnie noticed he was no longer drinking, and his hands were clenched around the arms of the chair.

'I arrived into this scene rather late. Some journalists had been there from the beginning. If you want to know what it was really like to live through the entire siege, read Janine di Giovanni's book. She reported it all, but I digress. I arrived without my usual photographer. He'd decided to stay in London after we returned from Iraq. I asked around to see if there was a freelance photographer who'd be willing to work with me and I remember my friend Saul Berens saying with a grin, 'You could try asking Mia O'Keefe, but she's one hell of a tough cookie. Don't expect her to fall for your charms, Rawlings.' Undaunted by this, I decided to investigate more about her before I made my approach. I learned she was Boston Irish, early thirties, had quickly made a name for herself, was ambitious and didn't like to be tied down to one paper, or one person. She was also tough, brave and, as I was repeatedly told, didn't suffer fools gladly. She'd already had a sniper bullet in the top of her shoulder, which had been removed without anaesthetic.' He gave a humourless laugh, 'My approach was, therefore, both cautious and respectful. One evening I caught sight of her across the room, drinking with the male journalists. There were very few females in the hotel, and they mainly kept to themselves. Mia, on the other hand, seemed to prefer male company. She mingled in well. From a distance, she looked more like a man anyway, very tall and thin, with her hair hidden in a baseball cap and always wearing jeans and a bomber jacket.' He gave a laugh. 'I remember the shock when she first took off the cap and revealed her long blond hair. Our first conversation was brief. I introduced myself and asked if she would be interested in taking some photographs for me. She looked a trifle annoyed at having her evening interrupted and told me to meet her in the morning and discuss it then.' Rawlings allowed himself a brief smile. 'It certainly wasn't a *coup de foudre*, if that was what you were expecting. That came later.'

'She agreed to work with you?'

Rawlings nodded. 'She was interested in the same aspects of life under siege as I was. I quickly realised she was expert at her job; in fact, she was brilliant. For the first six months, our relationship was entirely professional. She liked the way I worked, and I was certainly impressed by her'… he paused, 'and that's how it would have continued if it hadn't been for one extraordinary day.'

He stopped, and for a while, they sat in silence. Marnie waited, unwilling to push him on. She could read nothing from his expression. Quite suddenly, as if he'd made up his mind to continue, he took a deep breath and plunged in.

'We'd been out on a particularly…' he hunted for a word, 'challenging assignment. News had reached us that an orphanage had come under fire and there were many wounded. At some danger to ourselves, the snipers were out in full force; we reached what was left of the building. One side had been completely demolished, and bodies were everywhere. One unrecognisable child had his head split in two, and his brains were splattered on the blackboard. I already anticipated my editor would reject my description of this scene, but I continued to make notes…' he added grimly, 'some of them will be included in my memoir.' Another pause, another deep breath. 'Mia quietly went about taking photographs, but her face was white as chalk, and I could tell she was in shock. We thought there was nobody left alive; we must have counted at least thirty bodies of children and two or three adults; some you couldn't tell… and that was when we found him. This small boy, almost hidden by the body of a larger boy who very definitely dead, but this child was breathing. We dragged him out, and Mia wiped his face, which was covered in blood. I have never seen eyes so big on anyone. This child seemed to be all eyes, but they were expressionless. It was a miracle, but he didn't appear to be wounded. He was painfully thin, like a small rag doll, not a young boy. Mia found a piece of chocolate and handed it to him. He took it from her but didn't eat it, just clasped it in his hand. It was one of the strangest things that I remember about that terrible day. The child was starving but didn't eat the chocolate. Maybe he was just too much in shock. I checked around what was left of the building, while Mia held on to the child. There was no other sign of life. As I returned to Mia and the small boy, I shook my head, and she understood. She told me the boy's name was Luka but had given no further information. He was shivering now, so we laid him in the back of our jeep and covered him with our coats before discussing what we should do with him. Our hotel would not be a suitable place for the child to stay. Mia then suggested a family she knew nearby. The father had been a professor at the

University but now stayed at home to look after his wife and two small children. He and Mia had become friends, and she often visited them. She hoped they might take Luka in. It was worth a try, as nothing else came to mind. Again, dodging the snipers we drove to the house. Thankfully the Professor let us in. He spoke good English and quickly took in what had happened. Taking Luka from Mia, he called for his wife. Little was said, but we understood they would do their best to look after the boy. This was good of them. Their house was constantly under attack, and each day was a dangerous challenge to find what little food they could. We promised to help with provisions when we could.'

Marnie did not comment as he lit a cigarette. She could see his hands were shaking. He didn't look at her as he went on, 'Mia and I went out to the jeep. I drove to the safest place I could find and then stopped. She sat with hunched shoulders, and I knew she was crying. I took her in my arms, and she cried herself out. After about half an hour, when she'd recovered enough, we returned to the hotel. Mia had blood down her shirt. Someone saw this and said, 'Grim day?' I nodded and then we went to our rooms to clean up.'

He stubbed out his cigarette, grinding it fiercely into the ashtray.

'That evening, it was particularly noisy in the drinking area. I grabbed my usual tipple and took myself off to a quiet corner, needing to be alone. Suddenly the chatter ceased, and the only sound in the room was that of the piano being played. Nobody to my knowledge had touched the old upright before that moment. It stood in the far corner of the long room. When I stood up, I saw that it was Mia who was playing…' Another long pause. 'It was the most beautiful sound I'd ever heard. I learned later it was a piece called *"Lieberslied"*, that Schumann had written for his wife as a wedding present. She not only played like a professional pianist but with so much feeling that I was overwhelmed. Later she told me she'd studied music, before taking up photography. I sat down, stunned, and then the tears came. In spite of all the terrible things I had witnessed over the years, this was the first time I had cried since I was a very young boy. The combination of the harrowing scenes at the orphanage and the pure beauty of the music was too much to bear. My body was wracked with sobs, and I couldn't stop. The playing came to an end, and there was a burst of applause, and then the usual chatter started up. It must have been minutes later I looked up to find Mia sitting opposite me. She took my hands in hers, and we just stared at each other.' He paused and then sighed. 'That was it. For the first and only time in my life, I fell passionately in love. Before Mia, I think my soul had been dehydrated. I'd had no deep feeling or affection for anyone.'

He stopped unable to go on and dropped his head in hands.

Marnie knew instinctively it was time for her to leave. There would be no more from Rawlings tonight. Thanking him for supper, she quickly let herself out and returned to the boathouse.

★

Two days later, taking advantage of the summer sunshine to paint her garden furniture, Marnie was interrupted by loud shouting. Rawlings stood on the path in front of the boathouse, obviously in a rage.

'Do you know what that bloody woman has done Marnie?' Without giving her time to reply, he shouted, 'She's called an Election! She apparently wants a proper mandate for Brexit. I can't believe it! Doesn't the stupid woman understand what has happened? Brexit has already taken the lid off this country. It's now a seething sewer of nationalism, racism, corruption and unashamed vileness. Believe me, the world has seen this and won't forget. This country may never recover.'

'Maybe, Mrs May won't get back in,' Marnie ventured nervously.

'Of course, she will,' he barked, 'that's why the bloody woman has done it.'

Marnie not wishing to say more while he was in his present mood, called out, 'Isobel's actress friend arrives today...'

'Well don't expect me to be sociable,' Rawlings replied angrily and stumped off up the path. 'I'm going to see the man at the garage. He thinks he's found me a car.'

He returned a couple of hours later in a calmer mood. Marnie looked up from her task and put down the paintbrush.

'Good timing. I've just finished. Would you like a drink?'

Rawlings produced a bottle, looking a little contrite. 'It's by way of an apology, for barking at you earlier.'

'There was really no need. I actually agreed with you.' She pointed at the furniture. 'We'll have to go inside as the paint on the chairs is still wet.'

He looked at her and laughed. 'You've got a lot of

white paint in your hair.'

'It's odd,' she said, 'I'm the messiest sort of painter when it comes to things like this, yet meticulously neat in my art classes. These chairs were looking very shabby and needed a coat.' Smiling, she said, 'My mother always used to say I was the only person she knew who painted to avoid dusting and I suppose that was true. I've always hated housework, such a waste of time.'

She took the bottle from him and went into the kitchen. 'I've made an egg salad. Shall we have it with the wine?'

Once they were settled, she exclaimed, 'God, I'm bushed, and hungry. Painting always gives me an appetite, although one shouldn't eat too many boiled eggs. My mother said they were fearfully binding.'

Rawlings looked at her, amused. 'Your mother seems to be much on your mind today. That's the second time you've mentioned her in the last five minutes.'

'Have I? I've no idea why. She made very little impression on me when she was alive. Most of the time, she just infuriated me. It's probably the only two things I remember her saying.'

They passed a pleasant hour, with no further reference to Brexit or the Election, and then Rawlings declared he had to get back to his work.

A day later, his morning writing session was interrupted by what sounded like an Indian war dance. He limped to the door and went outside. Looking towards where the noise was coming from, he saw a tall woman dressed in flowing robes with a long scarf around her head, evidently addressing the river, making loud wailing noises, with hands raised. The chanting ceased, and she now embarked on 'The quality of mercy' speech. Rawlings, now intrigued, walked over to the garden. She caught sight of him and stopped.

'I'm so sorry,' Rawlings said at once, 'I didn't mean to interrupt. I was actually enjoying the performance!'

'Darling boy,' she said with a throaty laugh, 'no performance this, merely my morning vocal exercises. We call it a warm-up in the profession.' She held out her hand and went towards him. 'You must be Rawlings. Isobel has told me about you.'

'And you must be Fanny Markham. Isobel has told me about you,' and he kissed the proffered hand, which made her laugh again.

'I'm sorry if I disturbed you. I understand you are writing a book. Very annoying to have someone wailing and spouting Shakespeare when you are trying to concentrate.'

Rawlings smiled. 'I can think of no more pleasurable way of being interrupted. I feel honoured to have been given a private performance.' She rolled her eyes at this.

'Isobel did tell me you were charming, and a wicked flirt. And now I've met you, darling; I can see she was right.' She turned to go. 'Oh, I nearly forgot. She said if I did see you, to say you are bidden to join us for drinks tonight, around 6.30.'

Before he could reply, she had wafted her way up the garden.

He reflected that he seemed destined to be surrounded by this ever-increasing regiment of women. Was this a good thing? Not knowing the answer, he returned to his book.

Chapter Seven

May 2017

Early in the month, Rawlings received a call from the garage saying a car had been found for him, and on his way back from collecting the vehicle, he called in on Marnie to tell her of this new acquisition.

'It's not as exciting as I might have liked, but it's a good price and an automatic, which I'm obliged to have now, on account of my wretched leg.' Marnie flashed him a look of concern.

'I'd noticed your limp was getting worse, do you think you should see a doctor?'

He shrugged. 'Not a lot they can do. Isobel offered to take me to see her man, but I don't think there's much point. The consultant warned me arthritis would set in and he was probably right. I have pain in the other leg now too. I expect to be in a wheelchair by Christmas,' he added gloomily.

'For goodness sake, Rawlings,' Marnie snapped. 'Stop being so hopeless and get yourself to see someone before it gets worse. I am sure there's something they can do.'

He gave her a grudging nod, 'You're probably right. Next time I go to London I'll return to my consultant and ask him for an update, so stop being so cross.'

She poured him a glass of wine by way of an apology. 'I meant to ask you about your evening with Fanny? Was she entertaining? Were you absolutely fascinated?' He took the glass from her and gave a smile.

'No, I wasn't "absolutely fascinated", but yes, she was certainly entertaining. I couldn't quite gauge how old she was; I'm pretty sure she's turned seventy, but she has enormous energy and of course that wonderfully strong voice.' He gave a chuckle, 'Her heavy make-up disguised most of the lines of her face, and she wore this great slash of violent red lipstick, which added to the whole dramatic effect. I don't usually like women who wear a lot of make-up, but it somehow suited Fanny. Mia never wore any, but then she had great cheek bones and didn't need it.' Marnie was a little surprised that he had brought Mia back into the conversation so easily but made no comment as Rawlings continued the description of his thespian encounter. 'I've only met a few from the theatrical profession. They seem to me to fall into two categories; the shy ones, who only come to life when performing a character, and then the Fanny's of this world who give entertainment with equal vigour, both on and off the stage. She was in full throttle that evening, scattering famous names like confetti, and embarking on some amusing anecdotes, hardly drawing breath. I enjoyed it, but as I left, I wasn't sure if she had aimed that performance at me, or Isobel, or just couldn't help herself. Maybe she just likes performing and being the centre of attention. It was an enjoyable experience for one night, but the thought of living with such a person filled me with utter exhaustion.'

Marnie smiled at this and then, taking advantage of his mentioning Mia, asked if Mia had ever played the piano to him again.

'Not in Sarajevo', he said, 'but afterwards, she would quite often. She had a large repertoire, ranging from Bach to Bartok, but I would never let her play the Schumann. It brought back too many unhappy memories…' He paused. 'After the Siege was lifted, we both needed a complete break, not from each other, but from war zones. For a short while, we did go our separate ways, due to family commitments. Gerald had died while I was away, and a visit home was overdue. Mia went back to Boston, to her family. She was also putting together a book of her Sarajevo photographs. She'd approached me about writing the narrative, but I told her the photographs spoke for themselves and needed no further explanation…' He broke off and for a while said nothing.

'God, I missed her!' he burst out. 'I didn't think it was possible to miss someone so much that it was an actual physical pain.' He gave a shrug. 'The atmosphere at the Manor didn't help. Gillian seemed to have shrunk into a depression and was finding it difficult to come to terms with her father's death. Hugo wasn't helping either. I tried to keep the hostile exchanges to the minimum, but he was outraged that Gerald had left me a large sum of money in his Will, still with the proviso that I remained married to his daughter.' Rawlings gave a sigh. 'Difficult for me to explain to Hugo that I had made a promise to his grandfather on this score, a promise which I had kept. Gerald was an honourable man and had indeed kept his side of the agreement, although I hadn't expected him to be so generous. But it wasn't as if either Gillian or Hugo were not well provided for. They were. Gerald had been extremely rich and also shrewd with his money, avoiding death duties by putting most of his wealth offshore in a family trust.' This produced a gesture of annoyance. 'Families and bloody money it always produces problems. Lord preserve me from it!' And he glowered into his now empty wine glass.

Marnie stood up and filled it. 'Did the thought of divorce occur to you now that you had met Mia?'

'I did consider the idea, but apart from anything else, it wasn't the moment to discuss it, not with Gillian in her depressed state. I was fond of the woman and didn't want to add to her suffering. In any case, Mia came from a devout Catholic family; marriage was out of the question, even with a divorce. We did talk about marriage once, in Sarajevo. It was in the dying embers of the Siege, after paying a last visit to Luka. The kid had made a surprising recovery since being dragged from the orphanage. I wasn't sure he'd ever get over the shock of that terrible day, but he now seemed happily settled. This was entirely due to the great kindness, generosity and no doubt sacrifice of that family. It was the sort of gesture that made the Siege bearable and kept alive some faith in the human spirit; specks of humanity found amid so much inhumanity.' He smiled. 'The Professor had taught him English. Luka was a bright boy and surprisingly quick at picking it up. Mia had paid him almost weekly visits and inevitably allowed herself to become attached. Luka was very affectionate with her, almost treating her like a second mother. I worried about this, knowing there wouldn't be a good outcome, and frankly I was dreading the moment of our leaving. One night she finally admitted she couldn't bear the thought of being parted from Luka. Was there a possibility we could adopt him? I had anticipated this question and knew there would be insurmountable problems. We were not a married couple, and we had no home together. That was just for starters. It was then that marriage was discussed. I told her I would be happy to ask Gillian for a divorce, but even then, there would be huge problems getting the boy out of the country. I think in her heart, she knew this to be true, but it didn't stop the terrible pain she experienced when the time came to say goodbye. It was an agony for me to watch. After we left Sarajevo, she never mentioned Luka again, or indeed the subject of having children. It was if she deliberately suppressed all her maternal instincts…'

There was a long silence after this. Finally, Marnie asked, 'But you were still happy together?'

Rawlings looked at her and smiled. 'You are such an incurable romantic, Marnie. Yes, I think we were happy together, right up until the end. But it wasn't a conventional relationship…'

Marnie couldn't let it go and persisted. 'Did Gillian know about Mia?'

'Yes. I told her once she was over Gerald's death. It was the first, and last time I asked her for a divorce.' He paused. 'Her reaction was somewhat unexpected, almost one of panic. She told me flatly I would forgo Gerald's settlement if I went through with it. I assured her the money really didn't matter to me, but I was curious why she should be so adamant about no divorce. I presumed she had a relationship with a married man and discretion was necessary. When I asked her about it, the answer was not what I expected…'

'She was in a relationship with a woman.' Marnie said, interrupting him.

'Was it that obvious to you?' Rawlings looked surprised. 'It wasn't to me.' He gave one of his abrupt laughs. 'I suppose at the time I had a definite idea of what lesbians should look like, and Gillian just didn't fall into this category. Stupid really, I should have guessed, because it was someone I'd known for a long time and I'd seen them together. Jenny Roberts was joint manager of the stables and lived in a cottage which was part of the stable block, not far from the main house. If I'd seen more of Gillian, or I'd been closer to her, I would have noticed their relationship. As it was, I just thought Jenny's continual presence was because she was important in her work with the horses.'

He leant back thinking about it. 'What was really puzzling was why divorce would have mattered so much to her. But it obviously did. She was normally such a passive and unemotional person. On this occasion, she became completely panicked, telling me that if it came out about her lesbian relationship, it would harm her father's reputation and ruin her relationship with Hugo. I really didn't understand this, or agree with her, but as it upset her so much, I let it go. I suppose deep down I did mind that Hugo put all the blame on me, for what seemed to him ill-treatment of his mother. After all, I had behaved honourably, so it seemed unfair, when in fact she was very happy with Jenny. It ruled out any possibility of me having a civilised relationship with my son.' He gave a deep sigh and stared into his glass. 'I've always tried to avoid scenes. The only rows Mia and I ever had, were about her damned religion. I failed to understand why it was perfectly all right for us to live together, but we couldn't be married because if I were divorced, it would be a sin! It made no sense. I also hated the idea that a few 'Hail Mary's' in the confessional were enough to have all your sins wiped out.' He sighed. 'In the end, we agreed to differ. To be fair, she didn't understand my being an agnostic either. I think if all married couples made a vow never to discuss politics or religion, there'd be far fewer divorces.' He knocked back his wine with a gesture of defiance.

Marnie laughed. 'You're probably right.' Refilling his glass, she asked, 'Where was it you lived together? Did you have a house somewhere?''

'The longest time we were settled was in an apartment in New York. We spent about six years there, on and off, between Sarajevo, the second Iraq war and then going to Afghanistan. The late nineties were a time of comparative peace. There were pockets of unrest, but nowhere that I was sent to. I was relieved to have missed the Rwanda Civil War, a couple of my friends who had witnessed all the atrocities and horrors in that bloody conflict were badly affected by it.'

He stood up, shook his leg and then sat down again.

'So, there we were together, living a fairly normal, settled life. Mia was involved in publishing her photographic journal. I kept reporting, mainly on life as an Englishman in America, notes from across the pond, you know the sort of thing. Those were quite dramatic years in the States. 1997 saw the death of Princess Diana, which made a huge impact on the Americans. They're a sentimental lot. The following year Clinton was impeached but got away with it. There always seemed to be plenty to write about. As long as I was occupied, I was happy. And there were diversions. Mia had a large circle of friends, mainly in the arts world. That was the time I met some actors, but she also knew painters, writers and musicians as well. Once again, I was the outsider, but content to listen. Mia was at her happiest when surrounded by these people. She and I were still haunted by the images of Sarajevo, both of us had nightmares, but gradually they began to fade a little, although never leaving us completely. Our lives might have gone on like that forever...'

He stopped, drained his glass and looked at Marnie.

'Ironically what brought it to a halt was a date, my birthday. My birthday happens to be on the 11th of September.' Marnie reacted to this but made no comment. 'In 2001, I was due to celebrate my 50th and Mia had arranged an evening celebration. Then 9/11 happened. Out of our window, we watched the whole horrific scene unfolding, or at least I did. Mia grabbed her camera and went down to where it was happening...'

'I remember that day.' Marnie broke in, 'Isobel called me over, and we watched it unfold on television. It seemed so unreal, like a film…'

Rawlings looked at his watch. 'Good God, my writing schedule has gone to pot. I only meant to come in and tell you about my car.'

He stood up, limped to the door, gave her an airy wave and was gone.

Marnie was becoming used to his abrupt departures, but she was intrigued by the fact that he no longer needed prompting to talk about the past. It seemed to happen naturally and, as with today, when she least expected it. Maybe he needed to get it off his chest. She presumed more wars were to follow, and then there would be that fatal accident. Would he talk about that? She hoped so.

★

May turned out to be a glorious month. For Marnie, it was her favourite time of year. After the long drab winter, the colours were vibrant again, and she now spent all her spare time outside, either planning her arts project or just with her sketchbook. The great willow tree on the opposite bank had become a brilliant lime green, and the river sparkled in the sun. The boats going up and down the river had also returned, and although there was a strict speed limit, many of them still went too fast causing smaller birds, coots and ducks, to bob violently up and down in the wash. Swans and Canada geese sailed calmly through the ripples, but she was convinced the swans gave the departing boats a look of annoyance.

One morning, she had a moment of pure joy when she saw a flash of blue darting among the reeds, which meant the kingfisher was back.

Little was seen of Rawlings for the next three weeks. Now that he had his car, he'd taken to visiting London at least once a week. He told her he went to catch up with his cronies at The Frontline Club. There he'd meet other correspondents and, as far as she could gather, drink the afternoon away. These days always seemed to leave him in a morose mood, and as he passed her door, he would make some angry comment about the way the election was going and then limp off.

A week away from the election result, she received a

cryptic message asking her to join him for the night of the results. She thought about it and then decided to accept, but with the proviso she would only be there for the start of proceedings. By then they would presumably know which way the wind was blowing. She certainly didn't want to sit through angry comments from Rawlings until the early hours of the morning.

Chapter Eight

June 2017

Marnie began to regret her decision to join Rawlings on Election night and thought up many excuses to stay away; exhaustion, food poisoning, even going away for the night. The latter seemed rather too drastic as she had absolutely no idea where she would go. She wondered what Isobel would be doing. They had never talked politics, and since the start of the election campaign, Isobel hadn't even mentioned it. She was well trained in diplomatic skills, and it had become a habit to keep her private opinions to herself. It was unlikely she would stay up all night to listen to the results. Lydia wasn't an option, even had she been around, but she was away on a cruise with a friend. A cruise! The news of this had surprised her. It seemed a frivolous choice of holiday for such a severe and serious-minded woman. Isobel had smiled when she mentioned this and explained that it was one of those academic cruises where lectures were given, and visits made to ancient sites in Greece and Turkey.

The only other solution for her election night dilemma was a party with one of the teachers at the school. An invitation had been given, but she had quickly declined saying she was bidden elsewhere. There was nothing for it.

An evening with Rawlings ranting and raving it was going to have to be. At any other time, she would have welcomed his company, but lately, his obsession with politics and Brexit had turned him into something of a bore. It was therefore with some trepidation she set out on June 8th to join him for the dreaded results.

On arrival, she immediately noticed he appeared to be in a surprisingly jolly mood and before she'd had time to get through the door, he exclaimed, 'Have you seen the exit polls, Marnie? What a slap in the face for those ridiculous people.'

Marnie handed over a bottle of wine and a quiche telling him it might be a good idea to soak up the alcohol if it were to be an all-night session. She didn't mean to sound severe, but he looked at her and said shrewdly, 'You're not enjoying this at all, are you? Don't worry. I won't insist on you staying. Just wait for the first few results and then I will release you.'

Marnie thought again how annoyingly charming he could be when he wanted.

He added, 'I am so unused to seeing British politics in action. It comes as a shock after having been away for so long. I apologise if I have been boring on about it. After tonight it can become a taboo subject.'

The television was on low. Rawlings poured a glass of wine and assured her nothing interesting would happen until after midnight. The usual pundits were airing their views, but they left them to it, Rawlings merely commenting that this result was going to be more exciting than he'd expected. There was something satisfying in seeing the polls proved so drastically wrong. A landslide had been predicted, and a landslide wasn't going to happen. Marnie smiled. He was almost treating it as a personal victory.

The conversation turned to other topics. She told him of Lydia departing on an academic cruise.

'That figures,' he said, adding, 'She's always struck me as a cross between a crusty university lecturer and a prison warder.' Marnie laughed.

'That's a bit harsh. To be fair, she was a rock through the last six months of Peter's illness. Isobel would have found it unbearably hard without Lydia's caring skills. She made it possible for Peter to stay at home right to the end, rather than go into a hospital. He was adamant about not wanting that.'

Rawlings was surprised by this sudden mellowing of Marnie's attitude towards Lydia, she had previously been so hostile, but again privately thought the woman's humourless expression would have been of little comfort to a dying man.

'How long have you known Isobel? Does your friendship go back a long way?'

'It does seem like a long time. I met her when she was a J.P. My husband was being given a restraining order.' She shrugged. 'Isobel was very kind to me at the time, and we became friends after that. When I lost my boat, I told her about the situation, and she and Peter immediately offered me the solution of the boathouse. They saved me really. She seemed unwilling to go on, and Rawlings decided to probe no further. They were silent for a moment, and then he glanced at the television.

'Hey up, something seems to be happening. I think the first results are coming through.'

For the next three hours, they listened with growing

astonishment. The polls, which had previously predicted a Conservative landslide, now looked utterly wrong. The government, at this rate, would be lucky to have any majority at all. As Rawlings gleefully pointed out, not for the first time that night, Theresa May had gambled on increasing her vote and instead was going to lose badly. As the long night wore on, the reporters became more excited and voluble, the experts shook their heads in disbelief over their statistics and predictions, and Jeremy Vine and Peter Snow leapt round their models of parliament explaining the changes that would now happen in the seating plan. At 3 a.m., a grim Theresa May, wearing heavy make-up to cover her blotched face, arrived at her constituency in Maidenhead. Marnie decided it was the moment for her to depart. There was something almost indecent, watching a person go through such humiliation, however much you may have wished for it. She left Rawlings to it.

The next morning, he rang her, earlier than she would have wished.

'Who'd have thought it,' he declared, a note of weary triumph in his voice. 'The Conservatives lost seventeen seats, so they are now short of an overall majority. What a mess. They'll call on May to resign, but my guess is she won't.' He gave his bark of a laugh. 'Someone described her as 'a dead woman walking.' I think that about sums it up. What a terrible mistake to call the election. That's what comes from greed and over-confidence. She is hoist with her own petard. On top of which she ran a dreadful campaign.' He paused. 'Sad about Nick Clegg though…'

Marnie interrupted his flow. 'Did he lose? I'm sorry to hear that.'

'Yes, he did. And he was one of the few good guys. It's going to be an interesting week. The knives are out for May.' And with that, to her relief, he rang off.

Marnie didn't see or hear from him again that week. Just as well. She was utterly sick of the whole subject; the election, Brexit and the entire stupid mess. Her only thought was that David Cameron had a great deal to answer for, and then she deliberately turned her mind to other things.

Isobel informed her that she had her sixteen-year-old great niece, Selena, coming to stay for a few days. Apparently, it was her half-term. Marnie had met Selena only once before. The teenager was trouble, totally spoiled and her many expensive boarding schools seemed to have no control over her whatsoever. Isobel had told her this wild behaviour had put a great strain on her parents, who had no control either. Her mother was desperate to have her out of London for half-term, where Selena would have spent her time going to unsuitable night clubs and parties, so poor Isobel had been chosen as the solution. The child, therefore, looked on this stay with her great aunt as another kind of imprisonment. Marnie felt annoyed. Although Isobel wasn't old, nevertheless a rebellious teenager was a stressful responsibility, especially one as devious and difficult as Selena.

She was soon to be proved right. The day after Selena's arrival, Marnie was on her way up the garden to see Isobel, when she was stopped in her tracks by an altercation coming from the direction of the terrace.

'I know staying here is not to your liking Selena,' this was Isobel's voice, 'but there is nothing that can be done about the situation and you will just have to put up with it for a few days more. Your parents are away, and they don't want you to be in London unsupervised.'

'I don't see why.' Selena's tone was petulant. 'After all, I am sixteen and perfectly capable of looking after myself.'

'I am quite sure you are,' Isobel said dryly, 'but that is not really the point. Your parents are mostly concerned with what you'd be doing with your time, who you'd be seeing, and where you'd be going. I think nightclubs and late parties were mentioned.'

'For goodness sake, it is my half-term. I'm meant to be enjoying myself, not shut away with a lot of old ladies for company.'

Marnie gasped at the rudeness. She certainly didn't consider herself 'an old lady', and you could hardly include Rawlings in that description. And it was so insulting to Isobel. How on earth was she managing to keep her temper?

'I am sure you could manage to find plenty to do while you're here Selena…'

'Such as?'

'Well, it's lovely weather. You could go for walks by the river, or lie in the garden and read.'

This produced an angry snort. 'What do you suggest I read? I tried that quaint newsagent yesterday. They hardly had any magazines in stock, not even a copy of *Vogue* or *Hello Magazine*.'

Isobel persevered. 'I could take you shopping. There are some interesting local shops.'

Another snort. 'It's hardly the King's Road.'

This produced a lull in the conversation, and then, ever patient, Isobel tried again. 'If you like, we could go out to lunch later.'

'Big deal.'

Marnie was so angry at this she could hardly refrain from marching up to the terrace and giving Selena a good slap. Isobel too had obviously had enough. Her voice became sharp.

'Well, you'll have to find something to amuse you, Selena, as you are here for three days and that is that. Now, as it's getting late, I'd be grateful if you'd take your breakfast things to the kitchen as Maria will be waiting for them.'

With very bad grace, the girl stood up, picked up her cup, saucer and plate and left the terrace. Marnie watched her go and decided it was definitely not the moment for a visit.

The following morning, she did manage to see Isobel, who admitted that Selena's visit was turning out to be a joyless struggle. The resentful girl was continually rude and uncommunicative and spent most of her time on her mobile, where she talked in a bewildering language to her friends. Isobel understood little of what she overheard but presumed it was an endless moan about her situation, or 'imprisonment' as she called it. She had tried everything she could think of, and now, having run out of ideas, she finally left Selena to her own devices.

The weather changed, turning out to be scorching hot, a brief Mediterranean heatwave, with cloudless skies and sun burning down all day. Marnie took advantage of her half-term to sit outside and work on her arts project. It was therefore irritating, just as she was happily settled, to have her peace shattered by her mobile. She was almost tempted not to answer it, but in the end, gave in.

It was Rawlings, sounding outraged. 'Marnie, there's a

Lolita-like creature lying on the lawn. Have you any idea who she might be? She is clad in very few clothes and is doing her best to distract Jake from his work. I would go out and rescue the poor lad from her clutches, but my strong inclination is not to get involved with this nubile nymphet.'

Marnie patiently explained who she was, but advised him to stay well clear.

Rawlings sounded exasperated. 'Well, I need to go to the Post Office later, and it might be difficult to avoid her. She looks as if she wants a diversion and teenagers with raging hormones are not in my line.'

This made Marnie laugh, and she told him not to be such an old bear. It was only after she'd returned outside that she remembered she had a parcel that needed posting and could save Rawlings the worry of a Lolita encounter. She grabbed the package along with her purse and went over to the boat. Calling out several times but getting no answer, she made her way to the rear deck. Rawlings was sitting with his back to her, bent over the table working. He was clad only in a pair of shorts. She noticed at once what a great tan he'd acquired in the last few days, but when he turned around, she received something of a shock. There was a long scar running down the entire right side of his body from just below his arm to the waist. She must have stood with her jaw dropped because he said, 'I see you're admiring my war wounds'.

She quickly recovered and stammered out, 'That's certainly an impressive scar.'

He gave a grim smile. 'Yes, I gather it wasn't only my leg that needed attention. This, however,' he pointed to his scar,' doesn't give me any grief, unlike the leg.' He looked at her, 'Were you wanting something, Marnie?'

She was beginning to wish she hadn't come. 'Yes, well, I'm sorry to have bothered you. It's just that I have to go to the Post Office myself and I thought I could save you the trouble…'

He burst out laughing. 'You wanted to save me from the clutches of the seductive Selena! It's very kind of you, but I decided to make a couple of alterations to the manuscript I'd been going to send, so the postal errand can wait until tomorrow.'

Later that day, the image of Rawlings' half-naked body came back to Marnie. She puzzled as to what could have caused such a massive operation. Was it shrapnel, broken ribs, a collapsed lung? Previously she'd thought it was only his leg that had been damaged in the explosion. With his clothes on he'd always appeared to be in great shape. Therein lay a paradox. Instead of revealing Rawlings as a physical wreck, that scar made him even more interesting and somehow even more attractive.

The next day, to everyone's relief, Isobel took Selena up to London to see a matinee and then thankfully handed her back to her mother. She reported to Marnie that Selena had sulked her way through the entire three days and only brightened up and became vaguely pleasant on the way to the theatre. She was disinclined to offer the child hospitality ever again; however, desperate the mother might be.

'Rarely have I taken such a dislike to anyone and never want to see her again,' she said with feeling, 'even if she is the only relation I have of that generation.'

Marnie saw little of Rawlings for the remainder of that month, apart from one brief encounter on the way back from one of his London trips.

'You're looking a bit haggard,' she said by way of a greeting, 'have you been ill?'

He shook his head and explained that his 'haggard' condition was due to a lack of sleep. The problem being, that if he did manage to nod off, he was beset by nightmares, but if he just lay awake, his mind became filled with disturbing images — some nights he just gave up lying in bed and went back to work. Marnie felt at a loss to know what to say to this. He smiled at her anxious expression. 'Don't worry, all will improve I trust when I finish the bloody book.'

With that, June moved without further dramas towards July. Marnie presumed that the calm routine of their lives was now re-established. Rawlings would finish his book, Isobel would recover from her recent visit, Lydia would return from her cruise, and all would be calm again. How wrong she was. On the last day of the month, an event occurred that would profoundly affect all their lives, especially Rawlings.

Chapter Nine

July 2017

It was a Friday. Marnie had just returned from her morning class and with no further teaching to do that day, decided to use the afternoon clearing up the boathouse, a task she had neglected of late. Her early progress was suddenly interrupted by a knock at the door. With a sigh, presuming it would be Rawlings, which would mean abandoning her spring clean and opening an early weekend bottle of wine, she flung it open. To her surprise, it was not Rawlings standing in front of her, but Isobel. And an Isobel looking ashen-faced and in shock. Marnie negotiated her past the hoover and the piles of paper on the floor, sat her down and fetched a glass of water. After taking a few sips, Isobel looked at Marnie with an anguished expression.

'Something terrible has happened, and I think I am going to need your help, Marnie.'

'Of course,' she said instantly, 'I'll do anything. You only have to ask.' She sat down and took Isobel's hand, which was very cold. Her voice was shaky.

'Two policemen arrived, just after lunch, asking for Rawlings.' Marnie's eyes widened, but she let Isobel continue. 'I asked them what they wanted to see him about, and then they told me.' She paused. 'Hugo and Susanna, his son and daughter-in-law, were killed late last night in a car crash.' Marnie gave an involuntary gasp. Isobel went on, 'It seems the car was going very fast on a minor country road, Hugo lost control going around a corner, and smashed into a tree. They both died instantly.'

Marnie sat in shock and could say nothing, and then a realisation hit her, and she burst out, 'Oh my God! There was a child. Rawlings is his guardian.'

Isobel nodded. 'That is precisely why the police came. The boy is in a prep school about an hour's drive from here. Rawlings now has to be told about this awful tragedy, and then he'll have to go and collect the child from the school and bring him back here.' She made an effort to pull herself together and said firmly, 'Of course the boy can't stay on the boat with Rawlings, it isn't suitable, and there isn't room. I think it best if we get Rose's old room ready for him. I'm just relieved I've had it re-decorated.' She looked at Marnie. 'I need you to go over and break the news to Rawlings. You seem to have struck up a good friendship with him and will know how best to do it.'

Marnie wasn't at all sure this was true, but in the circumstances, she didn't argue.

Isobel returned to her practical self. 'You had better persuade him to change into a suit, or wear a blazer, something less casual. We don't want him to give a bad impression at the school. Oh, and tell him he can take my car, it's bigger, and the boy will have a trunk and a lot of other stuff, you know, school equipment. I'm so sorry to land this on you Marnie. We all have to do what we can.' Her expression changed, 'That poor child, what a terrible thing to have happened. Does he have no other family?'

Marnie shook her head. 'Not in England. I believe there was mention of an aunt, but she lives in Australia. It's why they asked Rawlings to be the guardian.' She thought grimly that he didn't know the boy at all. How on earth would it work out, having the boy living with him? But there was no other solution, so this is how it would have to be. She stood up.

'I'll go over and tell Rawlings now. I have no idea how he is going to take it.'

Isobel handed over her car keys, along with the directions to the school. 'It won't be easy. Outwardly he will probably cope. Inwardly? Well, that's anyone's guess.'

As Isobel had predicted, Rawlings took the news quietly and made almost no comment, merely saying rather stiffly, 'Please thank Isobel for her help. I'll get changed and then leave for the school. I'll let her know when we are on our way back.'

As he climbed into Isobel's car and drove off, his mind was in a whirl. He thought back to the day he had signed the papers of guardianship. At the time he had suggested that he should at least meet the boy. He hadn't seen Felix since Gillian's funeral when the child was only five, and then it was a very brief encounter. Graham, the solicitor, had put a call through. Hugo had abruptly turned down the idea of his seeing Felix, saying it was so unlikely his services would be called upon, there was no need for it. His meaning had been clear, if unsaid. He had been an absentee father, and he would remain an absentee grandfather. But now the fates had spoken. Felix was to be saddled with a guardian who was a complete stranger to him. He wondered about Susanna's sister in Australia. She was also a guardian. Would that be a better solution for the boy? Obviously not immediately, but it might be a solution in the long run. His thoughts then turned to Hugo. Marnie was probably surprised he'd shown no emotion over the death of his only son, but to be honest, he felt none. There had never been a relationship between them, and his main feeling now was one of irritation and anger at the sheer irresponsibility of his behaviour. It was something of a relief he'd only killed his wife and not involved others in the crash. It was sad about Susanna, but he hadn't really known her either. From the little he saw of them together, they had struck him as a selfish, ambitious couple who'd probably neglected this son they'd dumped in a boarding school. Now he was left picking up the pieces and the care of this poor orphan. He shook his head, angrily. Hugo had always been spoiled, allowed to drive fast cars from an early age. As soon as he'd passed his test, he'd started collecting speeding fines. Rawlings suddenly glanced at the speedometer and noticed he was also driving too fast. He made a mental note to stay calm and slowed down.

How on earth was all this going to work out? Marnie had said that Felix could stay in the house with Isobel. Would the boy be all right with that, among complete strangers? And how would he occupy his days? Rawlings then thought about his own life. What would happen to his book, if he was busy looking after his grandchild?

The questions were still coming as he drove through the school gates. Parking outside the main building he realised that in his hurry he had forgotten his stick. Lately, he had come to rely on it. Standing for a moment, trying to regain his balance, he watched some small boys in the distance playing cricket. Otherwise, there was no sign of activity at all, and he presumed they were all in afternoon lessons. He glanced around at the grand building with its portico and immaculate grounds. It was somehow all so English.

A security man was standing inside the front door. On giving his name, Rawlings was directed to the headmaster's room. Outside, he took a deep breath, knocked on the door and went in. The headmaster, Mr Caxton, came from behind his large desk to meet him with a studied expression of sympathy. They shook hands.

'Mr Rawlings, it is good of you to have come so quickly. I just wish we could have met in happier circumstances. Please do sit down. My wife Linda will be here shortly with some tea. Or would you prefer coffee?'

Rawlings assured him tea would be fine. The headmaster settled back behind his desk and paused for a moment, obviously finding the situation difficult. He then eased back into the usual clichés.

'This is an appalling tragedy. We are all devastated by the news. I hope you don't mind, but I took it upon myself to break the news to Felix and told him you would be coming to collect him.' He looked at Rawlings for comment, but as none came, he cleared his throat and continued. 'I understand you haven't seen Felix for a long time, which is a great pity as he won't really know you – difficult for him at a time like this.' His tone was slightly reproachful, and Rawlings decided it was time to intervene.

'No, sadly I don't know the boy, something I will do my best to remedy as quickly as possible. Until recently, I have been working abroad, and I haven't seen Felix since my late wife, his grandmother's funeral. He must have been about five then. He's now…?' He looked questioningly at the headmaster.

'Felix is ten. He would be doing the entrance exam to his father's old school next year.' Mr Caxton broke off, looking suddenly uneasy. 'Of course, all that is now under consideration. Plans may, of course, change.' Pausing yet again he looked to see if Rawlings was going to say something, but as he still didn't, he went on, 'I had a long talk with your family solicitor. He mentioned an aunt who lives in Australia. I gather she has recently given birth to a child and wouldn't be able to come over to England until the end of the year. It may be that in the long run, Felix could live with her family out there?' Still no comment from Rawlings. The headmaster pushed on. 'But we now have to think of immediate plans for the boy. As it is near the end of term, I think it best if Felix skips the last ten days. Most of the activities are winding down. He would have been sad to miss the house cricket match, but luckily that took place last week…'

Rawlings thought how mad all this was. Here was a child that had just been orphaned and this man was burbling on about house cricket matches. He said gruffly, 'This news has been rather a shock, and it will take a while to work out the best long-term plans for Felix. For the moment, he will return with me and stay until we have something firmly in place for his future.'

The headmaster put his hands together, almost in a praying position, and his tones were calming as if addressing an unruly schoolboy. 'Quite right, I do agree with you. That would be best.' He leant across the desk. 'Of course, if the boy is not to return to this school for the next term, we would need to know as soon as possible. Places here are at a premium and filled very quickly.'

Rawlings began to dislike the man intensely and thought if he had anything to do with it, Felix would never go near this school again, but merely said, 'I understand. I will be seeing Graham Pennington early next week, and we will discuss all aspects of Felix's future, including his schooling.'

At this point, further conversation was interrupted by the arrival of the headmaster's wife with the tea. Introductions were made, and further condolences exchanged. Once seated again, Rawlings asked, 'How did Felix take the news about the accident and death of his parents?'

The headmaster and his wife exchanged glances.

'It's difficult to say,' he said, 'He went very quiet. In fact, he hasn't really spoken to anyone since or shown any outward signs of emotion. It must be his way of dealing with the situation. Felix has always been quite a reserved boy, not shy exactly, but certainly not as outgoing as some of our boys.'

'He excelled at cricket,' his wife intervened. 'I think he was at his happiest with a cricket ball in his hand.'

Rawlings smiled. 'I am a great fan of the game myself. Maybe we could go to a Test match together.'

'An excellent idea,' the headmaster beamed at him and Rawlings felt he had just been given a gold star.

After another awkward pause, broken by his wife saying, 'Matron has packed up all his things. I think he is all ready to go.'

'Right, my dear,' the headmaster was back on safer territory. 'I'll send for him, and you can be on your way.' He picked up his telephone and asked for Felix to be brought to the room. Rawlings waited nervously, just relieved the headmaster hadn't asked him where he lived. If he'd told him he resided on a houseboat the man might have looked even more disapproving than he already did.

There was a knock at the door and a small boy came into the room. Rawlings stood up, towering over him. His first impression was that the boy was all eyes, and he was horribly reminded of Luka when they had rescued him from the orphanage. His other observation was that Felix was fair and slim, quite different from his father at the same age, who had been dark and built like a rugby player. This child was more Oliver than Artful Dodger.

The headmaster's voice cut through his observations, 'Felix, this is your grandfather, who has come to collect you.'

The child held out his hand, and Rawlings took it.

'Hello, Felix. I'm so sorry about what has happened.' He paused, 'You're coming to stay with me for a bit. I hope that is all right.' The boy said nothing but gave a nod.

Things moved quickly after that. Goodbyes were said, more sympathy given and the hope they'd see him next term, and then they went out to the car. The security man, who evidently worked as a porter as well, loaded the trunk and various other bits of luggage into the car. With a wave and a great sense of relief that this part of the ordeal was over, Rawlings drove slowly out of the school gates.

For the first few miles, not a word was spoken. Rawlings glanced sideways at the child. His face showed no expression, and he stared straight ahead. Only his hands clenched firmly in his lap gave any indication of what he might be feeling. Rawlings decided it was best not to ask questions, but instead told him about where he was going, explaining how he lived on a houseboat which didn't really have room for him to sleep, so he was going to stay at the house at the top of the garden with Isobel, who he would like and was a great friend of his. He also told him about Marnie and how she was a painter and lived in the boathouse. The child listened to all this, with no change in his expression. They moved onto the motorway. Rawlings noticed a sign for services and had a brainwave.

'We might stop soon. Would you like a McDonald's?'

Was it his imagination, or did the boy's eyes light up a little? In any case, there was a nod. Ten minutes later, they parked up and found a table.

'Would a Big Mac do you, and some French fries?' Another nod. He arrived back with the food and a Coke to drink.

'Thank you, sir.' It was the first time the boy had spoken, but 'sir'? Rawlings sat down opposite his grandson.

'Felix, I know we don't know each other yet, and I haven't been much of a grandfather so far, but I think we should find something better for you to call me than sir.'

The boy paused in his eating but made no comment. Rawlings tried again. 'What did you call your grandmother?'

'Grandma,' he said.

Rawlings smiled. 'I don't think Grandpa would really suit me.'

'What would you like me to call you?' Felix asked politely.

'Well, most people either call me E.G., or Rawlings.'

Felix thought about this for a moment. 'I don't think I can call you Rawlings as that is my surname, and it would seem a bit odd. I could call you E.G.'

Rawlings, relieved to have that sorted, nodded. 'E.G. it is.'

'What does E.G. stand for?'

Rawlings explained about not liking his names when he was a boy and, because of that, had always insisted on being called either by initials or his surname.

'I don't like my name either,' he said, adding 'at school they called me Catfood.' Rawlings looked puzzled by this, so the boy explained about an advertisement for cat food where they used a cat called Felix.

'Well I actually like the name Felix,' Rawlings told the boy, 'and advertisements come and go. People will have forgotten it in a few years. What's your second name?'

'Gerald. It was my great grandfather's name.'

'I knew him well. He was a very good man. That makes your initials F.G.' He thought for a moment. 'We can't very well have E.G. and F.G.; people will get confused.'

The boy suddenly laughed. 'If everyone else calls you Rawlings, I think E.G. would be a good name for me to call you.'

With some relief Rawlings felt he'd made a minor breakthrough, and went on, 'I looked up the meaning of the name Felix when you were born. It means, happy, lucky and prosperous. I should hang on to it if I were you.'

Felix gave him a curious look but didn't say anything. Maybe he didn't feel particularly lucky at this moment in his life.

The rest of the journey passed without further conversation, but the atmosphere had definitely relaxed. At one point, Rawlings looked across at Felix and was rewarded with a smile. He felt an emotion he hadn't felt in a long while, although he wasn't sure what it was.

'Here we are,' he said, as they turned into the gates and parked outside the house. Isobel was on the steps waiting for them. She held out her hand,

'Hello Felix, I'm so pleased to meet you.' He shook it rather solemnly and then followed her into the house. 'Maria has laid out a tea in the kitchen' she said, 'I hope you're hungry.' Rawlings limping behind them said they probably wouldn't need tea as they'd stopped for a McDonald's. Isobel laughed. 'Really, Rawlings! Feeding the boy junk food already?'

In the kitchen, more introductions were made, first to Maria, and then Lydia came in, and she was actually smiling.

'You're going to be in a room opposite mine, Felix, so if you need anything, you can just bang on my door.'

Felix looked a little bewildered by all this attention but managed to eat one of Maria's chocolate cakes.

Jake came into the kitchen, 'Would you like me to take the luggage upstairs, Lady Mallinson?'

Isobel nodded. 'Thank you, Jake. That would be kind.'

It struck Rawlings that this must all seem rather grand and like a scene from *"The Go-Between"* and wondered what the boy was making of it. Meanwhile, Isobel turned to Felix.

'Why don't you go with your grandfather down to the boat? I expect you're looking forward to seeing it. He can bring you back later and show you where you'll be sleeping.'

Felix stood up and thanked them politely for his tea. You couldn't fault his manners, Rawlings thought. At least that bloody awful school had done something. He led Felix down the garden.

Isobel standing on the terrace watched them go and noticed at one point the boy took his grandfather's hand. She wiped away a tear and said to no one in particular, 'That boy might be the making of Rawlings.'

To his relief, Marnie had tidied up after his rapid departure earlier, and the boat was looking immaculate. She had also opened all the windows to get rid of the smell of smoke. Rawlings made a mental note that from now on, he should probably smoke outside. Felix declared himself delighted with the boat and said he was sad he couldn't sleep on it as well.

'It just wouldn't be practical,' Rawlings told him, 'but you can come down each day after breakfast.'

They sat on the front deck as the sun sank lower in the sky. A procession of Canada geese made their way upstream, and Rawlings told him they did that every night. They had their leader in the front and then followed him two by two, like something out of a Disney film. It made Felix laugh. The heron also tactfully put in an appearance, along with an array of ducks and coots.

'I don't know any of these river birds,' Felix said.

'I don't either,' Rawlings admitted, 'except for the Canada geese, the swans and the heron. There are many different species of duck and a great many other birds you'll see as well. We'll have to get a book and sort them out.'

After this, the boy went quiet. Rawlings rightly surmised he was worried about being left alone in a strange room, which was scarcely surprising after such a traumatic day.

'Do you have a mobile?' He asked. Felix nodded and

produced it from his pocket.

Rawlings took it. 'I am putting my number in your contacts, with the name E.G. You can then ring me, any time, day or night.' As he tapped in his number, he noticed the next contact down was 'Home'. He had a strong urge to delete it, but then decided it was better not to and handed back the phone. 'Come on; we'd better go and see where you're sleeping.'

On the way back to the house Felix asked Rawlings why Jake had addressed Isobel as Lady Mallinson. He explained that it was because her husband had been a diplomat and knighted for services to his country, and that gave Isobel the title of Lady. With this, Felix seemed satisfied, and there were no more questions that day.

His room had been transformed since the last time Rawlings had seen it when the skeletal Rose had been curled up on a pile of newspapers. Now it was painted pale yellow, with white curtains at the windows. All was light and airy, and there was a good view out onto the garden and down to the boat. A bright patchwork quilt covered the bed and Felix's pyjamas had been laid out already. When the room had been re-decorated, Isobel had added a separate loo, basin and shower. Rawlings felt relieved about this. It would save the boy walking down the corridor in the middle of the night. The trunk stood under the window and had been partly unpacked and some of his clothes put in the white chest of drawers. His small overnight case was on a table, waiting for Felix to deal with it. Rawlings glanced through the books by the bed. There was a leather-bound copy of *"The Jungle Book"* inscribed 'To Peter, with all my love, Isobel'. Rawlings felt touched by this. Isobel had gone to such trouble and all for this boy she didn't know at all. He also noticed there was a beautiful pond yacht standing on the chest of drawers and guessed that must have been Peter's as well.

Felix was sitting on the bed. He suddenly looked very small and lost. Maybe he was frightened of being left alone with his thoughts. Rawlings decided not to prolong the goodbyes. He ruffled the boy's hair and told him not to forget to call him if he needed anything and that he would see him on the boat after breakfast. He then went down the stairs to thank Isobel for her help.

'He's a lovely boy, Rawlings. It will be a difficult time for him, coming to terms with all that has happened.'

Rawlings nodded, thinking grimly it was going to be a case of stepping into the unknown for both of them. Isobel, ever practical, mentioned the fact that everything they had unpacked was for wearing in school and there didn't seem to be any holiday clothes in the trunk. Rawlings thought about this.

'They are probably in the London house. I don't want to take him there for the moment. It might be a good idea to get him some new things for him while he is here. Maybe Marnie could help with that. She might enjoy a day out with the boy.' He paused. 'I'll have to go and see the solicitor early next week, Isobel. There is a great deal to discuss and sort out,' he paused, 'and then there's the funeral to be arranged. Lord knows how I'll get the boy through that.'

Isobel looked at him. He was exhausted. 'Try not to worry, Rawlings. The boy has taken to you already and obviously trusts you. It will be strange and new to him at first, but children are resilient. Give him a little time.'

Rawlings stood up and kissed her on the cheek. 'Thank you for everything Isobel. I'm very grateful. Will you send the boy down to me in the morning?'

'We'll give him breakfast first. Maria has it all organised. Now go! It's been a long day.'

This then was the start of the second half of that strange year.

Chapter Ten

July 2017

The first two days with Felix continued in much the same way. He was charmingly polite, did what he was told and didn't seem to put a foot wrong. The boy was almost too good to be true, and Rawlings remarked on this to Isobel. Her response was rather impatient, and to him, unexpected.

'For goodness sake, Rawlings, just be thankful he is such a beautifully mannered child. After the week I've just been through with my rude and churlish great-niece, I can tell you Felix is a delightful relief.' She looked at Rawlings' worried expression and said more gently, 'Quite honestly, the boy is probably still a bit bewildered by the huge change in his situation.' She paused before saying, 'I didn't know your son and daughter in law, but Felix strikes me as a boy who has been rather emotionally starved and is therefore extremely anxious to please, especially anyone who might give him a little affection. He's also been in a strict prep school where the good are rewarded, and the bad are punished. If you are a sensible child, you avoid being in the wrong and make very sure you stay in the right. Felix has obviously learned this lesson well.' She smiled. 'I think you will find, with a little patience, that he will start to open up.

I have a feeling there is a tough and interesting character just below the surface. Give it time, Rawlings'. She added, 'I may say, I find the boy quite enchanting and a breath of fresh air to have around the place.'

As usual, Isobel was right. Over the next week Felix did start to open up and Rawlings, taking Isobel's advice, was careful not to rush him. He just waited for Felix to bring up a topic and then deal with it as best he could. He was also pleased that he'd instantly struck up a friendship with Marnie. The boy told her that art had been one of his best subjects at school, so she gave him a drawing pad, and he seemed happy that first weekend, sitting on her balcony making sketches of the river and the boat. Rawlings bought him a book on river birds, and over the first week, he became very knowledgeable about the different species. A goose, not the Canada variety but large and white, had strangely turned up at the boat soon after he arrived, and to Felix's delight would spend hours just bobbing up and down in the water, waiting for the boy to feed him.

'You know you mustn't give the birds bread, E.G. It clogs them up,' he informed Rawlings one morning. 'My book says they like oats, peas and corn. Do we have any of those?'

'There are some frozen peas in the fridge. I'll get you a bowl, and you can defrost the peas first. Is there anything else they suggest?'

Felix studied the book, 'They can have chopped vegetables, peelings and salad.'

Rawlings smiled. 'I suggest you ask Maria for those. She should be able to keep you well-stocked.' The boy seemed pleased.

'That should make Harrison very happy.'

'Harrison?' Rawlings queried.

'My goose. I've called him Harrison.'

Everyone agreed that by the end of the first week, Felix had settled in far better than they could have expected. Rawlings watched with amusement as the women fluttered around him like a lot of doting aunts. Even Lydia had taken an interest in the boy, but what surprised him most was the relationship that had developed between Felix and Isobel. She seemed to derive great pleasure from his company and Felix informed him that Isobel and he would have long chats over breakfast.

'What do you talk about?' Rawlings had inquired.

'Oh everything,' the boy said vaguely. 'She tells me about all the places she has lived. She's been all over the world.'

The following week, while Marnie took Felix off to buy him some holiday clothes, Rawlings took the opportunity to go up to London. A long session was needed with his solicitor, Graham Pennington, who was executor of the Will. The sudden and unexpected deaths of two young people had produced endless complications in sorting out their estate, especially with a child involved. It was, therefore, with some trepidation that Rawlings walked into Graham's office. He was still feeling mildly irked by his last visit when he'd been made only too aware that he was the least favoured choice of guardian and his request to meet the boy had been flatly turned down. Well, he thought angrily, they were now hoist by their own petard or something of the sort. He sat opposite Graham Pennington and unlike the time before he now took the time to make made a study of the man. In many ways, he resembled his father, but his face was longer, and his melancholy expression made him look rather older than he probably was. Rawlings reckoned he could only have been in his forties, but he definitely looked older. From his general demeanour, it was likely he lacked a sense of humour as well. Not that there was much to laugh about in the present situation. A thought suddenly struck him. His father had been Graham too. Did that make this one Graham Jnr., or even perhaps Graham Pennington II? Or maybe that was only in America. Maybe if he had a son also called Graham, and he again followed his father, he would be Graham Pennington III. He gave an inward chuckle.

'My dear man,' the solicitor now said, cutting through his thoughts. 'This is such an appalling tragedy and a great shock to us all. You have my deepest sympathy.'

Rawlings thanked him and asked how they should proceed. Graham put his hands together and then studied the papers in front of him.

'I think you'll agree that the London house should be put up for sale, along with its contents, unless of course, you wanted to live in it with the boy?' Rawlings shook his head violently and stated firmly he didn't. Graham looked relieved. 'I rather presumed not. It makes things simpler. The proceeds from the sale will then be put into a trust for Felix, who will come into his inheritance when he is eighteen.' He looked over the top of his glasses at Rawlings. 'This, with the legacy from his grandmother, means he is going to be a very wealthy young man. The money, until he comes of age, will be looked after by the financial adviser, the same one I believe you use.' Rawlings nodded, feeling he had no contribution to make at this juncture. He'd inherited this financial man from Gillian and had left him to deal with the substantial sums left to him by Gillian and her father. He'd never touched his capital, having neither the inclination nor need to do so.

'Meanwhile,' Graham droned on, 'provision has to be made for his present welfare until he comes of age, and naturally generous allowances will be made available for whichever guardian he is living with, that is either you or his aunt in Australia.'

At this point, Rawlings did interrupt, protesting he had quite enough money of his own to provide for his grandchild. Graham frowned and said severely that would only confuse things. It was all a matter of keeping it orderly and legal. If the boy went to stay with his aunt's family in Australia, then the allowance would transfer to her. He looked at Rawlings and observed a faint look of mutiny on his face. With a sigh, he reflected that this man had, up to now, been the easiest of clients, previously agreeing to all arrangements with no argument. But now the situation would seem to have changed.

'I think we should take things one step at a time.' Graham said with studied patience. He had the sort of flat, unemotional voice that always sounded a trifle weary. Rawlings found it difficult to concentrate. All these matters were exceedingly tedious, but for the sake of the boy, he made an effort, and gave Graham an encouraging nod, letting him continue.

'There is the matter of the funeral to sort out first.' The solicitor looked down at his papers and frowned. 'There is also a Filipino woman who is in residence at the house. I gather she was a sort of housekeeper and looked after Felix in the school holidays.' Rawlings wondered what the hell the parents were doing in the boy's holidays? At least Hugo always had one parent around. But he kept these thoughts to himself. Graham was now in full flow.

'I think it best if we give her six months payment and suggest she looks for another job. I don't think she'll have a problem in that part of Kensington.' He again referred to a list in front of him. 'Do you think the boy will wish to go back to the London house before we put it on the market? He might like to collect some things that are personal to him.' Graham looked inquiringly at Rawlings who was now gazing out of the window. 'Rawlings,' he repeated patiently, 'will you be taking the boy back to the London house?'

Rawlings shrugged. 'I have really no idea at the moment, Graham, but I will ask him.' With an effort to be helpful, he added, 'Maybe we could make that visit one day after the funeral. Have any arrangements been made about that?'

'I had a visit from one of Hugo's friends, the best man at his wedding, I believe. He suggested the service should be held in the London church where they were married. Would you have any objection to that?'

Rawlings shook his head. 'I have no feelings about that at all. However, I think it might be a good idea if we made some arrangement with the church in Great Warley, where Hugo's mother and grandfather are buried. Maybe some sort of stone for the two of them could be organised, where their ashes are placed? It might be helpful to Felix in the future, to have a place he could visit,' and he added, 'even if he does end up living in Australia, he might occasionally return here.'

Graham nodded his approval. 'I think that is an

excellent idea,' and he made a note of it. He gave Rawlings a concerned look. 'How's it going with the boy?'

'Quite honestly, better than I expected,' Rawlings paused, 'but it's early days.' He suddenly needed to leave and stood up. 'There are of course many other things to discuss about his future, but for the time being, he seems to have settled in well enough. I suggest we postpone topics like his schooling and his possible life in Australia until after the funeral. Can I leave you to deal with the details of that? Perhaps that friend of Hugo's could help. You know how to reach me if there is a problem.' At the door, he said with a glimmer of a smile, 'Maybe I should see you soon about my own Will, Graham. I think my last one was made before Gillian died.' With that, he limped out of the office and with some relief returned to the boat.

The journey back was tiring, the train was packed, and his leg was giving him hell. To make matters worse, there was a thunderstorm, and the heavens opened as he left the station. He was already drenched by the time he reached his car, and the rain didn't let up as he walked from the house to the boat. Consequently, he was not in the best of moods as he opened the door and found an excited child jumping up and down and the floor covered in packages.

'Heavens, Rawlings, you're soaked! Marnie exclaimed.

'Give that woman a star for observation,' Rawlings said in sour tones, 'I'll just get out of these wet things if you don't mind,' and with that, he stumped off to his room.

By the time he returned, the packages had been tidied, and Felix was sitting quietly, looking a little apprehensive, holding onto a box on his lap. Rawlings made a determined effort to be pleasant and said with a smile, 'It looks as if I am going to have to take out a mortgage to cover this lot. You've certainly done a lot of shopping.'

Marnie said quickly, 'I know it looks a lot, but it's really only jeans and t-shirts.' She hesitated, 'There was only one real extravagance…' she looked at Felix, who opened the box on his lap to reveal a pair of trainers. Rawlings took the box from him to examine them and then noticed the price still stuck to the end.

'Good God,' he exclaimed, 'how could a pair of shoes cost that much?' An expression of guilt crossed Felix's face, and he said nervously,

'I'm sorry E.G. It was my fault. I persuaded Marnie to get them. I've been longing for these trainers for ages and ages and was going to ask my…' He stopped, and they both realised he'd been going to ask his parents for them. For a moment nobody said anything, and then Felix finished lamely, 'We could take them back, or I thought they could be a present for my birthday.'

Rawlings handed him back the box. 'When is your birthday, Felix?'

'August 18th,' he replied.

Rawlings smiled at him. 'I'm sure we'll manage something else for your birthday. You must let me know if those trainers are comfortable. You never know, I might get a pair.' The boy looked greatly relieved.

Marnie started collecting up the bags. 'We'd better get going, Felix. Isobel will be wondering what on earth has happened to us.'

After they'd left, Rawlings poured himself a large drink and slumped into his desk chair. He noticed a pile of receipts that Marnie had left for him, along with the credit card he'd given her. He did a quick tot up of the total. If he were to be given this allowance for the boy, he'd have to find a way of keeping all these bills separate. It was an idea he hated, but he didn't want to incur the wrath of Graham, so he pulled out an empty file and placed the receipts inside. This whole situation was a new experience, and if he were honest, he felt rather out of his depth.

The next day, Felix, wearing his new jeans and trainers, accompanied Rawlings to the paper shop. Sunil Patel was outside, cleaning his bicycle. Rawlings introduced them and left the boys talking while he went inside for his paper and cigarettes. Mr Patel immediately noticed the boy with his son. Rawlings explained it was his grandson and then told him about the car crash and how Felix would be staying with him for a while. Mr Patel's eyes filled with tears.

'That is a most terrible thing to have happened, Mr Rawlings sir. If my wife and I can do anything, anything at all, you only have to say.' Rawlings thanked him and then had a thought.

'Maybe Sunil could come over to the boat during his holidays. It would be good for Felix to have someone of his own age to be with.' This idea delighted Mr Patel.

As they walked home Felix said, 'Do you know E.G., Sunil is the same age as me. Well, to be exact, he is four months and twelve days older than me. Rawlings smiled at this precision as Felix went on, 'Sunil says you gave that bike to him.'

Rawlings explained. 'He'd had his previous bike stolen, in a burglary. I just made a contribution.' He looked at Felix, 'Do you have a bike?'

Felix shook his head. 'I did when we lived in the Manor

when Granma was alive. After she died and we moved to London, I couldn't have a bike anymore.' He added sadly. 'I missed that, and the horses. Jenny let me have my own pony, and we went out riding nearly every day.' He suddenly looked sad, and Rawlings again felt an anger at Hugo and Susanna's obvious neglect of the child's needs, once they had their London life.

'What did you do during the holidays in London?' he asked.

'I went out with Nula,' he replied, suddenly brightening. 'She is Filipino and lived with us. I really liked her. She took me to all sorts of places, museums and the parks. Once we went on the London Eye,' and he laughed. 'Nula didn't like that. She said heights made her feel sick. She wouldn't look out at the view at all but kept her eyes shut the whole time. Sometimes we'd go to films; only Nula didn't like anything frightening.' He walked on and then suddenly turned to Rawlings. 'What will happen to Nula now that…' He stopped.

Rawlings put his hand on the boy's shoulder and said gently, 'She'll find another job, but she will be well paid until she does.' This seemed to reassure the boy although he did say he would like to see Nula one more time, to say goodbye properly. Rawlings assured him this could be arranged.

'Sunil is going to a new school next term.' Felix said and looked at his grandfather. 'I suppose I will be going to a new school too, won't I?' He sounded as if this was what he hoped would happen, but Rawlings was unwilling to tackle this subject yet.

'We'll see,' was all he said.

The next day came the call Rawlings had been dreading.

Graham rang to say that all the arrangements had now been made and the funeral would take place the following week. Rawlings knew he would somehow have to get the boy through this ordeal and not at all sure how to do it.

Chapter Eleven

July 12th. The Funeral.

The day of the funeral duly arrived, and it was appropriately dark and overcast. The forecast was for rain. Rawlings thought gloomily that it always seemed to rain at funerals whatever the time of year. He hadn't slept well and was assailed by nerves, not so much for himself, but for the boy. Up to now, Felix had kept his emotions under control, but what would happen when he came face to face with the two coffins of his parents?

Isobel had insisted on lending Rawlings a black tie, one of Peter's he presumed. He wanted to resist, but she had been so kind it seemed ungracious to do so. Poor Isobel, she was also having a struggle getting Felix ready. He'd wanted to wear his new trainers, but she'd told him firmly they wouldn't be suitable. Rawlings wouldn't have minded, but again decided not to interfere.

They set out for the station, Felix clutching the large black umbrella, which Rawlings had grumbled he couldn't manage as well as his stick. The boy sat silent, and Rawlings noticed his hands were once more clenched in his lap. He wondered if there was something he should say or do, to make this day easier for him. But what? In the end, he comforted himself with the thought there was little that would be of any help. Thankfully the train was empty, and they had seats to themselves. The journey was only an hour, but that day it seemed far longer. Rawlings soon became lost in his own thoughts. He had a loathing of Church of England funerals, loaded as they were with such doom and gloom. He hoped this one would be short, and Felix wouldn't listen too closely to what was being said. Paradoxically he wished he could have gone to Mia's funeral, but that had been a proper Irish affair and apparently lasted three days, with a great deal of singing and drinking. A true celebration of a life, even in the terrible circumstances. Of course, it was possible to have good funerals in this country if you just organised them properly and didn't worry about breaking all the ridiculous conventions. One of his fellow journalists, the one who had committed suicide, had been given an outdoor wake in the middle of a forest, in a beautiful leafy glade. They'd sat around, remembering their times together and shared experiences. Their black humour returned as they drank, sang, laughed, cried, and then, the sunset, streaking the sky with colour, and they scattered his ashes beneath a large oak tree, and all hugged as they remembered him. It was somehow perfect and the way he would like to go. Rawlings sighed. Today would not be like that. They were back to dear old C of E, with everyone in black; long faces, solemn words, dust to dust, ashes to ashes.

'Do you think there is such a thing as heaven, E.G.?' The voice of Felix cut through his thoughts. This question had obviously been on the boy's mind, so Rawlings considered carefully before answering.

I think,' he said slowly, 'I think if we were meant to

know for certain, we would have been told about it, but we haven't.' He looked at Felix, who was unusually pale and had a worried expression. Rawlings felt it incumbent upon him to come up with a better explanation, that could be of comfort to the boy. He decided on something he'd told Mia, after witnessing so many mangled and dead bodies of children in the traumatic incident at the orphanage.

'My theory is,' he said, looking at the boy with a steady gaze, 'that there is a spirit world out there, that provides each new life with an individual spirit when it is born, and then that spirit stays with that person until they die. Although it leaves the body, that spirit, when it returns to the spirit world, is now changed because of the body it has inhabited. That way, I like to think we take something individual with us into the next life…' he broke off and looked at Felix. 'Does that make any sense to you?'

Felix considered this and then nodded. Suddenly he said, 'My mother had a baby, but it died before it was born. Maybe they are all together now.'

The thought seemed to please him, and he looked less worried. Rawlings was both surprised and shocked by this news. He'd never heard about a lost baby; presumably, it had been a miscarriage. Maybe that would explain why Hugo and Susanna hadn't had more children.

Felix was talking again. 'I'd have liked to have had a brother or sister. It would have been someone to play with in the school holidays.' Once again Rawlings felt an immense sadness sweep over him, but the boy looked straight at him and said, 'But now I have you, and Isobel and Marnie.'

Rawlings felt himself choking up and turned away so

the boy wouldn't see. After a moment he said, 'And now Sunil can visit you too...' and then hesitated. It hadn't been his intention to mention it so soon, but now might be just the right time, something good to think about while facing the ordeal of the day. 'Felix, I thought next week we might go and buy you a new bicycle. Then you and Sunil could go out for rides together.'

The boy turned to him with shining eyes. 'Could we E.G.? I would really like that. Maybe it could be an advance birthday present.'

Rawlings nodded and said, 'Maybe.

After that, Felix went back into silent mode, and nothing more was said until they reached London. Felix had really wanted to take the tube, but Rawlings decided on the extravagance of a taxi. In truth, his leg was already painful, and he dreaded the thought of all those stairs, up and down, to the stations. The boy looked so disappointed he promised him they'd take the underground on the way back.

In spite of the traffic, they reached the church in good time. The rain had held off, and a few people were already standing outside. They climbed out of the taxi and Felix broke away, rushing towards a small woman, who he instantly recognised and was very obviously Filipino. He flung his arms round her, and they clung to each other. Rawlings limped slowly towards them and held out his hand.

'I think you must be Nula. Felix has told me a great deal about you.'

'Nula, this is my grandfather...' Felix said. As they shook hands, the boy continued, 'Nula you must sit with us in the church. Can she? Please E.G.'.

'I think we must let Nula sit where she wants to, Felix,'

Rawlings told him gently.

The woman looked relieved. She spoke in perfect English, but slowly and precisely. 'Thank you, Mr Rawlings. I think I would prefer to sit at the back.' Then, turning to Felix, she added, 'I am so sorry about this terrible thing that has happened to you. We will speak afterwards, yes?' Her eyes had filled with tears, and before Felix could say anymore, Rawlings steered him away towards where Graham was standing. He made the introductions and Felix politely shook his hand. Rawlings looked at his watch.

'I think we should go in now, Felix. It looks as if it might rain.' His real reason was that he didn't want the boy to be outside when the hearses arrived with the two coffins. It was going to be traumatic enough when they went past them up the aisle. They were handed service sheets and shown to the front pew.

As they sat down, a horrified look came over the boy's face. 'E.G., I am so sorry. I think I left your umbrella behind in the taxi. I will buy you a new one out of my pocket money.'

Rawlings relieved it was something so minor said at once, 'Don't worry about that Felix. It was a very old umbrella. I will get a brightly coloured one next time.'

The boy relaxed again and then asked, 'Why wouldn't Nula sit with us. I really wanted her to.'

'I know,' Rawlings explained, 'but I think she would have felt awkward. This isn't her religion, you know.'

That seemed to satisfy him, and they both studied the service sheet. With some relief, Rawlings noticed the service had been kept short. There were a couple of hymns that Felix would probably know from school. Who on earth had chosen 'All things bright and beautiful'? It was a child's hymn and the lines 'The Lord God loves them all…' jumped out at him. He thought grimly the Lord God hadn't done much loving in the case of Hugo and Susanna, nor in leaving Felix without any parents. He glanced at the large black dais just in front of them. This was going to be a terrible ordeal for the child. Not that he was looking forward to it either. Looking around, he could see the church was pretty full, but very few people he recognised. There was no sign of Lavender, Susanna's mother, and there had never been any mention of her either. Maybe she had also died. He suddenly caught sight of Jenny and thought she could be someone for Felix to talk to afterwards. They could fix up a day at the stables for the boy. He'd like that…

There was a sudden hush, and the priest started intoning from the back, as the two coffins made their slow progress up the aisle. Felix didn't look round but kept his eyes resolutely fixed straight ahead. He was holding himself very straight and rigid. Rawlings put his arm around the boy and felt him relax a little and then tactfully removed it. The first hymn was announced, and the service began. Felix gave no sign of any emotion throughout the service but kept staring straight ahead. Rawlings couldn't help wondering if this was a good thing. Was he holding it together for his grandfather's sake? From what he knew of the boy already, that would be quite possible. Or was it because he had been brought up not to cry in public? Or, was it simply because the feelings he had for his parents just weren't strong enough to make him break down? Rawlings had the uneasy feeling that if it had been Nula lying in the coffin, Felix would have shed plenty of tears.

The priest gave condolences, both to Rawlings and to Felix. There was still no reaction. Eulogies were made to Hugo and Susanna, enthusing about what a talented and popular couple they had been, and how tragic it was that their successful lives had been cut so short. Felix listened to it all, but his expression never changed. He didn't even look round as the coffins were finally carried past them down the aisle and out to the waiting hearses. Rawlings sat down for a moment, wanting to wait until the coffins were well on their way to the crematorium before taking Felix outside.

'I like this bit of organ music,' he said.

'What is it?' Felix, at last, turned around in his seat.

'It's a prelude by J.S. Bach. One of my favourite composers.'

Felix thought for a moment and then said, 'I like it too. It sounds very grand and powerful.'

Rawlings thought that an apt and good description of organ music and then, realising people were waiting for them to leave, he walked Felix out of the church. They'd been asked to a reception at a nearby hotel, and Rawlings felt it would be expected of them to attend, if only for a short while. In any case, he wanted to give Felix the chance to talk to Jenny. While he did so, Rawlings took the opportunity to thank Graham for making all the arrangements. Graham informed him he'd organised a couple of designs for the headstone to show him, and they agreed to meet the following week. Rawlings also arranged a time to take Felix back to the house. He crossed over to Nula to tell her, catching her just as she was about to leave. The poor woman seemed overcome with emotion. He called Felix over to say goodbye and explained to them both they would be meeting up soon. By the time he had fixed up a time for the boy to spend a day with Jenny and had thanked Hugo's friend for all his help and for the eulogy, he felt he'd done about as much as he could, and they should now leave. Felix had behaved impeccably. He'd shaken hands endlessly and always been polite, but Rawlings wondered what was really going on in that small head.

As promised, they went back to the station by underground. The stairs were hell, but Rawlings was so relieved the damned day was over, he overlooked the pain, just glad to give Felix a bit of pleasure, although how anyone could derive pleasure from the noisy, crowded tube was beyond him. The journey was uneventful. No reference was made to the day, but Felix did talk excitedly about the purchase of a bike. It seemed to be the one thing on his mind, which was perhaps, something of a relief.

Isobel opened the door as the car drove up. One look at Rawlings told her he was exhausted. She addressed the boy, who didn't appear tired in the least. 'Felix, why don't you go upstairs and change into your holiday clothes?' Felix looked as if he was about to argue with her but then changed his mind. 'Don't' forget to hang up your suit,' she called after him, and Rawlings smiled.

'You're very good at handling that child' he said. 'I fear I am far too lax and am in great danger of spoiling him.' He followed her into the drawing room, as she assured him that a little spoiling after all he had gone through, could do him no harm. Rawlings lowered himself into a chair, greatly relieved to be giving his leg a rest at last.

'How was the day?' she asked.

'Better than I expected. Depressing of course, but we

survived, and Felix behaved perfectly, right through the service and then afterwards at the hotel.' He took the drink she poured for him and took a gulp. 'He was very quiet, but otherwise showed no emotion at all. I don't know if this is worrying. Apart from a brief, philosophical discussion about heaven, we didn't touch on the subject of death or funerals, or indeed his parents. He must be feeling something, but he's certainly not showing it.'

Isobel sighed. 'I think we just have to let him deal with it in his own way. I am sure...' But they were never to know what Isobel was sure about, because Felix, now changed into jeans and trainers, burst into the room.

'Can we go down to the boat now?' he asked with barely suppressed impatience.

Rawlings got wearily to his feet and was about to make a move when Isobel said firmly, 'Not tonight, Felix. You've both had a long day. If you go to the kitchen, you'll find Maria has left you supper, along with some of those chocolate crispy cakes you like so much.'

The boy hesitated and looked at Rawlings, 'But what about Harrison? He'll be expecting me to feed him.'

Rawlings smiled and told him Harrison would be perfectly happy waiting until the morning. Felix still hesitated, now looking a little mutinous, until Isobel once again came to the rescue, saying firmly, 'Once you've had your supper, Felix, we can have another game of Mah-jong. Would you like that?' He nodded, silently admitting defeat, and after saying goodnight to his grandfather, he left for the kitchen, noticeably dragging his feet a little.

When he'd gone, Rawlings said with grudging admiration, 'Thank you for that. I'll admit, I'm happy to be relieved of my duties. I've had just about enough for one day.' He smiled at her. 'I'm beginning to see what you mean about a tough little character lying just below the surface.' As he limped his way out, he added, 'I'll join you in a game of Mah-jong one day, haven't played for ages.'

Isobel watched him go and made a mental note to tackle him about his leg. His limp was definitely getting worse.

Chapter Twelve

August 2017

July slipped into August without further dramas. On the last day of the month, Rawlings had managed to purchase from one of his friends, who just happened to be a cricket correspondent, two tickets for the Oval Test Match. It had been a great day, with Felix in a state of high excitement throughout. England had beaten South Africa by 239 runs, and the boy took it as an almost personal triumph. He suggested that the cricket day, along with the purchase of his bicycle, should be advanced birthday presents. His birthday was obviously on his mind, so Rawlings mentioned this to Isobel, and she offered to plan a party for him. Rawlings was both relieved and grateful. It was a task that, quite frankly was beyond him.

There were still two other matters worrying him, that would need to be dealt with. One was to talk to Graham about schooling, and the other was an urgent visit to the London house. It was already under offer, the speed of this had come as no surprise to Graham, who informed Rawlings that it was because it was situated in such a desirable area. Rawlings reacted to this with annoyance; of course, it was desirable if you had the money to pay the astronomical asking price.

Felix, meanwhile, spent every day with Sunil. They would pass their time with their bicycles, riding up and down the towpath and exploring new areas of the river, or playing cricket on the nearby green. Maria would pack them a picnic, and they would be gone until late afternoon, regardless of the weather. This had the advantage of leaving Rawlings time to get on with his book, something he had rather neglected since the arrival of the boy.

When Rawlings suggested a trip to the London house, Felix showed a great reluctance to go, asking if it was really necessary. On being told firmly that it was, the pill was made more palatable by the suggestion he would spend one last day with Nula. Isobel had suggested they went by car, in case Felix decided he wanted to bring stuff back. Reluctantly Rawlings agreed. He hated driving in London, but they found the house quite easily, Felix following Graham's very precise directions. The next problem was finding a parking space, and then they both had to turn out their pockets for money for the meter. Rawlings grumbled about the expense, but Felix had already gone on ahead and was at the front door ringing the bell impatiently. It was opened by Nula who seemed overjoyed to see him, and the two of them disappeared down the stairs, presumably to the kitchen.

Rawlings didn't follow them immediately but started to wander around on his own, finding it a depressing sight. The packing was already well underway, and there were boxes stacked everywhere. Even so, he could see that the décor had been both chic and expensive. In the large living room, Rawlings sat on a sofa, already covered in dust sheets, and looked around. He reflected gloomily that it wasn't a lived-in family home, but more like a showcase house, straight out of a smart interior's magazine. The heavy curtains, the newly painted walls in fashionable soft grey, the elaborate fireplace and the central chandelier all smacked of a fashionable social existence but was somehow quite impersonal. He could have been in one of the smarter London hotels. At the far end, there was an antique desk which was open, but had been emptied, no doubt by Graham, and there was not a paper in sight. Dragging himself up, feeling distinctly uncomfortable, he made his way up the stairs to find Felix's room. Once again, there was nothing homely about it. Nula had put some clothes in neat piles on the bed, otherwise, the room had been stripped of any evidence of the boy. There was one tasteful picture still on the wall, a painting of the sea with some boats on the shore. Rawlings wondered if it was of particular significance. He would ask. There was also one photograph, in a silver frame on the bedside table. He picked it up. It had been taken when Felix was about four, and he was standing between his parents. Rawlings stared at it. It was a formal picture of a smart family group, but their expressions were blank, not one jot of life or joy emanating from them.

Nula had left an empty bag on the bed, presumably for Felix to choose the things he wanted to take back with him. Rawlings noticed a small laptop on the desk and presumed he would want to keep that. There were only a couple of books. One was the first Harry Potter, and there was an inscription inside, 'To Felix from Dad, Christmas 2015'. Not overly affectionate Rawlings thought sadly. He put these in the bag. There seemed to be nothing else for him to do in this room, and he made his way down to the kitchen where Felix was happily talking to Nula.

'We are going to go to the Science Museum,' he said. 'Is that all right, E.G.?'

Rawlings smiled and said it was a great idea because he had several errands to do and would return about four to collect him.

'Before we leave Felix,' he said, 'you might want to go up to your room and pack any things you want to take with you. I have already put some books and your laptop in the bag.'

Felix frowned. 'It is only a notebook. I am saving up for a proper laptop.'

'Well, the notebook might be useful until you do.' Rawlings said patiently and turned to Nula. 'You might see if any of his clothes should be packed up as well. Any he doesn't want can go to OXFAM.'

Nula looked at Felix and smiled. 'I don't think many of them will fit him now, Mr Rawlings. He has grown so tall.'

'There is a picture on the wall of some boats on a beach.' Rawlings told Felix. 'We could take that with us if you like.' The boy gave a shrug indicating he didn't really care. It was one less thing to take back with them.

Rawlings handed over some money, telling them to have a lovely day and went off for his appointment with Graham. Yet again he had trouble parking and was rather late. He apologised, but Graham greeted him more affably than usual.

'I have some news,' he said, as soon as Rawlings was settled. 'At last, I've heard from Susanna's sister Sarah, who has now written at some length. I gather the reason she couldn't come over from Australia earlier was that her last baby was born prematurely, just before her sister's accident. The baby is now doing well, but she doesn't feel she will be able to visit here before December.' He looked at Rawlings to see how he was taking the news, but when there was no comment, he continued. 'She is very keen to have Felix live with their family and to take him back with her at that time. As she is joint guardian, there should be no problem to this unless you have any objections.' Once again, he looked anxiously at Rawlings, but again there was no comment. He now spoke more briskly. 'There will be documents to sort out, arrangements with the Australian Embassy and so forth, but I foresee no real difficulty. The boy will need a passport, I presume up to now he has been on his parent's passport?'

Rawlings said, 'I have no idea about that. I rather thought all documents and papers would be with you.'

'Quite.' Graham sat back and studied Rawlings. His expression hadn't changed, so he said a little nervously, 'How would you feel personally about this arrangement?'

There was a moment of silence. This news had been a shock. In all honesty, Rawlings hadn't even considered it. He had somehow become used to having the boy with him. Now that he was faced with the prospect of the boy leaving, a terrible feeling of loss swept over him. Felix had filled an emotional gap in his life that had been empty since Mia died. It may only have been a short time, just six weeks, but he'd grown very attached to the boy and now dreaded the moment when he wouldn't be around. He glanced down at his leg. He was due to see the specialist later and knew the verdict on that might not be good. How could he look after the boy, if he was to have another operation?

Graham was watching him, and during the long silence, he'd begun to look increasingly worried. Observing this Rawlings felt an answer was required. He spoke slowly, trying not to let his emotion show, 'I will miss the boy, there is no doubt about that. But thinking sensibly about his future, Felix might be better off living with a family...' and he added with slight distaste, 'even if it is in Australia.'

This drew a thin smile from the lawyer. 'They live in the Barossa Valley above Adelaide. I am assured it is a beautiful place. Sarah informs me her husband Brad has a winery, and they have three children, the eldest is a boy called Shane.

'Named after the cricketer, I presume.' Rawlings remarked drily.

'I expect so.' Graham replied, annoyed at the trivial interruption. Referring to the letter he continued, 'Shane would be about the same age as Felix. Then there is David, who is eight and the new baby Ella. I have a photograph here.' He handed it over to Rawlings, and he studied it. They were grouped together informally, all laughing, one child making a silly face. It was a proper family group, so different from the one he'd seen earlier, and he sighed.

'It might be a good idea if I talked to Sarah before it is all finally settled. Can we use Skype?'

'I am sure that will be possible.' Graham said, adding, 'Oh the joys of modern technology.'

Rawlings thought testily he wanted this meeting to end as soon as possible; Graham was starting to annoy him. He'd obviously presumed he would be relieved to be shot of the boy, and this was very far from the case. He tried to concentrate on what needed to be said before he left.

'The immediate problem is to sort out schooling for Felix. I don't want to take him back to his old school.' He paused, not wanting to tell Graham he'd thought the school snobbish, narrow and had taken an immediate dislike to it. But some explanation was needed, so he pointed out that Felix had settled into his present life very well. It would seem a great pity to send him away again, adding pointedly that all the upheavals should be kept to the minimum. Graham nodded, and Rawlings continued, 'I understand there is a good Academy nearby, which might give him a place for one term, until his departure in December. I think Lady Mallinson is a member of the Trust, and that could help.' He was pleased he had done his homework on this. There was another advantage which he didn't have to mention to the lawyer. It was the school Sunil was to start next term. They could be new boys together, and Felix would like that.

Graham seemed content with this suggestion. 'You have done well with the boy, Rawlings.' He sounded faintly surprised at saying this and added, 'I was extremely impressed with his behaviour at the funeral.'

With that rather underwhelming endorsement, Rawlings departed, his mind filled with mixed emotions. He dragged a parking ticket from the front of his windscreen and set off for the hospital.

Two hours later, he sat in the hospital carpark, eating an unappetising sandwich and contemplating the outcome of his visit. His doctor had been kind but firm. Either he had an operation to have the bones of his damaged leg fused, in a final attempt to get them to hold, or, if nothing was done, the good medical man couldn't answer for the consequences. It was said so starkly and sounded so dire that he'd reluctantly agreed to go through the procedure and made a provisional date for January. The only positive in the situation was that he was still covered by his health insurance, which would also pay for his convalescence afterwards. This would be a necessity, although it went against his every instinct. The boat was certainly not a suitable place for a man with his leg encased in plaster. Here he gave a wry smile. The regiment of women who now surrounded him would have leapt to his aid, but that was the last thing he wanted. Privacy was what he needed. His recovery must be made in isolation, with only the impersonal ministrations of the nursing staff.

He finished his sandwich, which had tasted like a soggy piece of towelling, and left the car to put the packaging in the bin. One thing he'd found difficult to get used to, since his return to England, was the endless packaging. Everything was covered in cling film, plastic casings and cardboard. Was nobody thinking of the planet? Once more, he felt the black cloud of gloom descending. He looked at his watch. Time to make his way back to collect Felix or they would be caught in rush hour traffic leaving London. He started the engine and sighed. The fates had spoken; there was no way round it. If he were to be confined to a hospital bed for at least six weeks, he certainly wouldn't be able to look after the boy, let alone himself, so Australia it would have to be. He was already dreading the huge hole it would leave in his life. The boy had so quickly become part of it. And then, how would Felix take the news? Would this cause another major upset in his life?

He made an effort to put these thoughts from his mind and instead returned to his conversation with Graham. One minor victory had been the decision over the school. It had been surprisingly easy, although Graham might have been swayed by the fact that Lady Mallinson was on the Trust of the Academy and this gave him a moment of amusement. The man was such a snob. But his main relief was for Felix. It worried him that the boy had been so sheltered and over-privileged — smart schools, smart areas of London in which to live. The boy could have turned out as spoiled as his father, unaware of how others had to live. It was something of a miracle that at the moment he seemed untouched by this, but it would be good for him to go to a school with all classes and all races to contend with. The Academy was also co-ed, and this made him chuckle, a chuckle which stopped abruptly when he noticed he'd taken a wrong turning. Cursing his stupidity, he went around the block to get himself back on track. Once more on the right road, he returned to his musings.

Since his return from long years abroad, the divisions in English society were far greater than he remembered and had come as a shock. There was a new underclass, not like the solid working class of his childhood. The simplistic view was that the poor now seemed to fall under the radar, and the welfare system was failing them. At the other end of the scale, the rich were becoming richer, and there was a ghastly new class of nouveau riche, who didn't seem to give a damn about anyone, carefully putting their money safely offshore to avoid paying their taxes. Bloody Brexit was only going to make things worse. Rawlings cursed the politicians, along with the endless traffic lights.

Somewhat later than he intended, he drew up outside the house, left the hazard lights on for the benefit of any passing traffic warden and rang the bell. The door was flung open by an over-excited Felix, but before he could start on his chatter, Rawlings told him they had to make a fast getaway to avoid another parking ticket. Nula handed the child a small bag of his things, and after tearful farewells from her, they made a quick exit.

'How was your day?' Rawlings asked. Felix assured him he'd had a great time and proceeded to go into a detailed account of everything they'd done. When he finished, he pulled some money out of his pocket.

'Nula didn't spend much of your money E.G., although I tried to insist that she did. There's still quite a bit left over.'

Rawlings smiled. 'That was very generous of Nula,' and then added, 'Why don't you put it towards your laptop fund?'

This suggestion obviously pleased the boy. 'Wow, thanks, E.G.,' he said, and carefully returned the money to his jacket.

They had now reached the outskirts of London and were back on the motorway. Rawlings inquired if Felix was hungry. He shook his head. 'I had loads to eat. We went to Patisserie Valerie, and I had the largest chocolate éclair you've ever seen. I don't think I have room for anything else.'

'Lucky you.' Rawlings said. 'I had a horrible sandwich.'

After that, they drove on in silence for quite a while.

The boy looked anxiously at him. 'Are you all right, E.G.? You're very quiet. Is your leg bothering you?'

Rawlings was touched by this inquiry. To be honest, yes, his leg was giving him bloody gyp, but that wasn't what was bothering him. He assured the boy he was fine, just concentrating on the driving, as there was a lot of traffic. They arrived back early evening, and Felix went to put his bag in his room. Rawlings noted he'd brought very few things back with him. It wasn't much to show for a life, even if he was only ten years old.

'How was your day?' Isobel asked him.

'Interesting,' was his short reply. He looked at her. 'There is something I would like to discuss with you, which came out of the meeting with the solicitor. Not now. Can I come over tomorrow morning?' She looked curious but nodded.

The next day was overcast and gloomy. Undaunted Felix rode his bike over to Sunil telling Rawlings that if it rained, they would watch a DVD. Mr Patel had a great collection of old films. Reminding him to put on his helmet, Rawlings watched him go and then made his way over to Isobel. She watched him hobbling his way painfully up the garden.

Coffee?' she asked as he reached the top of the steps. He nodded. He'd had a rough night. When Isobel arrived back with the coffee, she insisted he put his leg up on a stool and then looked at him. 'Well, what did the specialist say?'

He told her the gist of it, and she listened quietly, without interrupting, as he went on, 'I also had an interesting meeting with the solicitor. He'd heard from the aunt in Australia, Susanna's sister, Sarah.' He paused and then took a deep breath, saying gruffly, 'It seems she is now anxious to have Felix live with them and will be coming over in December to collect him.'

Isobel looked startled by this news and gave him a quizzical look. 'And how will you feel about that?'

Rawlings gave her one of his wry smiles. 'I think I must bow to the inevitable. I hate to use the phrase, but it's 'probably for the best'. The outcome of my operation means I'll be out of action for at least eight weeks. I certainly won't be able to manage my recovery on the boat, let alone look after the boy, so I will be going into a convalescence home.' He held up his hand. 'Before you give me offers of help Isobel, which I know you will do, I have to tell you it's realistically not feasible.' He looked at her. 'I have to face it. The facts are plain. Felix needs a family and stability. Once he is out in Australia, I think, and hope, he will settle down and be happy.' Pausing, he added, 'It would be nice to think he will come back to England occasionally, but however much I hate the idea of losing him, Australia has to be his new home.' Isobel still said nothing, so he continued. 'They apparently have three children; the eldest is a boy of Felix's age. He has adapted so quickly to being here; I just hope he will do the same there.' He made a face and added with a flippancy he was far from feeling. 'My greatest concern is that Felix will get an Aussie accent.'

Isobel smiled at this and after a moment said, 'It's a shock. We're all going to miss him quite dreadfully. It will seem so odd not having him around, even though he has only been with us a short while.' She took his hand. 'You know Rawlings, the boy will always be welcome to stay here, on his visits to the old country.' He thanked her, saying yet again he was grateful for her generosity and understanding. She let go of his hand and offered him more coffee, but he shook his head, shifting in his seat. 'Is there something else Rawlings?'

'I'm afraid there is,' he said, sounding apologetic, 'and

something for which I again need your help. I believe you're on the Trust of the new Academy school near here?' Isobel nodded. 'Well, I wondered whether it would be possible to get Felix into it, just for one term. I don't want to send him back to boarding school now he seems so settled here. And his friend Sunil Patel is starting at the school next term as well.' Isobel raised her eyebrows questioningly, and Rawlings explained that Sunil was the son of the Patel's who ran the paper shop. 'Felix has struck up a friendship with the boy; they spend nearly all their time together.'

Isobel considered this for a moment. 'I think that sounds a very sensible plan,' she said. 'and I'm sure it should be possible to get him a place at the school. It's a fairly new Academy, and the results so far have been excellent. I will talk to the headmaster, who seems an enlightened man and doing a great job. I'll explain the situation and see what can be arranged.'

Rawlings was greatly relieved. It had been worrying him because he could think of no alternative other than to send him back to the previous school, which he was dead against. He thanked her again and stood up ready to go. Isobel walked with him to the door,

'Marnie and I have arranged a birthday party for Felix in the garden. We could invite the Patel's, and Jake and of course Lydia, Maria and Paul. I'm hoping it will be fine. If it's not, we'll all have to repair to the house.' She sighed. 'You can just never tell with August.'

Isobel's kindness never ceased to surprise him.

Chapter Thirteen

August 18th 2017. The Birthday.

Rawlings woke early on the morning of Felix's birthday, thankful to have had a reasonable night's sleep and one that unusually had been free from nightmares. Recently he'd been suffering from a recurrent dream which would have him waking him in a sea of sweat with his heart racing alarmingly. Because he'd had it so often, unlike some of his other nightmares, this one was etched on his memory. He'd be walking through a huge desert area that was littered with bodies, body parts, abandoned weapons and burned out tanks. With him, there was always a woman, someone he didn't know and who was definitely not Mia. He was aware that they were both desperately looking for the same small child. They'd turn over the dead remains and call out to each other there was nobody they recognised. Suddenly in the distance, they would catch sight of the child, he was never certain of the sex, sitting on an outcrop of rock. They'd immediately start running through the dead bodies, calling out for the child to stay there, saying that they were coming. But as hard as they ran, the child remained as far away. Rawlings could feel he was getting tired, and the terrible pain in his leg was making it difficult for him to move. As the child started to fade into the distance, the panic set in. And then, quite suddenly, it would be over, he would jerk awake, crying out in frustration and despair.

Rawlings closed his eyes. Stupid to think about it now, especially as he'd just had a good night's sleep for once. He wondered if the boy had slept at all. Felix had been in a state of high excitement the night before. Were birthdays so special at that age? He tried to think back to his birthdays when he was a young boy. They were uneventful, as far as he could remember. His mother always sent him a card, 'To my son', which she rather pathetically would sign, 'Love Mum and Dad', even after his father was long gone. Her present was usually something useful for school like a new pen or satchel, so not much excitement there. He glanced across at the fishing rods in the corner of the room. It had taken him a long time to decide what to buy. One thing was sure: Felix was going to be quite spoiled. Isobel, Marnie and Maria had talked of little else but birthday plans for the past week, their ideas for the boy's party being mapped out to the last detail. They'd tried to include Rawlings, but he'd assured them he was perfectly happy to leave them to it.

Looking out of the window, he noticed the sky was overcast and grey, not really suitable for the day that had been so carefully planned. He hobbled across the room and peered out. A thick layer of mist made it difficult to see to the other side of the river. If it didn't clear up, the garden picnic would have to be abandoned. He started to pull on his clothes. Bloody English climate! How could you ever plan for anything? Thunderstorms ruined summer weddings, cricket matches were washed out, Wimbledon had courts under water, and then, when everyone longed for a white Christmas, the sun perversely came out, and it was as mild as a spring day. And it was noticeable that the weather conditions appeared to be getting more extreme. The sun was hotter, the snow lasted longer, and the rainstorms ended up as disastrous floods. All due no doubt to 'Global Warming', which the present bunch of politicians were happy to ignore, far too busy with bloody Brexit and 'making America great again'.

Grumbling his way into the kitchen, he made a large pot of black coffee, taking it back to his desk. The card he'd bought for Felix yesterday was still in its envelope in front of him. Patel's had a somewhat limited choice, but he'd managed to find one decent picture, of a river scene with some boats, which had the advantage of being blank inside without the obligatory trite greetings and terrible verses. He took it out of the envelope and stared at the blank page, wondering what the hell he should write. At last, he settled on, 'For Felix, August 18th 2017, from your loving Grandfather.' And then with a flourish, he added 'E.G.', with an inky squiggle underneath. He waited for the ink to dry and then put it back in the envelope, addressing it to F.G. Rawlings.

His mobile, which he'd left beside his bed, started to ring and he glanced at his watch. It was only just eight o'clock, so he was not in the best of moods as he picked it up.

'Yes'? he said abruptly.

It was Isobel, sounding apologetic. 'I'm sorry to be ringing you so early Rawlings, but I have one very excited boy here, wanting to know how soon he can come over to the boat.'

'Well,' Rawlings paused, 'what about in half an hour? That will give me time to have some breakfast.' He paused again. 'Are we giving him presents now, or waiting until this afternoon?

'I'm afraid I've given him mine already.' Isobel sounded apologetic again. 'I think we could spread them out, maybe a few now, and then some this afternoon. I leave it up to you.'

'Right,' said Rawlings, feeling that this didn't help him much. He added gloomily, 'I'm a bit worried about the weather. It doesn't look very promising for a picnic.'

Isobel laughed. 'Don't be such a pessimist. It's only early morning mist; it'll burn off by eleven. The forecast is for sun and cloud today, so I'm sure it will be fine enough for his picnic this afternoon.'

Rawlings didn't have the same faith in weather forecasts that Isobel did, but all he said was, 'Good, well, tell the boy I'll see him soon. And thank you, Isobel. I hope he didn't wake you too early.' He rang off before she had time to tell him if he did.

Thirty minutes later, on the dot, Felix appeared, clutching a large pair of binoculars.

'Look what Isobel gave me,' he burst out. 'They are the best binoculars ever, really powerful. She told me they had belonged to her husband.'

Rawlings took them from the boy and made an examination. He was right. They were the best, which was no great surprise if they'd belonged to Peter. It was a generous gesture, and he was touched that Isobel had parted with them. 'That's very kind of Isobel. You're a lucky boy. You must take great care of them,' and he handed the binoculars back. 'When the mist clears, you can sit on the deck and try them out.' He then handed him his card, which the boy opened and read. For a moment he seemed overcome, and then he simply said, 'Thank you, E.G.,' but Rawlings could tell he was pleased. He looked at the boy. 'I wasn't sure whether to give you my present now or later. Maybe now would be good, as you may get other presents when people come to your party. What do you think?'

Felix said a little shyly, 'I think I'd like to have your present now.'

Rawlings nodded and went into the bedroom, coming back minutes later with the fishing rods and handed them over. 'I'm afraid I didn't wrap them up in fancy paper. I bought two so that you and Sunil could try fishing together.' He gave a laugh. 'I don't know much about fishing myself, but I believe Jake does, so he can give you guidance.'

Felix looked at him with shining eyes. 'Thank you, E.G. That is the best present ever,' and he flung his arms around Rawlings, nearly knocking him off balance.

'Glad you like them,' he said gruffly, disentangling himself. 'Now, sit down and tell me your plans for the day.'

Felix sat on the sofa and explained he'd been invited to have lunch with the Patel's and then they would all come over together for the party about three. He looked anxiously at Rawlings. 'Would you mind if I went over to Sunil now? I want to show him the binoculars and tell him about the fishing rods. I'll leave them on the boat for now, if that's all right?'

Rawlings told him it was, and in truth, he was relieved to be left in peace. It would give him time for some writing. There was a minor dispute when Felix was told not to take his bike because of the poor visibility. The boy was about to protest, but Rawlings explained he had no lights on his bicycle and it could be dangerous. Thankfully the boy seemed too happy to argue and clutching the binoculars and his card he left soon afterwards.

Isobel, as usual, was right. The mist burned off, and the skies cleared. There was the odd cloud, but these only blocked the sun intermittently. It was certainly warm enough to sit outside. By early afternoon the garden had been turned into a festive picnic area, with rugs spread out over the lawn and the long table under the trees already laden with sandwiches, cakes of all kinds and jugs of lemonade. A large chocolate cake, Maria's triumph, took pride of place in the centre and was made in the shape of the boat. Instead of the name Esme Jane, she had piped in Felix in white icing. Rawlings inspected it and was amazed by the detail.

'Someone should take a picture of that,' he said. Marnie assured him Paul would bring his camera.

The guests began to assemble, Maria and husband Paul, Jake, Lydia, and then the Patel's arrived, with an excited Felix. He immediately ran over to Rawlings and showed him a saddlebag for his bicycle.

'E.G., look what Mr and Mrs Patel gave me for my bike. It is large enough to put picnics in and everything. And Sunil gave me bicycle lights, so I'll be able to ride my bike even when it's misty.'

'They are wonderful presents, Felix. I hope you thanked them.' Rawlings smiled at the boy and said, 'Have you seen the cake that Maria has made?'

Felix and Sunil went over to the table, while Isobel made general introductions. On a small table by one of the rugs, there was another pile of presents. Rawlings felt anxious and murmured to Marnie that he hoped they weren't overdoing it. She vehemently shook her head and told him it wasn't possible to overdo a birthday.

'It's only one day a year Rawlings and the boy looks so happy.'

'Tomorrow is going to be a terrible anti-climax,' he said with a touch of gloom, and Marnie laughed.

'You're such an old Eeyore. He'll be far too busy, playing with all his presents.'

Isobel had automatically fallen into the role of gracious hostess. Rawlings was reminded of all the Embassy gatherings he'd attended. She now suggested they sat down while Felix opened his presents. The white cane garden chairs had been brought down from the terrace, and the Patel's, Isobel and Lydia sat on them, while Rawlings was given the largest to sit on, a beautiful peacock chair with coloured cushions.

'I feel like an old emperor enthroned on this,' he told Felix.

Everyone else sat on the rugs and then Isobel told Felix it was time for the present opening. The boy carefully opened each one, and Rawlings was overwhelmed by the care everyone had taken over their choices. Marnie had given him a large set of drawing materials, with crayons, pastels and water-colours. Lydia had bought him a small camera and Paul and Maria had brought him a photo of the boat in a frame – no doubt used as a guide for making the cake. Lastly, he opened the bulky package from Jake. It was a cricket set, bat, stumps and a ball. Immediately he wanted to play a game in the garden, but Isobel mildly pointed out that there was too much of a slope. Jake added that if anyone hit a six into the river, they would lose the ball. Everyone laughed at this, and Mr Patel tactfully said there was a good green space on the common near him, where they could set up the game, and Jake said he would join them.

The sun had come out from behind a particularly large cloud, and Isobel suggested they should have tea. Rawlings looked around and thought the gathering resembled a beautiful Edwardian scene. He hadn't felt this contented since his arrival back in England. It almost revived his hopes for the country. Mr Patel was in deep conversation with Isobel. Beata Patel was chatting to Lydia, while Marnie was with Maria and Paul on another rug. Sunil and Felix, their plates laden with food, were sitting with Jake, on a rug beside the present table and near to Rawlings.

'Well, it appears from this pile of riches that you've been very spoiled, Felix,' he told the boy, who gave a broad grin. 'I have been lucky, haven't I.' And then added rather solemnly, 'I've never had a birthday like this before. This had been the best day of my life.'

Isobel was just about to suggest cutting the cake when there was a sudden noise and commotion which came from the river. Jake pointed to a helicopter circling overhead.

'Something must have happened,' he said. 'Most likely there's been a collision, or a boat has overturned.'

'The helicopter might mean they are looking for bodies,' Paul added.

Everyone, except Rawlings, stood up.

'Do you see anything?' Isobel asked.

Jake shook his head. 'A lot of people are gathering down there. I might go down and see if they need any help.'

'Can I go with him?' Felix asked, and Sunil asked his

parents the same question. They all looked at Isobel, who smiled.

'I don't see why not, but you boys must stay with Jake.'

The three of them set off, and those that were left settled back, while Maria went around with the teapot and refreshed their cups. Rawlings took the opportunity to thank everyone for their kindness and generosity.

'He is a most lovely boy.' Mr Patel said, and his wife nodded in agreement. 'We do like having him visit us. I think he and Sunil have become great friends.'

'Well, I have some news,' Isobel suddenly declared. 'I only heard this morning and haven't had time to tell you yet Rawlings, but I had a letter from the headmaster of St Bede's Academy. He would like to see Felix for an interview next week, but I think it is very likely they will find him a place at the school for next term.' She turned to Mr Patel, 'That is the same school Ravi, I think your son Sunil is to go to.'

He beamed. 'It is indeed Lady Isobel. That will be such good news for the boys if they can be at school together.'

This exchange mildly amused Rawlings. It was so typical of Isobel to call Mr Patel by his first name, whilst he still addressed her deferentially as 'Lady Isobel', which of course was incorrect, because she was merely Lady Mallinson, not Lady Isobel Mallinson which would have meant she was the daughter of a duke or some such nonsense. He suddenly realised they were all looking for a response from him, so he quickly said, 'That would be a great relief to me Isobel, and a weight off my mind,' adding, 'but I would be grateful if nobody mentioned this to Felix, as I haven't told him yet. He hasn't actually mentioned next term to me, but I can't help feeling he will be relieved not to be sent back to boarding school. The boy seems happy and established here.' He gave a gruff laugh, 'And selfishly I think we'd all miss him if he left us.' There was a murmur of agreement, but Isobel looked anxiously at him, knowing now that Felix would be leaving for Australia at Christmas and already worried about the effect this would have on Rawlings.

The helicopter left the area and a short while later Felix, Sunil and Jake returned.

'Two small boys had overturned their boat,' Jake explained. 'They were both picked up, so no harm done. One of them couldn't swim. He was lucky there was a boat passing by. The stupid kids, neither of them had life-jackets on.'

'That makes me so annoyed,' Isobel said, 'we have incidents like this every year. Life jackets should be made compulsory wear for every child on the river under ten. Last year there were three drownings.'

The sun disappeared behind a cloud, and the party atmosphere turned noticeably solemn. Marnie leapt to her feet. 'Why don't we light the candles on Maria's wonderful cake?' she suggested, and at once the mood brightened.

'You should take a photo of the cake, Felix, with your new camera,' Jake said.

Lydia looked pleased with this suggestion. 'Shall I show you how it works, Felix?' she asked and went over to him.

While they were occupied getting the camera ready, the eleven candles, with some difficulty because of small gusts of breeze, were finally lit. Photos were taken, and Felix was then instructed to blow them out, which he managed in one go. Everyone clapped, and they all sang "Happy Birthday".

'You must make a wish, Felix, when you cut the cake,' Marnie told him, 'but don't tell us otherwise it won't come true.' He did this, closing his eyes very tightly. Rawlings wondered what he wished for and fervently hoped it wasn't to stay with them forever. He still had to break to him the news about his move to Australia.

Slices of cake were taken round, and there were general murmurs of appreciation.

'What a very silly tune "Happy Birthday" is,' Rawlings remarked, 'yet everybody knows it. I went to a birthday party in Sarajevo some years ago, and they even sang it there.'

'It was said to have been composed by two American women, at the end of the nineteenth century,' Lydia spoke in her precise tones, 'but this attribution has been greatly disputed. I believe it to be the most recognised song in the English language, but there have been translations into many other languages. I once heard it sung in Japanese.'

'I seem to remember there was some dispute over the copyright?' Isobel looked at Lydia for confirmation, and she smiled, which was a rare event in itself.

'Indeed there was, Isobel,' she said, impressing the assembled company with her great knowledge of the topic. 'It would have made somebody very rich indeed to have managed to claim the copyright, but last year the claim was finally turned down in court, and the song declared to be in the public domain.'

'That is most fascinating,' Mr Patel said admiringly.

The afternoon drifted happily on. Rawlings sat on his own, happy to listen to the general murmur of chatter. Lydia was now in deep conversation with the Patel's. Maria and Marnie were discussing recipes, while Paul was talking about fishing to the boys. Isobel and Jake walked around the garden and Rawlings could hear them discussing where to plant new roses. Names like Cecile Brunner and Zepherine Drouhin floated on the air. It was to him a uniquely English afternoon.

Finally, the clouds blotted out the sun, and a definite chill descended. The Patel's announced they had to get back to their daughter Carmen, who'd been staying overnight with a friend. With their departure, everyone started to leave. Lydia packed up the wrapping paper and offered to help Felix take his presents to his room. Jake took the garden chairs back to Isobel's terrace, while Marnie and Maria folded the rugs and took the tea things back on trays to the kitchen. Rawlings went over to where Isobel was standing, supervising the exodus. He kissed her on the cheek.

'I can't thank you enough for what you have done today, Isobel. I could never have given him such a wonderful party. Whatever happens, he will always remember this birthday.'

He looked emotional, so she smiled at him. 'Truly Rawlings, we will all remember it. Felix is such a lovely boy and has given us all so much pleasure.' She paused and said gently, 'But you, alone, must take the credit for how happily he has settled here. Think of the lost and lonely child you collected from that school. You have now given him a trust in people, and I don't think he will ever lose that.' Rawlings seemed unable to make any comment in reply to this, so she added briskly, 'I must leave you and go to the kitchen to send Maria and Paul home. Bless them; they have been here all day. That cake was a triumph and a total surprise to me.' She held onto his hand for a moment and then turned and went back into the house.

Later in the evening, Marnie delivered a bowl of soup to the boat. 'I know you are probably too tired to make something for yourself Rawlings. This is very light, especially after all that cake.'

He smiled wearily and thanked her. The soup was taken to the kitchen, and when she returned, he poured her a drink. 'I think the boy had a great day,' he said as she sat down opposite him. 'Everyone has been so kind and generous. When I went over just now to say goodnight, Felix was lying in bed with all his presents laid out in a neat row in front of him, just staring at them. He told me that usually he only had new clothes for his birthday. Isn't that the saddest thing you ever heard? It's odd that a child with such wealthy parents could be so deprived and unloved. In some ways, I feel it's my fault. I failed my own son and he, in turn, failed his. But Gillian was a good mother and always there for Hugo, even though she did spoil him. Susanna, on the other hand, seems to have neglected Felix as much as Hugo did, much too taken up with her own career.' He looked at Marnie. 'Maybe I've got something right at last. Felix told me it had been the best day of his life, and I truly think he meant it.'

'Well, of course, he did.' Marnie told him firmly. 'I'll tell you one thing, Rawlings. I am really pleased to hear about the school too. It will be ideal for Felix to remain here, now he has settled in so happily.'

Rawlings put down his glass and looked at her, a strange expression on his face. 'Sadly, it can't be for long Marnie.' He told her about Australia and the impending departure of Felix in December. It was a struggle for him to get through it. He'd found it hard to come to terms with this decision himself. When he finished, Marnie appeared in shock. Nothing was said for a while. She finally burst out, 'Why are you letting this happen, Rawlings? He is happy here with you, with us…'

He held up his hand to stop her. 'It goes without saying I am reluctant to let the boy go. It is the last thing I wanted to happen. But in the circumstances, I am convinced it's the right decision.' He paused, 'I haven't had a chance to tell you, but I'm to have a major operation on my leg in January, and this will put me out of action for at least eight weeks while I recover. And before you offer to look after the boy, I have to tell you Isobel has already done that. But quite honestly, I have no idea what the prognosis on my leg, and indeed my general health, is going to be. My body has taken quite a battering in the last few years, and I already have the beginnings of rheumatoid arthritis. It will be far better for Felix to make the change now so that he can settle down to a stable future. I selfishly wish it wasn't in Australia, but maybe it will be good for him to have a completely fresh start. He has a cousin who is the same age, and there are two other cousins as well. It will be the family life he has never had, and which I couldn't possibly offer him…' He broke off as a wave of exhaustion came over him. 'I don't think I can discuss it anymore today, Marnie. Why don't you come over for supper sometime soon, once the boy has gone back to the house?'

Marnie looked pleased with this suggestion. 'Why don't you come to me? You haven't been to the boathouse for a long while.' She stood up. 'Have your soup Rawlings, and get some rest. You look dead beat.'

After she'd gone, Rawlings thought about Marnie

with slight feelings of guilt. There was no doubt about it, since the arrival of Felix, he'd neglected her, and their evenings spent together had been few and far between. She'd never once complained when his time had been taken up looking after the child, but that night, with her departure, came the sudden realisation that he'd missed their evenings together, and he suspected she had too. Unlike evenings with Isobel, with Marnie, he always felt totally relaxed. She was like some old sweater that you pulled on for comfort. It wasn't that he didn't enjoy the company of Isobel as well, but with her, it was somehow more formal, and most times, he was asking the poor woman for further help with the boy, or her invaluable advice. He gave an inward sigh. There was really no reason for not doing both his caring for Felix and seeing Marnie as well, especially once the boy was at school. He could finish writing the bloody book in the day, and see Marnie in the evening, once Felix had gone to bed.

With this decision made, he limped off to the kitchen to warm up the soup.

Chapter Fourteen

September 2017

The proposed evening with Marnie didn't materialise until the beginning of September. Events in the last week of August suddenly piled up, making it a particularly busy time for Rawlings. There was the interview with the headmaster of the Academy, which Isobel had organised. She reported it went well and they now had to hope for an offer of a place. Rawlings was just relieved that Felix appeared pleased with the idea; in fact, his reaction to being told he would not be returning to his old school was nothing short of joyful.

After the interview, they had supper with Isobel, and later the three of them had played a game of Mar-Jong, which Felix won. 'He always wins,' Isobel told Rawlings, smiling indulgently. 'He insists on only collecting circles and green dragons, but it makes no difference. He still wins.'

Rawlings observed the two of them together. Despite their age difference, she and the boy were remarkably at ease in each other's company. Felix often made her laugh and on occasion could be positively cheeky, but she never seemed to mind. It made him wonder if, in Felix, she saw the child that she and Peter were never able to have. Whatever the reason, it was clear that Isobel already had a great affection for the boy. Maybe he filled an emotional gap in her life that had been lacking for a long time, especially since Peter's death. Seeing them together made him question yet again whether it was right to let Felix go to Australia. But now there seemed to be no alternative.

Soon after that, there was an unexpected invitation for the boy to spend the night with Jenny at her cottage beside the Manor Stables, which necessitated driving him up to Essex. Rawlings had quickly decided the train journey and taxis would be too complicated to arrange. After dropping Felix off, he returned to London and paid Graham a further visit, as it seemed there were yet more papers to sign. The whole process of sending the boy to Australia had become enormously complicated, but he patiently did as he was instructed. Graham's office had a stuffy, Dickensian feel, and as always, he found the lawyer dry and humourless.

It was therefore with a feeling of relief he arrived at the Garrick Club, to meet up with his agent, Jolyon Jordan-Smith, ostensibly to report on his progress with the book. Jolyon was a member of this august establishment, and Rawlings enjoyed the occasional visit to the club, with its theatrical portraits, elegant rooms and excellent food. Jolyon was in his element, talking throughout the meal in his high-pitched affected drawl and scattering the conversation with famous names. He was a man who liked to collect celebrities, particularly those in the publishing and literary worlds. Since his companion hardly drew breath, Rawlings had plenty of time to make a study of him. Jolyon was certainly a decorative character. Maybe with a name like his, you were obliged to be. Flamboyantly dressed in a brightly coloured shirt and polka-dot bow tie, he topped off this eccentric vision with blonde hair, which presumably was dyed, and worn in Byronic curls. Having never stinted on his love of all things epicurean, he was what his Scottish aunts would have referred to as a 'wee tubby man'.

'My dear,' he complained, at the start of the meal, 'I am the first to admit that this club is really not what it used to be. Nowadays it is not so much high-brow as positively middle-brow.' He gave a tinkling laugh. 'And I fear we are positively hurtling towards the low-brow, with the recent intake of members. Gone are the days of the great actors and lawyers. Far too many now are minor celebrities, arriving from the media and the lower end of journalism.' He looked up from his dish of oysters, 'Of course, Rawlings, I don't include you in that category. You would be most welcome at the Garrick, with your long, distinguished career as a war correspondent.' Rawlings winced at this suggestion and pointed out that he understood the waiting time to become a member now stood at twenty years or more, by which time he would be in his grave. Privately he wouldn't have wanted to join this club; it was too elitist for him and full of snobbery, plus the absence of female company. All in all, quite frankly, not worth its huge annual fees.

A few hours, and several ports later, he repaired with some relief, to the more motley assortment to be found in The Frontline Club. He'd left Jolyon happy with the promise that the book would be finished and delivered by the end of the year. It was therefore with a light heart that he entered the club and walked up the familiar narrow stairs, glancing at the brick wall adorned with Topolski sketches. It struck him, with some amusement, of the contrast between this and the sweeping stairs of the Garrick Club with all the lavish portraits of great thespians. On entering the Members Room, the differences struck him even more. Here was a plain square room with black sofas and stripped pine tables, a world away from the opulence and grandeur of the Garrick dining room. No portraits here; just books, a display of hats worn in foreign parts, and a board displaying photographs of famous correspondents. He limped towards the familiar bar and found a new barman. For some reason, they seemed to change with great regularity. This one was a languid specimen from Brazil. Rawlings patiently explained his usual tipple, took his drink and, as was his habit, raised his glass in a silent toast to the photo of Marie Colvin, before joining two cronies on the far side of the room.

It was somehow inevitable he should proceed to have far too many drinks, and the carousing went on into the small hours. Consequently, he was tired and somewhat irritable when he returned to the stables the following morning to collect Felix.

While the boy went to take a last look at the horses, Rawlings took the opportunity to tell Jenny about Felix's impending departure for Australia, explaining he was now to live with his aunt's family. She seemed genuinely upset by this news, and once again it struck him that the upheaval of the boy leaving was going to distress a great many people, not least Felix himself. He thought grimly that he had to break it to the boy soon; it couldn't be put off much longer.

In spite of his throbbing head, he decided to make a small detour, taking Felix to Great Warley churchyard, to see the spot where the urn with his parent's ashes had been placed. It was next to the gravestones of Gillian and Gerald. Rawlings stared at Hugo and Susanna's stone and grudgingly admitted Graham had done a good job in organising it. The elegant gothic shape was in dark slate, engraved in tasteful lettering with their names, the date of their deaths and the inscription, 'Tragically taken from us far too soon'. The marble urn containing their ashes had been placed on a stand at the base of the stone. Rawlings had managed to buy two bunches of flowers at a garage, one of these he now placed at Gillian's grave and the other he gave to Felix, instructing him to put them in front of his parent's stone. The child did as he was told, showing absolutely no emotion; he just seemed relieved when they returned to the car. Rawlings wondered whether he should ask the boy how he felt about this visit to the graves, but observing the set expression on Felix's face, he decided this would not be the moment to pry. Instead, they drove on in silence. Rawlings didn't mind at all for if he were honest his hangover was worsening by the minute. They had nearly reached home when Felix finally began to talk, telling him about the great time he'd had with Jenny. His parent's gravestone was never mentioned at all.

★

On the first day of September, they received the news that Felix had been offered a place at St Bede's Academy, starting on September 10th. He seemed genuinely delighted by this news and Rawlings gratefully accepted an offer from the Patel's to take him to buy the school uniform at the same time as they shopped for Sunil's. It took the whole day, and

Felix returned in the evening with a pile of receipts and a message from Mr Patel that it would be fine for Rawlings to settle up with him in the morning. Rawlings glanced through them, making a vague calculation of the damage and gave a 'whew!'. It seemed to be a large amount of money for one small boy's uniform. How on earth did parents of the poorer children manage? It was his understanding that this Academy was open to all backgrounds and classes. Marnie would have to be asked about this. He looked up from the bills to see that Felix was staring at him anxiously, so Rawlings smiled at him reassuringly.

'Shall I come over and inspect what you have bought?' The uniform had been laid out on the bed, ready for him to see. The school colours were grey and bright green; the trousers were dark grey, and so was the blazer, which was adorned with the St. Bede's badge in green on the pocket. The light grey sweater had a green band round the neck, and there was a dark grey fleece, again with the badge. All very tasteful. Rawlings thought gloomily that it seemed a lot of kit for one term, but he was keen not to dampen Felix's spirits, so he said, 'You're going to look extremely smart. You must take good care of your uniform. I suggest you hang it up in your wardrobe and when you get back from school each day you can change into your jeans, so you keep it looking good.' He turned to go and then stopped. 'Now that you are going to your new school, I think we should get you a proper laptop. Shall we go shopping for it tomorrow?" Before the boy could answer, he'd left the room.

★

A few days later he accepted a supper invitation from Marnie and duly arrived at the boathouse, carrying the obligatory bottle of wine. He noticed at once she was looking flustered, so he gave her a hug, which left her even more flushed. She took the wine from him and hurried into the kitchen.

'Are you all right?' He called out after her, 'you're looking harassed. I can go away and come back later if you like.' He heard a cork pop, and she returned with two glasses of wine.

'No, I'm fine. It's just that I'm trying out a new recipe and it's taking rather longer to cook than I thought, and I'm not at all sure it will work.'

Rawlings settled into his usual chair assuring her it would be delicious and anyway he was in no hurry. She handed him his wine and gave him another worried look, 'I bought some Australian wine,' she told him, adding nervously, 'from the Barossa Valley. I thought you might like to see how their wine tastes.' He smiled and took a sip, closed his eyes and kept the wine in his mouth for a while before swallowing. 'It's actually rather good, mellow and fruity. I look forward to testing more of their bottles. How clever of you to find it.' Marnie was greatly relieved with this reaction and decided not to tell him how much it had cost.

'I want to pick your brains about this school Felix is going to.' Rawlings said, 'These Academies are a completely new system to me, so please enlighten me about them. How do they differ from other state schools?'

She didn't answer immediately. 'I think the main difference,' she said slowly, 'is that they are independent of local government control. They're still state-funded and examined by Ofsted, but they're run solely by an Academy Trust, which is a charitable body.' She looked at Rawlings. 'This means a great deal depends on the quality of the Trust, and the ability of the headmaster. A few Academies have failed because of this, but others have been successful in that they have been lucky with both. St Bede's is a case in point. It has an excellent headmaster, and of course, Isobel is in on the Trust, so Felix should be fine.'

'I've just paid for his uniform,' Rawlings said grimly. 'I can afford it, but how on earth do the poorer families manage? I can tell you it wasn't cheap.'

She shrugged. 'I think they run a very good second-hand shop.'

He was looking straight at her, and she suddenly noticed how very blue his eyes were. Why had she not noticed this before? She'd always thought they were greyish blue. Maybe it was because they were mainly masked under his thick eyebrows. The colour was really startling. Realising she was staring at him, she covered her embarrassment by saying quickly, 'I've never seen you wearing glasses Rawlings. Don't you even need them for reading?'

'My eyes seem to be the only bit of me still working,' he said gloomily. 'I fully expect them to give up on me soon as well.' This made Marnie laugh. Things were back to normal, and she told him not to be such an old pessimist.

After the meal, which Marnie had thought lacking in flavour, but Rawlings declared delicious, another bottle was opened, and they settled back around the log burner.

'How strangely autumnal it already feels,' she said. 'summer seems a distant memory. I miss those long days...'

'What summer?' Rawlings interrupted huffily. 'I can't

remember a single hot day in August. The English always think August is a summer month because it's the summer holidays. Instead, we usually get four weeks of absolutely atrocious weather. You can observe the wretched result of this every year, sad little English families huddled together on the beaches, in the driving wind and rain.' Marnie was about to protest that this was a total exaggeration, but Rawlings turned his attention to the wine that he'd brought. 'This claret is also a decent red, but quite different from your Barossa bottle. It was good to try something new Marnie, and excellent with your beef and black olive stew. My claret is also excellent with cheese.' Marnie at once apologised for the absence of cheese, but he waved an airy hand. 'Please, it was no criticism; I was just stating a fact. You have fed me so well I really couldn't eat another thing.'

Marnie sipped her wine. This had to be the moment, she decided, to ask a question that for some time had been on her mind.

'What happened to you and Mia after 9/11?'

Rawlings sighed. He had half expected this. It was inevitable Marnie would want to bring his story up to date. Once again, he inwardly chided himself. He should never have embarked on it in the first place. Now it would have to be finished, and that meant talking about…

He glanced across at her as she waited patiently for him to say something and was momentarily distracted. She was looking rather marvellous, clad in a cerulean blue kaftan, which was a wonderful contrast with her unruly red hair. It made him think of one of those Pre-Raphaelites paintings. There was certainly something about her he found very endearing and yes, loveable, and for some inexplicable reason that he couldn't fathom, he had told her things about himself he wouldn't have dreamed of saying to anyone else. With a weary sigh, he launched into what would definitely be the final episode of his saga.

'After 9/11' he began, searching his memory, 'Mia and I actually had two further years in New York. It was an unsettling time for the American people, and consequently an interesting time to be there. They were suffering from the shock of having been invaded, and it caused a loss of their usual confidence and bravado. It was particularly evident in New York, where the main attack had occurred. The empty shells of the twin towers daily haunted them, and us...' He paused. 'But funnily, Mia and I were probably at our happiest, and it was the nearest we ever got to having a settled relationship. She was finalising the book of photos she'd taken on 9/11 and the aftermath. These pictures were brilliantly caught and made the whole event horrifyingly real. Meanwhile, I was still writing for my paper, giving an Englishman's view of the effect of 9/11 on everyday life in the city.'

He broke off. 'Do you mind if I smoke? I've been trying to give up, or smoke less, but I think I will need one to get me through this.'

Marnie fetched an ashtray and Rawlings lit up. He blew the smoke out slowly, before continuing.

'I suppose it was inevitable it would end. I think it was about March 2003 when I was dispatched to report on the second Iraq war, the last thing I wanted to do, but my usefulness in New York had come to an end. I was presented with an ultimatum; to break my contract with the paper, or bite the bullet and go to Iraq.'

He smoked quietly for a minute as if gathering his thoughts.

'That second Iraq debacle was a particularly nasty war, even though the actual conflict only lasted a few months. People in the UK and America had rightly been uncertain about it, and many of those reporting, strongly against the idea,' he gave a grim smile, 'but those blood brothers, Blair and Bush, were determined to push it through. As we now know, there were no weapons of mass destruction, the main reason given for entering the war. It is certainly true Saddam was a particularly nasty dictator, but good God, the world is full of nasty dictators, and we can't fight them all.'

He angrily stubbed out his cigarette and immediately lit another one.

'I had arrived in March when 'shock and awe' took place, and Iraq was blasted into defeat. The whole bloody business was over by December. That should have been the end of it, and I could have returned to Mia, but it wasn't. It was only the beginning of a disaster that continues to this day. None of our useless politicians, or military, had thought through the consequences of their actions. We on the ground could see very well what would happen. After Saddam was executed, a power vacuum was left, and there was complete and utter mismanagement of the situation by the West. No plans for the aftermath had been considered, and it was no surprise to those of us close to the action that the result was widespread sectarian violence on a horrific scale. It's the sort of horror you don't forget in a hurry, remaining all too graphic.' His expression was grim. 'That was not the only problem I had in reporting this war. I won't bore you with the details, but the way in which journalists worked had now changed. We were embedded.'

Marnie interrupted. 'What did that mean?'

'It meant that instead of being free to report at will, on any aspect of a conflict, now, for our own safety, or so we were told, we had to be under the protection of the army and were only able to report on what they allowed us to. I disliked this intensely. It went against the grain. As a journalist, I wanted to give an eye-witness account on all aspects of a conflict, which meant uncovering untruths and destroying myths that could so quickly appear in these wars.' He gave a shrug. 'At first, I tried to resist this new way of working, but then an ITN crew went missing, and a friend of mine was killed making his way to Basra in an effort to be the first to enter the liberated city. So, I bowed to the inevitable, especially as my paper insisted on it. Even so, with the mounting incidents and atrocities, it was impossible not to report some of what we witnessed, especially when they were crimes committed by the Allies. We saw so many senseless deaths; civilians were bombarded, and, as you would have read and seen, bombs in Baghdad were a daily occurrence, particularly of the suicide variety. In 2004 I wrote a particularly graphic description of the terrible prisoner abuse by our troops, on the prisoners in Abu Ghraib.' He gave another grim smile. 'It was widely reported, but my account drew particular wrath, and I was recalled. This was actually a relief. Baghdad was a terrible place to be working, and now as things were, I didn't feel I could write as the honest journalist I'd always tried to be.' He was silent after this, apparently sunk in gloom, and Marnie was keen for him to return to his personal story. She re-filled his glass.

'Did you return to England, or go back to New York?'

Rawlings looked up at the ceiling as if trying to remember. Marnie waited. At last, he continued.

'It was an odd few years. Several major incidents occurred, which meant I was continually on the move. Hugo and Susanna decided to get married, and I dutifully attended their wedding – not that Hugo would have been upset by my absence – but Gillian would.' He wore a grim expression as if the whole thing was distasteful to him. 'It was another grand affair, in a smart London church. A total waste of bloody money. The flowers alone must have cost thousands, and I am pretty sure Gillian footed the bill. I remember Susanna's mother having a kind of film star glamour, very thin and brittle. She went by the name of Lavender, which seemed to suit her rather exotic persona.' He chuckled. 'She was another absentee parent. It seems she had divorced when young and gone to live with some Romeo in Italy, where she still resided. I left the jollities, as soon as was politely possible, and returned to New York.' He lit a cigarette. 'Two years later, I was informed that Felix had arrived. Strange to think of it now, but having a grandson didn't affect me at the time.'

He was silent for a while, lost in his own thoughts and then gave a sigh.

'I'd no sooner managed to return to New York than Mia and I were parted again. I was sent out to report in Afghanistan, where I was once more an embedded journalist.' Looking at Marnie, he said, 'I don't need to tell you about the Afghan war. It has been heavily documented and still fresh in everyone's memory. Suffice it to say our involvement was mismanaged yet again and therefore depressing to report. Those bloody politicians, they make a pig's meal of everything. Look at the mess we're in now.' He paused and finished his cigarette. Marnie looked at him expectantly, and he gave a shrug of resignation.

'Mia was about to join me late in 2010 when I was suddenly summoned back to England. The news reached me from Jenny, not Hugo, that Gillian had advanced cancer and had only a few weeks to live. This was a shock. Unlike me, she'd never been a drinker or smoker, and was still comparatively young, only just sixty. Apparently, she'd endured terrible pain for months, but told nobody, not even Jenny. By the time she sought medical advice, the cancer was too advanced, and there was nothing they could do.'

He gave a wry smile. 'I've never been good around ill people, but I think and hope I made an effort on this occasion. It was all pretty harrowing. The poor woman had shrunk to half her size, almost unrecognisable, but she remained incredibly brave and even cheerful, right to the end. On the last day of her life, we talked long and late into the night. I told her more about Mia and our life together. This prompted her to thank me yet again for not divorcing her. She obviously felt I'd made a great sacrifice in sticking by my promise, but in all honesty, I hadn't. Mia would never have married me if I'd been a divorced man because of her bloody religion.' He drained his glass in a savage gesture and Marnie quickly re-filled it. 'After the funeral and the reading of the Will, I went away for a few days on my own. It had been a bruising experience. I'd been fond of Gillian 'in my fashion', as the song says, and nobody should have to die that way. I'd rather take myself over a cliff in a bath chair.'

Marnie smiled at this and thought that probably true. She glanced across at him. He seemed to be sunk in his memories. 'What happened then?' she asked. 'Did you go back to New York?'

'I wanted to, but the paper insisted I return to Afghanistan.' He added savagely, 'I should have followed my instincts and packed it in, there and then. Gillian had generously left me a nice legacy. I could easily have retired. Looking back, I don't know why the hell I didn't. I think I'd made up my mind to postpone my decision until I reached sixty-five in 2016. That didn't happen, because Mia made the fatal decision to come out and join me.'

He shrugged. 'You know the rest. The army by that time was involved in trying to rebuild the institutions and protect the population. On the day we were blown up, we were out on an ordinary patrol, going up to a nearby village. Mia didn't need to come with me, but she thought there might be a few photographs in it. I should have stopped her...' He broke off and then said abruptly, 'I don't remember another thing except waking up in hospital and being told she'd been blown to smithereens. The great irony is, the night before, we'd had a wonderful evening. We'd even made plans to go back to Sarajevo and see the orphanage, which had now been rebuilt. I think Mia was keen to catch up with Luka as well...'

He stood up abruptly. 'The rest you know Marnie, there is nothing more to tell you.' Limping badly, he crossed the room, gave her a hug and left.

After he'd gone, she sat, filled with a mixture of emotions, some of guilt, because she'd more or less forced him into telling her all that, and some of sadness, because she now knew for certain that Mia had been the love of his life and her loss was something from which he would never recover. She picked up the dishes and went out to the kitchen, but a wave of tiredness swept over her, and she decided to leave the washing up until the morning.

Returning to sit by the fire, she drank the remains of her wine, musing about the latest revelations. Maybe, in some strange way, it had helped Rawlings to have this outpouring? It was evident he'd never discussed his life with anyone else, not even Isobel. Even so, she made an inward vow not to pry anymore, and in future would think only of cheerful topics to discuss.

Staring moodily into her empty glass, Marnie thought again of his very blue eyes and with a deep sigh finally accepted she had fallen deeply in love with this enigmatic man, which was a stupid and useless thing to do, as it was clear, there was no place in his heart for her.

★

Felix set off to his new school on September 10th. The previous night he'd been full of happy anticipation, but at breakfast, they noticed he was pale and silent. Rawlings had joined them, intending to accompany his grandson to the Academy, but the boy wouldn't hear of it. He told Rawlings firmly he had arranged to meet up with Sunil and they would travel to the school together. Isobel and Rawlings watched him go.

'He seems very nervous. I hope this is the right decision for him,' Rawlings remarked, as he disappeared from view. Isobel just laughed and chided him for being an old worrier.

She added that Felix would be fine, it was a good school, and he'd settle in quickly.

As usual, she was right. Felix returned in the afternoon, cheerful and anxious to tell them all about it. Rawlings listened indulgently to his chatter while reflecting that he still had to tell the boy about the move to Australia. For the moment he was only too happy to postpone this task, deciding it was best to let the boy settle in at the school for a few weeks and then break the news. He was still very uncertain how Felix would take to the idea of being moved to the other side of the world. He bitterly knew only too well how he would feel about the loss of his grandson. He could think of little else.

The next day was his sixty-sixth birthday. He had intended to keep it quiet, but this was scuppered by Marnie. He received a summons to go over to the house as soon as Felix returned from school, which he dutifully did, albeit with some reluctance. A birthday tea greeted him, and even a cake, discreetly adorned by a single candle.

Rawlings, although grumpy at all this fuss, thanked them for the trouble they'd taken, and was especially amused by the efforts of Isobel and Marnie to smarten him up with their presents. Isobel had given him a cashmere cardigan and Marnie a dark blue linen shirt, luxuries both. Felix had also been taken shopping and chosen his grandfather a large keyring with a painted dolphin.

'It's to stop you losing your car keys, E.G.,' he explained, having witnessed this particular incident several times. He'd also drawn a card, with a picture of the boat and the willow tree, and inside he'd written, 'Happy Birthday E.G., With all my love, your grandson, Felix.'

A few days after this, he had an unexpected visit from Lydia. She was carrying three books which she now gave to him, explaining she'd noticed Felix didn't really have anything to read beside his bed, so she'd consulted a friend who had a son of the same age and had been advised that Michael Morpurgo's books were the most popular reading for boys, so she'd ventured to the local book shop and bought Felix a selection.

'I have included "War Horse", she told Rawlings. 'I have read that one myself and last year went to see a performance of it in the theatre. I was quite overwhelmed and found it a most moving experience. There is a film as well, but in my opinion, it didn't do the book justice. Anyway, I just thought the boy might enjoy them.'

Rawlings was surprised and grateful, reflecting how badly he had misjudged her. He asked her to stay for a cup of tea, but she declined, seeming almost embarrassed, and saying gruffly she had to return to work. Strange woman he thought, but definitely intriguing.

Chapter Fifteen

October 2017

The suppers with Marnie now became a twice-weekly occurrence. They decided it would be fairest to take it in turns, although Rawlings pointed out this gave him a decided advantage, as Marnie was already an excellent cook. It did, however, encourage him to make an effort with his culinary dishes and on the day before he was due to entertain, Felix would borrow recipe books from the kitchen at the house and then pour over them making suggestions. His deliberations often resulted in Rawlings scurrying to the local delicatessen for complicated ingredients, and on more than one occasion, he had to reproach the boy for choosing something quite so challenging, but his efforts, much to his surprise, were generally successful, and always drew compliments from an appreciative Marnie. There was only one disaster, when they had to resort to wine and cheese, and this was only because the meal had burned while they were deep in conversation.

'Felix found this recipe,' he told Marnie, as they dug yet again into one of the more exotic dishes, 'although I had to improvise a bit, as some of the ingredients couldn't be found locally, but I think there are enough prawns and crab to justify calling it a seafood pasta.'

'It's delicious and clever of Felix to find it. I'm glad you used linguine. I prefer it to other pastas.' Marnie polished off another large mouthful and then gave a laugh. 'We're beginning to sound like one of those terrible television cooking programmes.'

'Don't watch 'em,' Rawlings said, finishing his plate and contemplating having more. 'I hardly watch television these days. I've even stopped watching the news, too bloody depressing, just endless discussions of Brexit. And to think we have another two years of it.'

Marnie looked at him and said severely, 'I refuse to spoil our meal by introducing politics into it.'

'Quite right,' he agreed almost meekly, but couldn't resist adding, 'Brexit poisons everything, even the digestive system.'

Marnie gave him a reproving frown and then burrowed in her large bag, producing several packages. 'I went to that new delicatessen on the high street today. They have a wonderful selection of cheeses,' she said as she unwrapped them. 'I don't know the names of half of them.'

'What a wonderful woman you are,' Rawlings exclaimed, delighted with the array of riches before him. He poured the remains of the white wine into their glasses, then cleared away the pasta plates. 'I think we should honour your cheeses with a bottle of red,' and he limped off into the kitchen.

As he stood by the sink, the thought occurred to him that he and Marnie had become like an old married couple. Was that a good thing? Opening the wine, he considered how easy it would be to fall into a relationship with her and just settle down. Then he quickly put the thought from his head. The complacent life had never been for him. There was a definite danger here and could lead to complications in the future and was best avoided. For the moment, he was content to let it continue, at least until the boy left. It was good everything was on an even keel, and to take the analogy further, he wanted nothing to rock the boat. Felix had settled into the school far better than he'd anticipated, he'd more or less completed the book, and even though his leg was bloody unbearable at times, at least he knew it would be dealt with in January. The one dark cloud hanging over him was the prospect of informing the boy about the move to Australia. He wrestled endlessly with this problem. The more Felix felt settled in here, the more difficult it was going to make it. But he couldn't put it off much longer. He decided the best time might be during half-term, which was due at the end of the month. Maybe it would be best to take Felix out for a meal and break it to him then. It was a moment he dreaded and was far from certain how he would take the news. Would he see it as a betrayal of trust, of abandonment on his part? Somehow, he had to make the boy see it was in his best interests to go and live with a family. But was it? He'd watched Felix develop happy relationships here. Could it be right to uproot him and send him across the world, so far away from them all? And to Australia? It was such a Philistine country.

★

'I have never met a child with such curiosity,' Isobel remarked a few days later. They were making the most of an Indian summer, and she and Rawlings were sitting on her terrace, basking in the last of the sun. 'He questions me about everything.' And she gave a laugh. 'He even wanted to know the makes of all the china in the drawing room cabinet and kept repeating the names as he examined them; Famille Rose, Meissen, Rockingham and so on.'

'Maybe he'll end up working in an auction house,' Rawlings chuckled, adding, 'I think we've all found that about his curiosity. He always asks me about the music I'm listening to; what instruments, what composers, endless questions. Sadly, my tastes in classical music are rather narrow; mainly Bach, Mozart and Beethoven. He loved the storm sequence in Beethoven's 6th, but I leave it to Marnie to broaden his musical education. She plays him Sydney Bechet and Scott Joplin. The other day I found them both dancing around the boathouse with great abandonment to 'I wish I could shimmy like my sister Kate'. They were like two kids in a playground.' He sighed, thinking she was someone Felix would miss as well and he added, 'He really loves spending time with Marnie.'

At the mention of Marnie's name, Isobel reacted and looked as if she were about to say something, but then thought better of it. Rawlings noted this and presumed Isobel was worrying again about their relationship, or more probably about Marnie's involvement. Her protective hackles were up, and she didn't want to see her hurt. Well, he didn't either. For the moment he was happy to keep it uncomplicated, just as a friendship. There was certainly no physical involvement, which would take it up a notch. At some point, he would try and reassure Isobel on the subject, but at this moment decided to talk about something else.

'Do you know Lydia came to see me the other day, with some Michael Morpurgo books for Felix? It was an unexpected and kind gesture. I'm afraid I rather misjudged her when I first arrived, after all that trouble over Rose.'

'Easily done,' Isobel said and sighed. 'Poor Lydia, she does have an abrupt manner, probably due to the fact she's had a difficult, and in many ways, tragic life.'

Rawlings looked at her questioningly, and she added, 'I don't know a great deal about her background, only the little she has told me. She opened up suddenly late one evening, while we were sitting with Peter. He was nearing the end, and I think she wanted to keep my mind off his suffering, so she told me about hers.'

'Had she been ill?' Rawlings asked.

Isobel shook her head. 'No, nothing like that.' She paused. 'Lydia apparently came from an extremely wealthy family, somewhere up north, I believe they made their fortune in cotton. Her early years were spent in what she described as a bleak, Victorian mansion. She was an only child and spent what must have been a very lonely childhood, with her head permanently stuck in books. She told me she would spend hours looking at all the old copies of *Punch* in her father's library, which seems quite an eccentric thing for a child of six or seven to do.' She looked at Rawlings who was listening intently. 'Quite early on, in her late teens, she came to realise she had lesbian tendencies, there was mention of her falling in love with one of her governesses. Against the family wishes, she managed to go to Cambridge to read medicine. Here I gather she soon embarked on a full-blown lesbian relationship. She and this student wrote passionate love letters to one another and Lydia stupidly left some of these in the desk drawer in her room. While she was back at University, her mother happened to come across them and after reading these, as Lydia put it, "the balloon went up". She was immediately summoned home, on the pretext that her father was very ill, which of course was untrue. There were terrible rows that followed. Her parents insisted she gave up this girl. The upshot was that she had a kind of nervous breakdown and didn't return to Cambridge on the grounds of ill health. Lydia was rather vague about the next few years, but from what I can gather, she became a recluse, shutting herself away with her books. One can only imagine how miserable it must have been for her. Thankfully, rescue finally came from a Godmother who invited her to stay in London. This woman was sympathetic and kind, and Lydia soon found herself pouring out her story, telling of how desperate she'd become, to the point of being suicidal. Her story obviously shocked her Godmother. Lydia was invited to stay permanently in London and enrolled in a nursing course. Her parents were just relieved to have rid themselves of the problem, and the solution seemed respectable enough to satisfy them.' Isobel shrugged. 'Eventually, the parents died, they'd had Lydia late in their marriage, both being in their mid-forties, which might explain a great deal about her strict upbringing. Thankfully she now became financially independent and decided to take up full time caring. When she came to look after Peter, she stayed on afterwards to see me through the worst of it, and then I suggested she made a permanent home here, or at least for as long as she wanted. She could afford a house of her own, but she seemed to feel settled here.'

There was silence as Rawlings digested all this. 'Did she

ever have another relationship?' he finally asked.

Isobel shook her head. 'Not as far as I know. But she does tend to get involved with the people she cares for, especially the lonely and vulnerable women. Rose was a case in point. I know she feels badly about landing me with that particular problem, but to be fair, none of us realised how desperately ill Rose was until we found her collapsed. Lydia told me the other day that Rose's mother had died soon after her first stroke, leaving Rose a small legacy which has given her some financial independence. I understand that as soon as she was allowed to leave hospital, she went to live near one of her brothers, somewhere in the Midlands.'

'I thought the brothers refused to have anything to do with her.'

Isobel's reply was unexpectedly sharp. 'Oh, I don't think they minded, once she could financially support herself and was no longer a burden on them.'

'It's ridiculous the way women like this are given no support and are unable to lead independent lives.' Rawlings burst out.

Isobel sighed. 'Alas, in these days of austerity, huge problems arise from exactly this kind of problem. Single women like Rose fall by the wayside and unhappy marriages drag on because wives can't afford to leave, having no way of supporting themselves or their children. It can lead to terrible consequences as I know only too well. Until last year when I had to retire because of my age, I was a J.P., and we had endless cases of this sort, involving physical and mental abuse, with the women just enduring the marriages because they had no alternative. It was hard to listen to.'

They were both silent for a while. Then Isobel said,

'Talking of Lydia, she informs me she has bought three tickets for a matinee of *War Music*, the Wednesday of half-term. I gather it is on tour and in Canterbury that week. I know she will offer a ticket to you...'

Rawlings shook his head. He wanted no more of war; he was already up to his eyeballs in it. Isobel smiled and said that if that were really the case, she would be happy to go with Felix, and rather looked forward to making a day of it.

The expedition to see *"War Music"* was a definite success. Felix was on a high, so it was with a sinking heart that Rawlings took him out to supper the following night to break the news to him about Australia. For the first half of the meal, the boy talked happily, embarking on a full description of the production, with not a detail left out. As he dug into a heaped plate of profiteroles, which had momentarily stemmed his narrative, Rawlings ordered a double espresso and took a deep breath.

'Felix, I have some news for you.'

The boy, noticing the serious note in his grandfather's voice, put down his spoon and looked warily at Rawlings. 'What sort of news, E.G.? Is it good or bad?'

How the hell was he to answer that? Rawlings decided to be truthful, 'It depends on what you think about it...' He paused. 'I know you have been very happy here with us...' He paused again, trying to remember how he'd decided was the best way to break the news. He'd rehearsed it so many times but now... The boy started to look worried. He tried again. 'Do you remember your mother has a sister, your aunt, who lives in Australia?' Felix nodded. Rawlings attempted to inject some enthusiasm into his voice, 'Well, she has a lovely house, and family, three children, one who is the same age as you…' This was bloody terrible. Whichever way he put it, this was going to sound as if he wanted to be rid of the boy, which was the exact opposite of what he really felt.

'Do they want me to visit them in Australia for a holiday?' Felix asked helpfully, seeing that E.G. was struggling.

'Not just for a holiday, they want you to live with them, permanently,' Rawlings blurted out. Felix gasped in shock.

'To leave living here with you? Is that what you want me to do, E.G.?' he asked.

Rawlings said almost crossly, 'No, of course, it isn't what I want. But it's not about me. It's what is best for you and your future.'

Felix looked mutinous. 'In that case, I want to stay here, with you and Isobel and Marnie and Lydia.'

This was worse than he'd thought it would be. He stared at the boy.

'Felix, I want you to listen to me for a moment and not interrupt, while I try to explain. Will you do that?' Felix said nothing, nor did he nod, so Rawlings ploughed on. 'I hadn't told you before, but one of the reasons it might be better for you is that I have to go into hospital after Christmas, to have a major operation on my leg and when I come out of hospital, it may take me weeks to recover…

Felix almost shouted, 'Isobel would look after me while you're away, I'm sure of it. And Marnie would help you to get better…' He sounded desperate, panicked. Rawlings held up his hand.

'Please Felix, just hear me out. I have thought about this carefully before making this decision. I am sure we could all manage while my leg heals, but it is not just next year, but all the years to come. Neither Isobel nor I are getting any younger…'

'I wouldn't be any trouble,' Felix said, desperation creeping into his voice.

Rawlings smiled. 'I know you wouldn't. You have given us no trouble at all. We've loved having you with us. That's not really the point.'

'But you're my guardian,' Felix persisted.

'I am one of them,' Rawlings told him firmly, 'your Aunt Sarah is the other, and she really wants you to make a home with them and become part of their family. They have a lovely house. Sarah has sent me pictures. I can show you. It has a swimming pool…' The boy gave no reaction to this, so Rawlings desperately ploughed on. 'The eldest boy, Shane, who is eleven like you, is very keen on cricket…' Still no reaction. 'Then there is David, who is eight and a baby, Ella. They live in a very beautiful part of Australia, near Adelaide. It's a lovely climate, not wet and windy like here…'

'When do you want me to go?' the boy asked dully.

'Felix, please try and understand,' Rawlings snapped, 'None of us wants you to go, we are all going to miss you terribly, but as adults, we have to try and decide what is best for you, for your future…' and he added, 'I am sure you could come back here for the summer holidays, if that is what you wanted.'

Felix sat hunched and defeated. 'When do I leave?' he asked, and there was a coldness in his voice that was hard to bear, but he could do nothing now but answer the boy directly.

'Sarah is thinking of coming over in December, and

then you will go back with her in time to spend Christmas with the family.'

Felix stood up. 'I think I'd like to go home now.'

Home, Rawlings thought despairingly, he thinks of here as home, and a wave of anger swept through him; anger with Graham for putting him in this situation, with Susanna for having a bloody sister and with Sarah for living in bloody Australia. Why did it have to be so far away? This wasn't just a small change of venue for the boy; it was a huge upheaval.

He hastily paid the bill and followed Felix out to the car. They drove back in silence. Once parked in the drive, Felix thanked him politely for supper and ran up to his room slamming the door behind him. Rawlings limped slowly inside, where Isobel was waiting for him.

'I gather that didn't go well,' she remarked drily, looking at the expression on his face.

'I need a large brandy,' he said, as he slumped onto the sofa. After a few gulps, he gave Isobel an account of the evening. 'He was desperate to stay here with us Isobel; said he'd be no trouble, as if...' Looking directly at her, he said, 'I feel I have betrayed the boy. He'll never trust me again.'

'Nonsense!' she replied briskly. 'For a clever man, you are being rather stupid. Felix has had a shock, and he's panicked. It's only natural for him to react like this. It's a great deal for the child to take in, so it's no good taking it personally. Let me talk to him tomorrow and try and put things in perspective.'

Rawlings almost shouted, 'It won't do any good, Isobel. He feels rejected. He thinks we don't want him. No, correction, that's not true, he thinks I don't want him, and the thought of that is killing me.'

She felt a mixture of irritation and sadness, but it would be wrong to let him simply wallow in his unhappiness. That would only make the situation worse. She said quietly, 'Go back to the boat Rawlings. You look exhausted. And try not to worry, I will do my best with him in the morning.' He nodded and wearily got to his feet as she added, 'Give him a little time to adjust to the idea. When you find a good moment, you could suggest to Felix he writes down any questions he would like to ask Sarah about life in Australia. It might help to make it more real and a possible alternative to here.' As he limped off, she called after him, 'You ought to skype Sarah too, now that you've broken the news to the boy.'

The next day Isobel watched, as Felix sullenly kicked a football around the garden.

'Would you like a hot chocolate?' she called out.

He hesitated, then followed her into the kitchen, for once not removing his muddy shoes. It was the definite sign of a rebellious mood, but on this occasion, she made no comment. After handing him the cocoa, she decided it was the moment to talk.

'I know you are upset Felix, about the news you heard last night…'

'I'm not upset,' he said almost rudely and then added stiffly, 'I just didn't know that E.G. found me a burden.'

Isobel spoke almost sharply, 'Felix, you are not a stupid boy, and you know perfectly well that is not true. You are also old enough to understand that your grandfather is terribly unhappy about having to make this decision. He is going to miss you dreadfully, as we all are…'

'Then why is he sending me away?' he shouted. 'I don't want to go; I want to stay here with him, and with you.'

Isobel tried a different tack. 'You know, sometimes the fear of the unknown is worse than the reality.' Felix looked at her obviously puzzled, so she tried to explain. 'You probably don't remember, but you were worried, at the beginning, about coming to stay with us here. It was all very new and strange. But look how quickly you settled in, and now you are happy with us because it has all become familiar. You might find it is the same with Australia. At the moment you don't want to leave here, because you feel settled and happy, but when you have been living with your aunt's family for a while, you might find you like it just as much.'

Felix thought about this. 'What happens if I don't like it. Can I come back here?'

'Yes, of course, you can. But you have to give it a try Felix. I hope in any case, you will come back and visit us often. You will always have a home here, I promise. And meanwhile, we can keep in touch via Skype.' She smiled, 'After a while, I expect you won't even have time to do that. There is so much to do in Australia. A lot of sport which you will really enjoy.' Felix nodded at this, and feeling encouraged, Isobel added, 'Try not to be angry with your grandfather. He really didn't want to do this, but you must understand, it wasn't just him. There are other people involved in deciding what is best for you and all of them thought that living with a family would give you a happy and stable future.'

There was a long pause after this, and then the boy said suddenly, 'Is E.G. going to die?'

Isobel was shocked. 'No, at least, not for a good while yet I hope.' She hesitated. 'He does, however, have problems with his leg and is in a good deal of pain.'

Felix nodded and said, 'I know. He has to have an operation. He told me last night, but I could have helped look after him.'

Isobel smiled. 'I know you could, but he'll have plenty of people to look after him, you really mustn't worry about that.'

Felix stood up, bringing their conversation to an end. 'Thank you for the hot chocolate, Isobel. I have to go and feed Harrison now.'

Isobel watched as he went down the garden and wondered if that had helped the situation at all.

His grandfather was also not in the best of moods that morning. He'd booked a long overdue skype with Sarah first thing, and felt churlish at finding her so bloody irritating. She came over as a jolly, homely sort of person, very different from her sister, who had plainly been a career girl and not motherly in the least. It wouldn't have been so bad, he told Marnie, when she dropped in on her way to her morning's teaching, if Sarah hadn't been so relentlessly cheerful and enthusiastic about the boy's imminent arrival. It was as if she had no understanding of Felix's reluctance to leave a place where he'd been so happy. It was bordering on the downright insensitive, the way she insisted he would have a wonderful home with them, as if he hadn't been well looked after here. Marnie noticed the indignation in his voice and patiently pointed out that Sarah was probably trying to reassure him. Rawlings knew she was right, of course, which only annoyed him more. In clipped tones, he informed her he'd done his best to put any hostile feelings aside while speaking to Sarah. He'd even remembered Isobel's suggestion to ask if it would be all right if Felix wrote down some questions to ask her. Rawlings made a face here, to express his distaste of the whole conversation, adding that the woman didn't hesitate for a moment, telling him she thought that a great idea. She went on to inform him of all the fantastic things Felix would be able to do, making their life sound as if it was conducted in the middle of a theme park. No superlative was left out, he'd growled. Marnie just laughed and told him not to be such an old bear. She then left for school, informing him Isobel had invited them all to Sunday lunch the following week, which was why she'd called in on him in the first place, not to have an earful of his moans.

Rawlings sat back and reflected that the only positive outcome of the whole wretched business was that Graham would sort out the financial side of things, so at least he didn't have to talk to Sarah about money. He had, however, suggested Felix should have pocket money and a savings account of his own. The boy would need some independence once he was out there. Sarah had immediately agreed to this. He had the distinct feeling she would have agreed to anything, so keen was she to please. Before finishing the call, she told him she'd sent some pictures to show Felix, which she hoped he would like. In all fairness, he could see she was doing her best.

He sat at his desk, exhausted. He'd hardly slept.

There was a knock on the door, and he yelled 'Enter'.

Felix came in. The boy never usually knocked, just barged straight in, but it was clear he was now going to make his displeasure felt in any way he could.

'I've come to feed Harrison,' he said abruptly, then adding over-politely, 'I hope that won't be a nuisance, interrupting you, while you're working.'

Rawlings told him it was fine, that he hadn't yet started work, adding there was a bowl of peelings for Harrison that Marnie had left in the kitchen. Felix went to fetch them and left by the back door to go out on the deck. Rawlings could hear the boy talking to the goose as he fed him, telling him off for being so greedy. That bloody bird was yet another thing Felix would hate leaving. He'd printed the pictures of the Australian house and wondered whether Felix would grow to like the place as much as here. So many doubts swirled around in his mind.

Felix returned. Rawlings was about to ask him to sit down for a moment, but the boy was moving quickly towards the door.

'You'll have to look after Harrison when I'm gone,' he said, almost rudely and left slamming the door behind him.

Rawlings looked after him with a feeling of despair. For once Isobel hadn't been right. The boy wasn't going to forgive him, and he was now to be deprived of the one person he'd felt any affection for since losing Mia.

Chapter Sixteen

The last week of October 2017

The following days were an agony for Rawlings. He hardly slept and ate little. Felix would come down each day after school in order to feed Harrison, and then would leave the same way, without a word, slamming the door behind him. Both Isobel and Marnie, worried at the state Rawlings was in, urged him to have patience, telling him the boy would come around to it in the end, but Rawlings thought despairingly that time was fast running out. He had barely two months left and then Felix would be gone for good. By the time Saturday arrived, his patience had given out. He'd had enough. As Felix returned from feeding the bird, and before he had time to cross the room, he thundered, 'Sit down, Felix!'

The boy was so startled by the raised voice of his grandfather, he obeyed, but still wore the same belligerent and angry expression.

Rawlings was past caring. He looked directly at Felix. 'I know you're still very angry with me, Felix, and you've convinced yourself that I don't care about you leaving. You must know, deep down, that's not true. I'll tell you one final time. I do care. I'm miserable at the thought of you going. I know it doesn't help, but I'm trying to be unselfish here and do what is best for you…' He broke off. The boy said nothing; his expression unchanged. Rawlings decided to try another tack. Changing to a more sympathetic tone, he said, 'I don't want you worrying about Harrison. I promise I will feed him when you've left, and I know Marnie will too when I'm away in hospital.'

Felix looked a little mollified by this reminder of the operation Rawlings was to have. After a moment he said almost defiantly,

'Isobel says I can come back here if I don't like it in Australia.'

Rawlings nodded, relieved that at last, he'd made some sort of contact. 'That is true, but I hope you will at least give Australia a try.'

Felix mumbled, 'Isobel said that too.' He stood up. 'Can I go to Sunil's now? We want to go out on our bikes, and his mother has invited me to lunch.'

Rawlings looked out of the window at the grey skies and ominous clouds. 'It looks as if it's going to rain, so you'd better go prepared.'

There were no more words spoken between them. Felix left, but this time didn't slam the door.

Rawlings had intended showing Felix the pictures Sarah had sent, but it was obviously too soon for that. Instead, he decided to ask Isobel to put the folder that he'd marked 'Australia' in the boy's room. Inside he'd placed, not only the photos but also a map of Australia, marking the area of where Felix would be living. He sat back in his chair, lost in thought. Had that been a slight break-through that morning? He desperately hoped so.

Meanwhile, Isobel was wondering if it had been a

good idea to ask everyone to Sunday lunch. Rawlings had accepted the invitation nervously. Relations between the boy and himself were obviously still raw and fragile. She just hoped there would be enough people present to act as a buffer state. But it could all go horribly wrong.

Happily, her worst fears weren't realised. Lydia had also been invited, and this turned out to be an inspired idea. Felix spent a good deal of the meal talking to her about *"War Horse"*. He then quite suddenly informed the company that he had been asked to take part in the Christmas concert at the school. There were murmurs of pleasure at this news and Marnie said she hoped they would all be able to attend. Isobel lamented the fact that Christmas seemed to come earlier every year and pointed out they were already playing *"Jingle Bells"* in the supermarket.

While all this general conversation was going on, Marnie glanced anxiously at Rawlings, who had been unusually quiet and made no contribution to the conversation.

As Felix thanked Isobel for the meal and asked if he could leave the table, he turned to Rawlings and said, 'I hope you will come to the Christmas concert E.G.'

It was a definite peace offering. Rawlings smiled and looked pleased with this invitation. He assured the boy nothing would keep him away and Isobel heaved a sigh of relief; her decision for the meal had been justified.

'I think Felix may be slowly coming around to the idea of Australia,' Rawlings told Marnie after their next meal together. 'He's certainly been less hostile to me lately.'

'Well he had to accept it really,' she told him, 'he realised it was a fait accompli, and this, unsurprisingly, was bound to leave him angry for a time.'

'An anger that was mainly aimed at me, as of course, it was left to me to tell him.' Rawlings stared gloomily into his wine. 'I was given no choice. I could hardly leave it to a crusty old lawyer to break the news to the boy.'

Marnie smiled and reminded him that it was natural to want to shoot the messenger. 'Felix showed me the pictures you'd left for him yesterday. It looks an amazing house, and he'll like all that outdoor stuff. Sarah looks the motherly sort too.'

Rawlings gave a grunt, adding irritably, 'Oh, she's definitely that. The sort of woman I've tried to avoid all my life. She can talk about nothing except her bloody husband and the exploits of her children, with occasional references to the country club they belong to, but that's about the extent of her conversation.'

Marnie looked at him crossly. 'Really Rawlings, sometimes you are impossible. You've only talked to the poor woman once. Give her a chance. She was obviously trying to put your mind at rest by showing you what a lovely life Felix will have.

'All cricket and swimming,' Rawlings retorted, 'completely devoid of any culture.'

Marnie sighed, 'Felix won't lose his love of books and music when he's out there. He'll just have other things to occupy him as well.'

Rawlings didn't look convinced but inwardly decided that when he helped Felix compile his list of questions for Sarah, he would insist on him adding in topics like music and theatre. Marnie could see from his expression he was still unhappy about his grandson's removal to the other side of the world. It would take time for him to get used to the idea.

'At least,' she said, 'in Australia, Felix will be away from all the terrorist attacks this country has endured this year. The Finsbury Park attack in June made it four. Even I'm nervous about going up to London now.'

'I hardly think they will attack this part of the River Thames,' he retorted sarcastically, but privately had to admit she'd made a valid point.

Chapter Seventeen

November 2017

The last vestiges of autumn were fast disappearing and the first week of November turned cold and foggy. On a day of particularly dense mist, Felix had his games period cancelled and returned from school early. Maria had made a ginger cake and dispatched him to the boat with slices for Rawlings. As they sat munching the cake, Rawlings said, 'You've never told me much about this school. Is it very different from your last one?'

Felix thought about this. 'In some ways, it is. The teachers call us by our first names at this school, not our surnames.' He grinned. 'There are twin sisters in my class, and they would have had a problem calling out their names with that.' Rawlings suggested they could have just added an initial on the end. Felix shook his head, 'that wouldn't have helped at all, they both have Christian names with the initial S, Sapphire and Scarlet.'

Rawlings looked startled. 'Good heavens, that's a bit exotic. What's their surname?'

'Evans,' Felix replied and then gave a laugh, 'Scarlet is mad about Sunil.'

'Is she indeed?' Rawlings regarded his grandson with

interest. 'It must make a change for you, having girls in your class. How do you feel about that?' The boy gave a shrug.

'I don't mind it, but some of them are a bit silly.' His expression changed. 'Some of the class seem to be angry about Scarlet and Sunil. I think it's because Scarlet is a white girl and Sunil is from India. Some of the older boys make really horrid comments as well. It makes me angry, but Sunil doesn't seem to mind.'

This piece of information worried Rawlings and he wanted to inquire about it further, but Felix seemed to have lost interest and changed the subject. Catching sight of the piled-up manuscript on the desk he asked Rawlings if he had finished his book. With a nod he replied that he had, or anyway the first draft. 'I take it up to my agent in a couple of weeks. The publishers may want some changes made before it goes to print.'

'Is your book just about wars?' Felix asked.

Rawlings thought about this before answering. 'Well, it is about wars of course, but it is more about my experiences reporting on those wars.'

The boy suddenly said, 'My father says you took unnecessary risks.' This observation came to Rawlings as a great surprise and with not a little annoyance. He hadn't been allowed to take risks dammit. But it was something of a shock that Hugo had even mentioned him, and a further surprise was to follow when Felix added, 'but he did say you were very good at your job and one of the best reporters going. I think he was proud of you. He told me you were brave as well.'

These revelations so startled Rawlings he was unable to speak for a moment, and then he said with a grim smile, 'I certainly wasn't brave when my leg was half blown off. Ask Isobel. I was reported to be one of the worst patients in the hospital.'

'I think you are being very brave now. Isobel says you are in a lot of pain.' And with that parting comment, Felix took himself off to meet Sunil, while Rawlings was left pondering the strange disclosures about Hugo. Had he misjudged his son? Could there have been some sort of relationship with him once he was an adult? In all honesty he didn't see how. Hugo had shown him nothing but hostility. And yet...

'It was so totally unexpected.' Rawlings reported to Marnie later. 'I had no idea Hugo held any opinions about me. But at least it indicated there's a definite thawing in relations between Felix and myself. I think, and hope, we are now more or less back to normal.'

'I knew that would happen,' Marnie said in an annoyingly smug voice. 'The boy isn't stupid. He realised you had to tell him and anyway, I think he is coming around to the idea. The fact that he showed me the pictures of the Australian house means he's accepting it. I must say, it looks very...' she paused, searching for the right word.

'Australian?' Rawlings offered. She looked at him reproachfully.

'No, I was going to say something like 'well appointed', but I couldn't find any words that wouldn't make me sound like an estate agent.' She refilled his glass. 'Felix tells me you've finished the book. That must be a relief.'

'I suppose it is, but I fully expect they will demand re-writes,' he said wearily. 'I have this extremely fussy female editor.'

'Aren't you being rather sexist? Does it really make a difference that she's female?'

Marnie was looking crossly at him, but he smiled charmingly back at her.

'Don't get on your high horse. This particular specimen of womanhood tends to be what I consider over-fussy.' He gave a sigh. 'You can't say anything these days without being accused of being sexist, racist, ageist, or some sort of 'ist'. Conversation has become almost impossible without offending someone.'

Marnie changed the subject. 'It must please you that Hugo thought you were so good at your job.' He made no comment, so she went on, 'I've often wondered how you became a war correspondent in the first place. Was it by accident?'

Rawlings sighed. 'Oh Lord Marnie, you and your inquisition. I don't know. Quite honestly, it probably was by accident, someone dropped out, and I replaced him, although I didn't object at all to being sent overseas and made it quite clear to my superiors it was what I wanted to do.' He gave a laugh. 'My early reading had been full of the exploits of Stanley – of Dr Livingstone fame – and Winston Churchill's account of his time as a war correspondent in South Africa. So, although I started as a jobbing journalist, when I was sent off to my first war, I was excited at the prospect.' This produced a chuckle. 'I'd be the first to admit, I was a complete novice and really thrown in at the deep end.'

He lit a cigarette, then looked at Marnie, 'Only my fourth today. I'm trying to cut down. Do you mind me smoking in your house?'

This made her burst out laughing. 'It's a bit late for me to start objecting now. You've always smoked when you're here. In any case, it's bitter outside, so it would be rather brutal of me to chuck you out.' She regarded him thoughtfully. 'You must have been pretty young to have been sent off like that without any training?'

I'd covered the Falklands war from home, so I was not entirely unprepared for it, but I had to learn the actual job of being a war correspondent on the spot.' Here he smiled disarmingly, 'Lucky I was a quick learner. I watched the others. They'd sit around with their laptops – it was when the first portable computers had just come in, not slimline like today but my God, they were a joy compared with the old heavy type-writers we used to lug around. Anyway, there we were, all fighting for the proverbial front page. I was up against some ancient hacks with years of experience, but I was young, ambitious and full of ideals, unlike some of my jaded colleagues. The constant fatigue, danger and hunger, tended to make ambition fade over the years, but I'm pleased to say my aims remained the same. I always endeavoured to make myself indispensable to the foreign desk by finding different angles, and I think I can say, more or less, I achieved that.' He stubbed out his cigarette. 'Inevitably, that sort of life came at a cost.'

'A cost?' Marnie questioned. 'You mean your leg injury, I presume.'

Rawlings gave a grim smile. 'Yes, that, but it wasn't just being wounded or killed. The life of a foreign correspondent is no bed of roses. For a start, the long absences make it difficult to have any personal relationships that work. It's a fact that a high percentage of journalists who work abroad have marriages that don't survive, and those that do, leave behind neglected offspring, Hugo being a case in point. I often wonder if I had been around more, things might have been different between Hugo and myself. It's something I'll never know.' He sighed and went on. 'For those reporting on wars, there is, as you know, the added danger of being maimed, imprisoned or killed. This has increased as conflicts have become ever more complex. One of the nastier things to have happened recently is that the enemy is deliberately targeting reporters. This hasn't been helped by the stupidity of our politicians, often inciting the violence and further endangering us; that idiot Donald Trump is the worst of the lot. It's the reason for the embedding, to try and protect us, as far as it's possible. As I explained, it meant we lost our freedom, but at least someone knew where we were and also where it was definitely unsafe for us to be.'

He lit another cigarette. 'Mia's great heroine, Marie Colvin, was one of those who was deliberately targeted and killed. It happened in February 2012, just before Mia and I were blown up. The tragedy shook us all. Marie was in Syria when she was murdered, which thank God, I never had to report on, because it must be the worst and most brutal conflict to date.' He gave a grim smile. 'Mia and I had one of our few arguments over Marie Colvin. I agreed with her that she was a true heroine, but angry that she refused to be embedded, insisting on always acting as a freelance, and to my way of thinking, although nobody could ever doubt her own personal bravery, she took too many risks and put those she worked with in danger as well. Mia maintained it was their choice to go with her. I told Mia that in the end, they paid the price with their lives. We were never going to agree on that. She shrewdly remarked that if Marie Colvin had asked me to go with her, I would have gone.' He shrugged. 'Probably true. It would have been a privilege to work with her. I'm just glad she never asked!' He gave a bleak laugh at this. 'Marie Colvin was an obsessive woman and completely driven, but there is no doubt she had countless major successes, which should never be overlooked. One of her greatest achievements was to search for, and find, the bodies of the Fallujah massacre in Iraq, which otherwise would have remained hidden. She also brought to public attention the terrible civil war in Sri Lanka, which before her, had been ignored and unreported. This was true war reporting at its best. Poor woman. She lost an eye in one attack, and I know she suffered from complex PTSD.' He sighed. 'Nothing new there. We all had the nightmares, but I remember seeing an interview with Marie Colvin once when she said the images in her head would not go away until there was a bottle of vodka inside her. I just hope I never reach that stage.'

Marnie privately thought that Rawlings was quite near that stage already. It was noticeable his intake of alcohol had greatly increased lately, especially in the daytime, which hadn't been apparent before. Whether this increase was due to pain, or the fact Felix was leaving, she wasn't sure. Maybe a combination of both, along with the irritation of his bossy female editor.

On this occasion, all she said was, 'If it was all so dreadful, why on earth did you do it?'

'I think what you are really asking is if I think foreign reporters make a difference and if the sacrifices are worth it?' He gave a bleak smile. 'The answer is a definite yes, on both counts. We are badly needed. At least we reporters can try to get near the truth and stop some of the mendacity that is put about back home. Being on the spot, we see the bigger picture, all sides of the conflict. I believe it is vitally important we should try to make people care about the things that we do, things that we know are happening, that they otherwise would never hear about, or understand.' He was talking seriously now, with an injection of unusual energy and passion. 'For instance, in war zones, people back home should know that parents have to go to bed every night, never knowing if their children will be alive in the morning. The public should also be informed that there are brutal dictators existing right now, who have deliberately started killing women and children, using them as human shields. It is one of many shocking facts that we correspondents witness. It makes us feel despair at the cruelty of the human race, but at the same time, we need to report on it.'

He paused, waiting for a reaction from Marnie, but as none came, he continued more calmly. 'There's another side of our work too. We can report on the bravery of the civilian populations and the often-witnessed, simple acts of humanity carried out by our forces and medical staff.'

He drained his wine. 'It's a grim world out there Marnie, and people need to know about it. Sadly, in these days of 24-hour television reporting from every part of the globe, we may be in danger of overkill. People have become so used to seeing horrifying images it ceases to be real, or to make an impact.' He sighed. 'Old hacks like me, who sent in their reports with all the graphic detail written down, may soon become a thing of the past. Newspapers are on borrowed time and may disappear altogether in the near future. I think I may be one of the last of a dying breed.'

★

A few days after this, Marnie had her worst suspicions about his increased alcohol intake, definitely confirmed. She'd gone to take his post over after lunch, only to find him passed out on the sofa, with an empty whisky bottle beside him. She tidied away the bottle, and the glass also on the floor, and then took some time to rouse him. He was disorientated, cross and his speech was slurred.

'What the hell are you doing here Marnie, and why wake me up?'

She decided on a practical approach. 'I have woken you up, because Felix will be home any minute, and it would upset and worry him to find you like this, passed out with an empty whisky bottle rolling about the floor. I have now removed that to the kitchen. It's none of my business how much you drink Rawlings, but it might be better if you try to keep it under control until Felix is gone.'

Rawlings sat up and rubbed his leg. It was extremely painful, and so was his head. There was something about the calm way she was reproving him that caused him to lose his temper, and he shouted, 'Felix! Felix! It's all about Felix these days. Well don't worry, he'll soon be far away from my bad influence, and you won't have to keep a check on me any longer'. Marnie gave a gasp of shock and Rawlings made an effort to pull himself together. 'It's all your fault anyway, Marnie,' he grumbled, 'with your damned endless questions about my past. Don't you realise it brings back the nightmares and then I don't sleep? Good God woman, no wonder I turn to drink.'

'I'm sorry if I'm the cause,' she said huffily. 'I certainly won't ask you anything else.'

'It's too bloody late now,' he yelled, 'the damage is done!'

Marnie stood there for a moment, and then something inside her snapped. For the first time in years, she lost her temper. 'You always have to blame someone else Rawlings. Nobody has ever had to suffer as much as you. Well, for your information, I have. I had a violent and controlling husband who mentally tortured me for eleven years until I was a complete wreck. I had three miscarriages and was blamed for those as well. When I finally escaped his clutches, it was to be landed with another bully, and I was brought to my knees by that bloody mooring landlord. By the time he'd finished with me, I'd lost my boat and everything I owned. So, you're certainly not the only person in this world who has suffered.' Her face was red with anger, her fists were clenched, and her eyes were welling up with tears. She then gave her parting shot, 'In spite of all this, I have tried my hardest not to feel sorry for myself or wallow in self-pity. I suggest you do the same. Here is your post.' She threw the letters on the desk and left, slamming the door behind her.

Rawlings sat for a moment, completely stunned by this outburst. Then he staggered slowly to his feet and went out to the kitchen to make some black coffee. Switching on the machine, he leant against the sink, trying to work out what had caused Marnie to flip in that way. In the foggy recesses of his mind, he remembered Isobel telling him that Marnie had been hurt in the past, but that outburst revealed far more. Three miscarriages. No wonder her suffering lay so close to the surface. It had actually struck him the first time he'd met her that she was somehow badly damaged. To give him his due, he'd tried to find out more, but she had never been forthcoming. With a shaking hand, he poured the coffee into a mug and then suddenly became angry. For God's sake, he might have had a chance to show the bloody woman some sympathy if she hadn't always been so persistent in probing into his past.

He returned to his desk and sat down. A gulp of coffee revived him a little, and his thoughts became clearer. If he were honest, there was an element of truth in what he'd shouted at her. Continual talking about the events in his life had brought to the surface many sleeping dragons. It had caused many nightmares to return and given him broken nights. He was suffering from a definite lack of sleep. No wonder he was irritable and yes, feeling sorry for himself.

He drained the last of the coffee. Annoyingly he also knew she was right. He'd noticed the empty bottles in his bin. His drinking had lately somehow spun out of control. It would have to be cut down, at least until Felix had gone.

Looking down, he noticed the letters she'd flung on the desk and opened them. One was a missive from Graham with medical requests for the boy. He'd enclosed up to date records of Felix's illnesses and vaccinations so far, but further action needed to be taken before his departure for Australia. Glancing through them, Rawlings could see Felix would need tetanus and diphtheria injections, eye tests, and doctor and dentist overhauls. He stared blankly at the documents. His head was throbbing, and his brain, still cloudy, barred him from making sensible decisions. He decided to turn the whole thing over to Isobel, who would know exactly what to do and make all the necessary arrangements.

His mind went back to the events earlier, and he reflected he badly needed to make his peace with Marnie. It would mean eating humble pie, and he sighed. After some thought, he took up his pen and wrote:

Marnie, please forgive my unforgivable outburst. Sadly, I am a recidivist and know my worst drinking habits are in danger of returning. My only defence is that alcohol seems to be the one relief I have from pain at the moment, but for the sake of the boy, I will cut it down and return to taking aspirin, which will probably give me a stomach ulcer. If all else fails, there is always laudanum. If you can once more overlook my behaviour, I should like you to come to supper, so I can make amends. I promise to be in cheerful vein, with not a sign of self-pity. Shall we say Thursday? Affectionately, R.

After their row, Marnie had returned to the boathouse still shaking with indignation. It took her over an hour and a small tot of brandy, to calm down. It was a complete mystery why she had lost her temper like that. Maybe it was because she hated seeing him in a drunken state, or that he put the blame on her, or it could have been that she felt he'd neglected her of late. Even so, with an inward reproof, she knew she somehow had to get her feelings for him under control. It was doing neither of them any good. What he'd said was true; she had been relentless in finding out about his past and now felt guilty about it. Would he forgive her or want to see her again? She thought probably not, and this made her miserable. In fact, she was in great danger of feeling sorry for herself.

It was, therefore, a surprise to find his letter on her return from school later that day. She read it with a mixture of amusement and relief. It also sent her diving for the dictionary to find out the meaning of the word 'recidivist'. She sent an immediate text back to say she'd be delighted to join him for supper and would bring a selection of cheeses. Feeling a good deal happier than before receiving the note, she resolved not to aggravate him further in any way, either with questions or reproaches.

★

The next day, on returning from school, Felix excitedly informed Rawlings that Jake had organised a bonfire in the garden for November 4th. He and Sunil were going to make a guy, and Marnie had offered to help them, especially with the face. Rawlings felt some misgivings about this. Guy Fawkes celebrations had previously passed him by. On the few occasions he'd been in England he'd been careful to avoid it, having a great dislike of fireworks and explosions of any sort. Now looking at Felix jumping up and down in front of him, he resolved to make an effort.

'Do you have any old clothes we could use E.G.?' Felix was on a mission and in a hurry. 'Isobel has given us some, but if you had any spare, it would make him extra fat.'

Rawlings hobbled to the bedroom and pulled out an old sweater and a pair of jeans.

'That's great,' Felix took them from him and ran to the door. 'We don't have much time as the party is going to be on Saturday.'

Saturday duly came, and in spite of a November drizzle,

the preparations went ahead. The boys had made a good job of the guy, and to Rawlings, it looked horribly realistic and struck him that it resembled someone he knew but couldn't immediately think who. He studied it more carefully and then he realised that Marnie had made a replica of the villainous landlord from the moorings. It was a private joke, her way of having a small revenge.

As soon as it became dark, the various guests assembled. There were the Patel's of course, and Maria and Paul. Rawlings saw Lydia and Isobel, and then he caught sight of two young girls, the same age as Felix. They were brought across to meet him and introduced as Scarlett and Sapphire, the twins Felix had mentioned. He wasn't given time to talk to them as Sunil yelled out that the fire was about to be lit and they rushed back to the action. There had been some worries that the damp might have caused problems, but Jake obviously had boy scout training, and soon it was dramatically ablaze. He'd built it so high the fire took some time for the flames to reach the guy perched on the top. The children had been given sparklers and were dancing around the bonfire like small demented demons. What a bizarre ritual it was. To Rawlings, it seemed somewhat abhorrent. He watched as the flames caught the bottom of the guy and people were cheering. A vision suddenly came to him of a fire in Baghdad, when, helpless to do anything, he had watched while women and children inside had burned to death with nobody able to reach them. Their screams were still horribly real.

The bonfire became too much for him to watch. He turned and hobbled back to the boat, locking the door behind him. Pouring himself a large drink, he sat at his desk chair, hearing the loud bangs as the fireworks started exploding. It started him shaking. Unable to stop, he put his hands over his ears in an effort to block out the noise.

Marnie noticed him leave and became concerned. While the excitement was at its height, she went over to the boat. Finding the door locked, she peered through the window. Rawlings had his back to her, but she could see he was bent over and had his head in his hands. Quickly realising the fire and explosions were causing him distress, she saw there was nothing she could do but return to the party.

'Where did E.G. go?' Felix asked her.

She replied vaguely that his leg was probably hurting from standing around in the damp, and this seemed to satisfy the boy. Marnie sighed. She was beginning to understand the extent of Rawlings' suffering.

Chapter Eighteen

Late November 2017

To his great relief, Isobel seemed only too pleased to organise all the medical appointments for Felix. Her previous diplomatic status meant she still had private doctors and dentists and could organise it all out of school hours. Rawlings yet again told her how grateful he was, but she smiled at him saying she enjoyed looking after the boy. It made her feel like a proper grandmother. He later reflected that bringing up children in the 21st century was no picnic. In a couple of years, Felix would be exposed to all the dangers of social media, drugs and yes, alcohol, and he wondered if the problems were as bad in the Barossa Valley as they were here. Marnie had already pointed out the horrors of terrorist attacks in London, but there was also the increase of gangs, drugs and knife crime. Up to now, Felix had lived a sheltered life, an innocent in all these matters, but how much longer could that continue? The Academy, although not entirely to his taste, was a good, middle-class school with good, middle-class values, but he was very sure, that at some point there would be bad influences around if he stayed. Reluctantly, he came to the conclusion, that Australia might well be a safer place for

Felix to live, and the blessed Sarah, bringing up another boy of the same age, would be far better equipped to deal with the many adolescent problems that loomed so largely ahead. Even so, he thought savagely, it didn't make up for the fact that he would miss the boy more than he had ever thought possible. It seemed particularly cruel that Felix had been allowed to become such a huge part of his life, only to have him snatched away and taken to the other side of the world.

In spite of these gloomy thoughts, he set off in cheerful mood the following Tuesday, relieved, finally, to deliver his book to Jolyon. Looking forward to a long and expensive lunch he decided to make a day of it, with a few drinks at the Frontline Club afterwards. Alas, these hopes were to be cruelly dashed. Jolyon sent him a text while he was on the train, saying, unfortunately, he had a very important meeting with some client from Hollywood who'd just flown in, and their lunch would have to be postponed, so would Rawlings mind a short meeting over coffee instead? Yes, Rawlings definitely would mind, but he couldn't compete with Hollywood, so reluctantly he decided to abolish his plans, curtail his trip, and return to the boat after the meeting, missing out on a visit to the Club on this occasion.

Consequently, he was not in a happy frame of mind as he limped down the path on his return. His irritation was further increased by finding the main door open, and the boat distinctly chilly inside. He slammed the door shut, turned up the heating and went into the bedroom to change out of his London clothes. He then noticed the back door was also open. Storming out onto the deck, he was stunned to find Felix, sitting on the steamer chair, and smoking.

The boy jumped up in alarm when he saw Rawlings

and flung his cigarette into the river.

'What the hell do you think you are doing?' Rawlings yelled at him. 'Why aren't you in school?'

'We were given free time this afternoon because the sports master is ill'. Felix looked at him nervously, 'I'm sorry, E.G., I came looking for you and...'

Before he could say any more, Rawlings said curtly, 'Come inside, and shut the bloody door after you. This is not the weather to be leaving doors open.' Once inside they sat opposite each other, Felix guilty, Rawlings trying to control his anger. After a moment, Rawlings spoke first, his voice cold and abrupt.

'Explain to me why on earth you thought you could smoke? Have you no idea how bad it is for you?'

Felix clenched his fists and said defiantly, 'Well you smoke.'

'Yes, I do,' Rawlings said. 'It's a filthy habit, and I wish I didn't. I started at an early age. Once you start, it is very difficult to stop, which is why I am telling you now. You must never smoke again. Do you understand this? YOU MUST NEVER SMOKE AGAIN.' He yelled the last bit.

The boy looked shocked at first, and then suddenly something else took over. He leapt to his feet, and he spoke half crying, half shouting as if all the pent-up worries and fears of the past weeks were now pouring out of him.

'You can't tell me what to do. You're not my father. You can't even be bothered to take care of me. You're sending me somewhere else the other side of the world, so in a few weeks you won't have to worry about me, ever again.'

And with that, he left the boat and Rawlings could only stare after him in bewilderment, as he heard the angry sobbing from the boy running up the garden and into the house.

What was the matter with everybody? They were all yelling and shouting at him.

For half an hour, he just sat, in a state of shock, going over in his mind what had just occurred and wondering what the hell he should do. He had now completely ruined all chances of a lasting relationship with the boy, and he felt despair. Finally, he reached for his mobile and rang Marnie. She could tell at once from his voice that something dreadful had happened, and she sighed. It was not a good moment for the interruption; she was in the middle of an important proposal for her work. But it was Rawlings, and he was in trouble, so of course, she dropped everything and made her way over to the boat.

Isobel heard the boy come in and called out to him, but unusually for him, he didn't go in to see her. Instead, he slammed the door behind him and ran up the stairs to his room, once again slamming the door. She frowned, wondering what could possibly have happened. Maybe it was something to do with the school. She left it for a while and then made her way up to his room and knocked on the door. There was no reply and having tried knocking again, she decided to let herself in.

The boy was sitting hunched at his desk, and it was obvious from the redness of his eyes that he'd been crying and she became seriously alarmed. She sat down on the bed.

'What has happened, Felix? Do you feel able to tell me?'

He looked at her as if deciding what to do. After a moment he said almost in a whisper, 'I have done something terrible.'

'At school?' He shook his head. 'What then?'

The words came in a rush. 'I did something bad, and E.G. caught me doing it, and he told me off, so I yelled at him, and now he'll never forgive me.' He was near tears again.

Isobel remained silent for a moment and then said gently, 'It sometimes helps to talk about it. Why don't you tell me exactly what happened?'

Then seemed to pour out of him; how he'd returned from school early and had gone to find Rawlings and when he wasn't there, he went out to feed Harrison, and after that, he sat on the deck. He noticed a pack of cigarettes on the table beside him. It was a spur of the moment action, and he wasn't sure why he did it. He went to the kitchen to find some matches and then lit a cigarette, just to see what it was like. It was then that Rawlings had returned and caught him.

'I know what I did was wrong,' he burst out, 'but I didn't like him shouting at me, which is why I said the awful things I did. I didn't mean it, and now I know he won't speak to me again.'

'What exactly did you say to him? Isobel asked.

He stumblingly told her his exact words and sounded so desperate she took great care in replying.

'There is an old saying, Felix, which I think applies to this situation, and that is, "you always hurt the one you love". It seems to me exactly what has happened here. Your grandfather was desperate not to see you take up the habit of smoking because he cares for you so much. He also felt guilty because he smokes, and that made him shout at you. You felt guilty about the smoking, but upset because E.G., who you love, had been angry with you, so you hit out as well. Can you understand that?' Felix nodded, and Isobel smiled. 'And now you're both feeling miserable, and we really can't have that can we? I suggest you come down when you've changed out of your uniform and have some tea. Then, in a while, you can go over to the boat and apologise. This will all blow over I'm sure of it. I'm also sure your grandfather will apologise as well.'

Meanwhile, Marnie had managed to calm Rawlings too, saying something pretty similar to Isobel's advice. She was sure the boy would be back, and after that, it was up to both of them to make the very best of the time that was left. She didn't stay long, explaining that she had a project to work on, and once Rawlings was in a better frame of mind, she left him.

After she'd gone, he stared out at the darkness of the river. The nights had drawn in so quickly it was now dark by five. He put the outside light on, just in case Felix should decide to come back. Then, putting on some Bach, he deliberately didn't pour himself a drink but listened to the music hoping to hear the approaching footsteps of the boy.

Two hours later he was rewarded by a timid knock on the door.

'Come in,' he called out, and Felix entered and stood in front of him looking contrite. 'I'm so glad you came back.' He smiled at the boy. 'I wanted to tell you how very sorry I was for shouting at you, but...'

'You were right,' Felix said, interrupting him. 'It was wrong of me to smoke. I was only trying it out to see what it was like. I won't do it again.' He paused. 'I shouldn't have said what I did. I didn't mean any of it, I promise, somehow it just came out.'

Rawlings sighed. 'I think we were both out of order.

These things happen. Shall we call a truce?'

Felix nodded and sat down. Neither spoke for a moment, and then the boy said, 'I like this music, what is it?'

'It's by J S Bach, one of the 'cello suites and the sort of music I never tire of.'

Felix considered this. 'I think I should like to play an instrument when I get to Australia. Do you think that would be allowed?'

'I'm sure it would.' Rawlings looked pleased. 'I think that is a great idea. Have you thought of the instrument you would like to play?'

Felix nodded. 'Although I like the cello, it's a bit big and clumsy to move around with. I think the saxophone would be a good one to try. Then I can play both classical and jazz.'

This was a rather surprising choice, but on thinking it over Rawlings thought it a clever one. He decided to speak to Sarah about it and make sure an instrument was bought for him. They talked on for a while and then Felix said he ought to go because he had school in the morning. As he left, he suddenly turned and hugged his grandfather and then ran back to the house.

Rawlings, not for the first time with this boy, felt overcome by emotion. It was a puzzle, but Felix had become more important to him than he ever could have imagined possible. He turned the music up and poured himself a drink.

★

November was fast moving into December, and as Rawlings stared at his diary, he realised that only a month remained before the departure of Felix for Australia. He fervently wished that time could stand still for a while so that he could spend more time with the boy. It was as if Felix felt the same, for now, every day after school he would come straight to the boat, and he and Rawlings would spend the time together, talking about anything and everything. Always, at around six, a call would come in from Isobel, telling him to return for supper and his homework. When the mobile rang, they would both look at each other and laugh, saying simultaneously, 'Isobel!'

At some point, Felix noticed that Harrison hadn't been around for a few days. This was unusual because although he occasionally missed his daily visit, he was a greedy bird and enjoyed the treats Felix threw for him. He mentioned his worry to Rawlings who assured him Harrison would soon turn up. But he didn't, and even he began to fear the worst. These fears were confirmed when Jake turned up one morning with the news that the body of a dead goose had been found further upstream.

'I'm very sorry, Mr Rawlings. I know how much this will upset the boy.'

'Do you know the cause of death?' Rawlings asked. Jake shook his head.

'I don't rightly know. Could have been old age, or he could have eaten something that poisoned him. Some swans have died of lead poisoning; lately, it could have been that. There's also been a lot of rain of late and bad stuff runs into the river off the farmlands, pesticides and that. It don't look like foul play. Sometimes the travellers do kill the larger birds, but they would have taken it away to eat it.' He looked at Rawlings, 'Will you tell the boy, or shall I?' Rawlings assured him he would do it and grimly thought of the task ahead. Jake was right. It would upset Felix and might seem to him like the last straw. He had grown very attached to that bloody goose.

'I just don't know how to tell him,' he confided to Isobel over a coffee. 'That poor boy has been through so much; the death of his parents, being told he was to live the other side of the world, and now this bloody goose has to go and die. Why couldn't the stupid thing have waited until after Felix had gone?' He added morosely, 'It's just something else the boy will blame me for.'

'Don't be so ridiculous, Rawlings,' Isobel spoke sharply, 'how could Felix possibly blame you for what was most likely the natural end to the goose's life? He watches all those nature programmes, so he knows how it goes.' Rawlings didn't look convinced and stared gloomily into his coffee cup. Isobel felt some sympathy for him, of course, the boy was going to be upset, and none of them wanted that. She was about to say something brisk and bracing when she had an idea.

'If it's all right with you, I'll tell him myself, this afternoon. It so happens I might have the perfect opportunity. I hadn't told you, but I've decided to get a puppy. It's a long time since there was a dog in the house. Peter had his Labrador, but Bosun died just a few months after Peter. Since then I hadn't really thought about having another one until a friend of mine sent me a picture of her spaniel puppies and asked me if I wanted one.' She smiled. 'The picture was enough. I couldn't resist. A spaniel is the right size of dog for me now, and it will force me to take plenty of exercise and keep myself trim.' Rawlings regarded Isobel as the picture of trimness already but made no comment. 'I'll take Felix with me to collect the puppy and break the news about Harrison on the way. The excitement of the puppy may help to soften the blow.' Rawlings looked at her with admiration.

'As usual, Isobel, you are the answer to every prayer and find a solution to every problem.' He turned to go and then added, 'Can I borrow one of your cookery books from the kitchen? I have Marnie coming to supper tonight.'

After he'd gone, Isobel sat thinking about the Marnie/ Rawlings situation. She knew they were now seeing each other almost every night and although for Rawlings it was mere companionship, she was convinced for Marnie it meant far more. Her keen observations, when watching them together, had led her to believe that she was definitely in love with him. As a typical man, he had no idea of this. It boded ill for the future, and she worried for her friend. For the moment, she had to concentrate on Felix until his departure. Rawlings would likely fall apart with the boy gone and then, in all probability would find consolation in the bottle rather than with Marnie. He might be charming, but he was also insensitive when it came to people's feelings. It was almost certain poor Marnie would feel neglected and hurt. She gave a deep sigh. Why did life have to be so horribly complicated?

Isobel and Felix set out later that day and, as she had predicted, the excitement of getting the puppy greatly softened the blow over Harrison. He became quite philosophical, telling her that animals chose the moment they wanted to die. It was sad he wouldn't see Harrison anymore but agreed they didn't really know how old the goose was, and it was good that he'd had a happy last few months of his life with plenty of food. Isobel was relieved by this reaction. She had anticipated tears.

It was only half an hour's drive to her friend's house, and they were taken straight to the pen in the garden, where the five puppies were playing. Felix's excitement knew no bounds.

'Which one are you going to choose, Isobel?' he asked as he climbed into the pen.

Isobel smiled. 'Why don't you choose, Felix? They all look lovely to me. Take your time. I'm going inside to have a cup of tea, so when you've made your decision come and tell me.'

Felix knelt down, and the five puppies jumped and crawled all over him while the mother looked on indulgently. One of the puppies sat on his foot and chewed the laces of his trainers. He gently removed it, but it came straight back and as Felix explained afterwards, gave him a cheeky look. That's definitely the one, he thought, and he carefully picked it up and carried it into the house.

'Oh, you have chosen Juno,' Isobel's friend declared. 'She is definitely one of my favourites, plenty of character, although she tends to be a bit naughty.'

Juno was taken home. Felix wanted her in his room, but Isobel said firmly there would be plenty of accidents, to begin with. The puppy should stay in her basket in the kitchen, where the floors were wooden, and newspapers could be put down.

'She'll feel a bit strange at first,' Isobel told him, 'it is the first evening away from her mother. I'm going to put a hot water bottle in her basket to keep her warm and comfortable.'

Once they'd settled her down, Felix ran down to the boat to tell Rawlings.

'You wouldn't believe how sweet she is, E.G., and she's really funny, she goes round and round in circles, and her ears are so long she trips over them when she runs. I can't take her for walks yet, but I can play with her in the garden. I wish I didn't have to go to school tomorrow.'

'But you do,' Rawlings said firmly. 'Cheer up. It is nearly the weekend, and then you can spend a lot of time with her.' He paused and added, 'I was sorry to hear about Harrison.'

Felix nodded. 'It is sad, but Isobel said he might have been very old, we just don't know. I'm glad we kept him happy for the last few months of his life.'

Rawlings felt relieved by this measured reaction, but as he remarked later to Marnie, this was mainly due to Isobel. The blow had been greatly softened by the arrival of that puppy.

★

Although Rawlings was only too aware of the time dwindling away before the departure of Felix, the boy had obviously put it from his mind and seemed happier and more settled than ever. He would rush home from school each afternoon to play with the puppy. Sometimes he would bring Juno over to the boat. Rawlings would complain mildly about the piddling on the floor, but Felix just laughed and was quick to mop up the puddles. As he watched the boy, he was uncertain if this great attachment to the animal was a good thing. Wasn't it going to be even more of a wrench for him to leave now? Maybe he should suggest getting a puppy in Australia, along with the saxophone. It was another conversation he would need to have with Sarah, although she would be arriving soon, and he would be able to hammer everything out with her in person. At least, he reflected, they would be handing over a happy and contented boy. It was, therefore, something of a shock when a couple of days later, he had a visit from Lydia.

'I don't know whether I am worrying unnecessarily,' she boomed out in her deep voice, 'but for the last few nights Felix has been suffering from what seems like extremely bad nightmares.' Rawlings looked startled but let her continue. 'He wakes up in a very distressed state. As I am nearest him, I am the one who hears it. I do my best to calm him down, but he doesn't make much sense and seems a bit bewildered by it. I give him a glass of water and sit with him, and after a while, he agrees to go back to sleep. For the rest of the night, all is quiet. I wouldn't be bothering you, but as it's still occurring, there must be something causing this, and you are probably the best person to find out what the trouble is.'

Rawlings thanked her for telling him and apologised for her broken nights.

'Please don't worry about that,' she said, 'I just don't like to see the poor little chap in such a state.'

After she'd gone Rawlings puzzled as to what could be upsetting Felix. Several things could suddenly have surfaced; delayed shock from his parent's deaths, the imminent departure to Australia, or even the demise of the goose. But why now? He seemed so happy and contented. More importantly, how would they find out the cause?

He paced about for a while wrestling with the problem, and then made the decision to consult Isobel before taking any action.

She was as surprised by this latest development as he had been.

'If you like, I can try and find out what is wrong, but I agree, it is strange it should happen now.' She thought for a moment. 'I might have a good opportunity to talk to him this afternoon. The puppy has to go to the vet to have injections. I will leave Juno at the surgery and take the boy out to the coffee shop while the injections are being done. I'm not promising anything. He may not even know what is worrying him, but I'll do my best to find out.'

Felix sat opposite Isobel in the café, happily tucking into a large éclair and trying not to let the cream spill down his school blazer. He was quite unaware of the interrogation that was about to come and pleased that Isobel had asked him to help with taking Juno to the vet.

'I hope the injections won't hurt her,' he said.

Isobel smiled and shook her head. 'I'm sure they won't. Mr Davidson is an excellent vet, and she will be well looked after.' She paused, wondering where she should begin. 'Felix,' she began, and he recognised her tone was different and looked wary. 'Lydia tells me you've been having some nasty dreams lately and I wondered if you knew what might be causing them.' He looked at her and shook his head. 'Sometimes,' she continued, 'we don't think about something that's upsetting us during the day, but then it worries us when we are asleep and turns into a nightmare. I feel there is something that is worrying you, which is causing this, and it won't really go away until you talk about it. Can you think of what it might be?'

He stared down at his plate. 'There is something that worries me, but… He hesitated, looking almost frightened.

Isobel added gently, 'This can just be between you and me Felix. I won't tell anyone else unless you want me to.' He looked up then.

'Promise?' he said. 'You won't tell anyone? I don't want to be a snitch.'

'Why don't you tell me first,' Isobel said, relieved that she might be making progress. 'If we find out what is troubling you, we can look for a solution.'

The boy struggled to find the right words to explain. 'It's Sunil,' he said at last. This was totally unexpected.

'Is he ill?'

Felix shook his head. The poor child was now looking desperate. 'There are some older boys at the school,' he finally burst out, 'about four of them. Three weeks ago, they started surrounding Sunil when we were walking home together. Now they do it in the mornings as well, and it is getting worse. It all began when Sunil became friends with Scarlet. She's a girl in my class.' He hesitated and then explained, 'I think it's because she is white and he isn't. These boys say terrible things to Sunil, swearing at him, calling him Paki and telling him he should go back to his own country. It's getting worse. They have started to push him around. I've told them to stop, and they just call me a Paki lover. And he's not even from Pakistan, he's from India, and his family has been in this country for years. I am so worried, Isobel because if I'm not there, they could really attack him and hurt him badly. Sunil won't fight back, I know, and he forbade me to report it when I said we should. He said it would only make things worse.' He looked at Isobel. 'I just don't know what to do.'

There was real fear in his eyes. Isobel was at first shocked, and then angry, but she was careful to speak calmly. 'You were right to tell me, Felix. It is brave of you to try and protect Sunil, but this is a serious matter, and it does need to be reported. Sadly, there will always be a few bullies, even in a good school, but what they are doing is very wrong, and they have to be stopped.'

'But I can't be seen to be a snitch.' He sounded panicked. 'I don't mind what they do to me, but they will presume it is Sunil who told on them and they will do something awful.'

Isobel was quick to reassure him. 'I promise, neither you or Sunil will be named. I am a Trustee of the school, and the Headmaster is a good friend of mine. I will go and talk to him, and he will know exactly what action to take without involving either of you. Will you trust me on this?' Felix nodded, looking relieved. 'Can you tell me the names of the boys, Felix?'

'I only know one of them,' he said. 'He's called Dominic Masters, and he's a big bully. Everyone in my class tries to avoid him, even the girls.'

'I will deal with this,' Isobel said firmly. 'Will you promise me to stop worrying about it? They won't harm Sunil in the future, I can assure you of that.'

Later in the day, Isobel asked Rawlings over and relayed the entire conversation. She added that she'd made an urgent appointment with the Headmaster for the next day in order to report the matter.

'Bloody racist bullies,' Rawlings growled. 'What a very

nasty country we've become. I blame Brexit.

'I think you will find,' Isobel intervened sharply, 'that regrettably, Felix will come up against bullies wherever he goes, even in Australia. They are a fact of life. And yes, they have problems there too, with racism.' She smiled at him. 'You should be proud of your grandson Rawlings. He was bravely trying to protect his friend, and he wasn't worried about himself. His great worry, and I think the cause of his nightmares, was that once he had gone, things would become a great deal worse for Sunil.'

Rawlings regarded Isobel with admiration and thought again what a wonderful woman she was. He also made a mental note to talk to the Patel's and tell them that if Sunil was targeted again, they should go and see Isobel about it.

The following day, as promised, she went in to report the incident to the Headmaster, and he, as she knew he would, took the matter very seriously. The school assembly the next morning was a long one. After the usual matters had been dealt with, the Headmaster came down to the front of the stage and addressed the boys. He cleared his throat and eyed the pupils before him with a stern expression.

'A matter has come to my attention, which has worried and upset me, deeply. It has been reported to me, not by one of the pupils, but by a distinguished Trustee of this school. She informs me that a small number of older boys have been seen bullying a new boy, taunting him with racist insults and making physical threats. This is **unpardonable** behaviour and abhorrent to all the principles we hold most dear. The pupils of this school make up a family, and into this family, we welcome all, whatever race, colour or religion. We live in a multiracial society, and our pupils represent this society. It enriches us to learn about other cultures. So, let me make this very clear. Every pupil in this school is of equal value, and every single one of you makes contributions to the life of the school in different ways.'

His voice became sterner.

'I know the identity of these boys, and I am putting them on warning. If I ever hear of them committing another racist act of this kind or an incident of bullying of any sort, they will be asked to leave the school immediately, and the reasons for their dismissal will be well recorded for future reference. This goes for anyone else who feels inclined to indulge in such abhorrent behaviour. We will not tolerate it in this place.' Here he gave a rueful smile.

'Sadly, we have to accept that we live in an imperfect society, and you may hear adults talking and behaving in this irresponsible way. There are laws that forbid such behaviour and adults can be brought to justice for such actions. Similarly, punishment here will be handed out if any sort of racism is brought to my attention.' He paused.

'I am extremely relieved this matter was brought to my attention but disappointed that it wasn't one of our own pupils who felt able to tell me about it. I know you feel great loyalty to each other, and you don't wish to be seen as an informer. But in cases like this, it is absolutely vital we know about such incidents immediately they happen so that behaviour of this sort can be eliminated once and for all. To make it easier for you to speak out, I am asking my secretary, Mrs Matlock, who you can always find in the office or in the staff room, to be the person you can refer to in future, should the occasion arise. Please report to her any such incident, and if necessary, action will be taken. That is all; you are dismissed.'

Later in the afternoon, Felix burst in on Isobel and Rawlings who were having a quiet cup of tea and reported all the events of the day, particularly the Headmaster's speech. He seemed jubilant.

'It was brilliant Isobel. Nobody suspected us, but a lot of people were trying to find out who were the boys involved. Luckily there was a long choir practice for the concert, so we didn't have to say anything. Sunil is very relieved. I didn't tell him I had told you, Isobel, he just thinks like everyone else, that a Trustee reported it to the Headmaster, so it was an ace plan. Can I take Juno out now and could Sunil come over at the weekend to meet her?'

'That will be fine, Felix,' Isobel said, 'I'd love to see Sunil again. If you are going out, it's rather muddy, so when you bring Juno back, take her into the kitchen and be sure to get her paws clean. We might give her a bath later. You can help me with that if you like.'

'Cool,' was his answer, and he ran from the room. Rawlings looked bewildered.

'Does cool mean yes or no?

Isobel smiled. 'I think it is the affirmative, an expression of approval.'

'How bewildering,' he murmured and stood up. 'Sarah arrives on the 16th. I wondered whether it might be a good idea for her to come down here, the weekend before they leave. It would give Felix the opportunity to get to know her a little before their departure, and easier here than in a London hotel.'

'Of course,' Isobel said at once. 'Does she want to come

and stay? There is plenty of room.' Rawlings shook his head.

'Kind of you Isobel, but I gather she has a lot to do in London; long sessions with the solicitor, a couple of shows, and Christmas shopping. It's a bit of a holiday for her, I imagine.'

Isobel watched him anxiously as he limped down the garden. He was holding it together for now, but she was well aware there might be a collapse once the boy had left.

Chapter Nineteen

December 2017

With the closing of the Sunil episode, December arrived and moved into calmer waters. Thankfully the nightmares had stopped and Felix once more seemed relaxed and happy. If he was worrying about his imminent departure, he certainly didn't show it. His time was fully taken up with concert practices, playing with Juno and spending time with Rawlings. Meanwhile Isobel, with quiet efficiency, was seeing to all the travel arrangements in such a discreet way Felix barely noticed them, although he did oversee the purchase of new luggage, which they chose together.

The day of the much-anticipated Christmas concert finally arrived. Felix appeared unusually quiet, almost nervous. He travelled with Isobel and Rawlings in one car, and Marnie and Lydia followed. Felix fidgeted nervously and kept coughing and clearing his throat. This irritated Rawlings.

'For goodness sake Felix, it's only a bunch of carols, not a performance of the "Messiah".

Isobel, more sympathetic, informed him there were some honey lozenges in the glove box, and he gratefully took one. Rawlings gave an inward sigh. School concerts were not the sort of event he was familiar with and he'd always done his best to try and avoid Christmas celebrations, but it was evidently important to the boy, so he determined to make an effort. Isobel had instructed him to smarten himself up for the occasion, and this he had duly done, even down to wearing a tie. The poor boy had been polished as well, with Maria beating his unruly hair into submission until it lay flat.

Parking in the place reserved for Trustees, Felix hurried off to join the rest of the pupils taking part. Rawlings and Isobel were greeted by the Headmaster as they entered the hall, who was all benevolence and bonhomie. Rawlings quickly summed him up: middle-aged, public school, possible ex-army and more politician than teacher.

'So very good to see you both,' he said in unctuous tones, as he kissed Isobel and shook the hand of Rawlings rather too vigorously. 'I am sure you will both want to sit at the front. I have reserved your seats.' He beamed at them in a way that made Rawlings wince, as he led them through the large hall, waving to various people as he went. Rawlings didn't like to be so conspicuous and was worried it might put Felix off, but he didn't seem to have much choice, so followed without protest as they made their royal progress to the first row. Once they were sitting, he looked around to see where Marnie and Lydia were and caught sight of them near the back. He sighed and put down their special treatment to Isobel being a trustee.

The boys taking part in the concert assembled on the platform and Isobel pointed out that Felix was right in the middle at the front. The headmaster stood up and welcomed everyone with his opening speech and it came as no surprise to Rawlings that he managed to scatter clichés like confetti. I'm going to hate this, he thought. I wish I was at the back with Marnie. I could even pop out for a quick fag.

The headmaster at last sat down and the lights were switched off in the hall, remaining only on the platform. There was silence. The choirmaster stepped forward and beckoned to Felix, who also took a step forward. Then something extraordinary happened. The boy began to sing, as a solo, the first verse of 'Once in Royal David's City.' Nobody had warned Rawlings about this, and he was quite unprepared for it. Felix had never mentioned a solo, but his nerves in the car now made sense and he felt guilty for being so irritable. As he listened to the beautiful pure voice reaching with ease the top notes, he could scarcely breathe. This was his grandson, making pure music. He had no idea the boy could sing like this, let alone make such a wonderful sound.

'Mary was that mother mild, Jesus Christ, her little child.'

The solo came to an end and only then did Rawlings dare look at Isobel. She had tears running down her cheeks and he found himself near to tears himself. He passed her his handkerchief and she smiled, taking it gratefully. When the audience joined in with the final verses, he whispered, 'Did you know about this?'

'No, it was a complete surprise.'

The rest of the evening passed him by. Rawlings didn't really listen to any of it, he could only think of the boy's solo voice. When it was over and the boys had filed out, the headmaster turned to Rawlings and told him how proud he must be of his grandson and how they were all going to miss him. Rawlings, now on his best behaviour, thanked the man for all he had done for Felix. Isobel added her thanks, saying what a wonderful evening it had been.

At the back of the hall they met up with Marnie, Lydia had apparently already left to wait for her in the car.

'She never struck me as being the emotional type,' Marnie told him, 'but when Felix was singing, she was quite overcome. I had to lend her my handkerchief.'

'I think we all felt like that.' Isobel said. 'He kept it very quiet.' She turned to Rawlings. 'Did you know he could sing like that?'

'No, I had no idea. It came as a complete shock.'

Felix was waiting for them by the car. There was a big hug from Isobel but he looked anxiously at Rawlings, waiting for his comment.

'Well, you are a dark horse Felix. That was wonderful, I am really proud of you,' he said, and he meant it. 'Why on earth didn't you tell us?'

'I was worried if I did, I might make a mess of it,' and they both laughed.

'Well you most certainly didn't do that. It was a triumph,' Rawlings assured him. As Felix climbed into the car he added, 'I expect all that singing has made you hungry. What about a McDonald's to celebrate?'

'Cool' the boy said. It was obviously the word of the moment.

★

The week came to an end and so did the school term. Felix rushed back, dropped off his games kit and ran down to the boat. Rawlings was going through the proofs of his book and didn't hear the boy until he was right in front of him.

'E.G., what do you think? I got a prize.' He handed his grandfather a leather-bound book. It was *The Oxford Book of English Verse*. Inside was the school logo and below that, was written in large print: 'This Prize has been awarded to Felix Rawlings. Star Pupil, Autumn Term, 2017'. It had been signed by the Headmaster.

'He told me it was for all round excellence,' Felix explained, 'but I think it was mainly for singing that solo.' He gave a grin. 'Nobody else wanted to do it, they were all chicken. Sunil kept telling me how brave I was, which was why I was so nervous.' Rawlings handed back the book.

'That is a great book to have, Felix. Congratulations. You've done well at that school. I'm proud of you.' He was about to add that he hoped he would do equally well at his new school in Australia, but then decided against this and instead told him to go and show his prize to Isobel. 'I know she'll be very impressed. Come back and see me later.'

After he'd gone, Rawlings limped over to the window and stared out at the river. The days were so short now the light had nearly gone. A couple of swans glided by, very white against the dark of the water. There were few birds about these days. Even his heron seemed to have given up, although that might have been because the parakeets would viciously swoop down on the bird, while he was standing on the bank. Maybe his heron had gone somewhere else to escape their persecution. It occurred to him that persecution was everywhere, even in the animal kingdom. He sighed and gave a shiver. Soon the boy would be gone and what then? His book was finished.

What would he be coming back to after the operation? He knew Marnie wanted him to stay. But wasn't that just one more complication he should try and avoid?

His musings were disturbed by the battalion of Canada geese beginning their evening parade upstream. He wondered if they took it in turns to be the leader. How could you tell? They all looked the same as they dutifully followed, two by two. He returned to his desk and stared at the proofs of his book. A few more minor changes had been suggested by his editor. Bloody woman. He wasn't going to argue. He didn't care enough about the work to refuse her suggestions, but he did need to sort out some photographs for them to use. He pulled a box out of his desk drawer. It was difficult to make a selection, there were so many. Suddenly, right at the bottom, he found a picture of himself with Mia. It must have been in Sarajevo. They both looked so young, and yes, happy, in spite of the dire situation they were in. God she was beautiful. He stared at it for a moment. Then removing the photo from the rest, he placed it on the desk. This was not one that he would allow to be used. He needed to keep Mia for himself. Putting the rest back in the box, he decided to hand over the whole lot and let the publishers make the choice.

It was almost dark now. He put on the lights and poured himself a drink. Felix would be back soon for their evening chat, and this started him thinking about the boy. Had he really done enough for him? He still had no idea what Felix thought, what went on in his head, or what worries he had deep down. Maybe he should have discussed the death of his parents with him, and how he felt about it. The subject had always been avoided between them, but was this damaging?

Should he have tried to draw him out on the subject? Would it affect him later on in life, to have buried it now? So many questions and he had no answers. He searched his memory, trying to think of his emotions when he was told his own father wasn't coming back. It was difficult to remember what he'd felt exactly, but like Felix he'd shown no emotion to the outside world, just got on with his life. Maybe this is what the boy was doing. But had it harmed him? He couldn't see how, although some might say it explained why he'd been such a neglectful father. That had to be bloody nonsense. Pure psychobabble. His neglect had been entirely due to the circumstances he'd found himself in. That, and the fact he'd never bonded with the child. He felt far closer to Felix in a few months than he'd ever been to Hugo. He knocked back his drink and poured another. The questions kept coming, needing answers, but he could find none. His fervent hope was that Sarah's husband would take on the role of a father figure, even if he was a bloody Australian!

Pushing back his desk chair he stood up, grabbed the bottle and removed it to the kitchen, to make quite sure he didn't have another drink before the boy arrived. Limping back to his desk, he gave a sigh. It was time to stop being so narky about Australia. He had to accept that Felix would be spending the rest of his childhood out there, although his great hope was that he would return to England to go to university and maybe stay on afterwards. It would all be fine, as long as the boy didn't return with an Australian accent. Meanwhile his aunt would be coming down at the weekend. He had to be on his best behaviour for that.

★

Sarah arrived by train and Rawlings went on his own to meet her, keen they should talk together before she met with Felix for the first time. He decided the best place would be a café within walking distance of the station.

It was a bright, but cold December day. Sarah greeted him affectionately. She was well wrapped up and admitted it was hard to adjust to the abrupt change in climate. Apparently, there'd been a heat wave in Australia just before she'd left.

'The high temperatures might come as a bit of a shock to Felix,' Rawlings told her with a smile. 'It will be strange for him to arrive in the middle of summer, especially at Christmas.'

He ordered them both coffees and then sat back, making a study of her. It was odd but she didn't resemble her sister in the least. Susanna had been sharp of feature, and also it seems, of character. Sarah's face was round, open and friendly. There was perhaps some similarity in the eyes, which were like Felix's, but there it ended. She was also plump, whereas Susanna had been fashionably thin. Sarah had removed her bulky coat, but still remained of ample build. In earlier years he would have referred to her as a jolly sort of girl, rather like Gillian.

'How has Felix been?' she asked. 'We were wondering how he'd reacted to his parent's accident? It was such a terrible thing to have happened to such a small boy. I mean, to lose both of them at once. That was just awful.'

Rawlings thought about this, wanting to put the boy's lack of emotion over the loss of his parents as tactfully as he could.

'Felix is a boy who tends to keep his feelings well

hidden, but outwardly he has dealt with the trauma as well as could be expected. Isobel, who you will soon meet, has been very instrumental in this. She's become like a surrogate grandmother.' He paused. 'I expect you will find Felix rather shy and reserved at first. He is not a very tactile child, given to hugging and general affectionate responses...

Sarah interrupted here, 'I know exactly what you mean. He'd get that from my sister. Susanna always found it difficult to show affection. Looking back, I think she was more affected by our mother leaving than I was. I was younger and, in any case, I had a real bond with my father, which she didn't.' She looked at him and smiled. 'We are rather a tactile family I'm afraid, but we will be careful not to force anything on Felix. I am sure it will take him time to adjust to such a new situation, but I'm really hoping we can give him a good home and a good life.' She spoke earnestly adding, 'Shane is looking forward to having someone of his own age and Brad has already put Felix's name down at the sport's club.'

Rawlings, in spite of himself, found he was warming to her, although couldn't help inwardly sighing. It sounded just as he'd imagined, and the heartiness made him privately shudder. Putting these feelings firmly aside, he tried to sound encouraging.

'To give the boy his due, and what we have all come to realise, is that Felix adapts quickly to situations, as long as he is allowed to do it in his own way and in his own time.'

Sarah nodded and he hoped this particular advice had been taken seriously.

'Do you have any pets?' he asked.

'Oh yes. We have two dogs and Davey has a tortoise.

Does Felix like dogs?'

Rawlings gave a laugh. 'He does indeed. Isobel has just bought a puppy, and he's devoted to it. I think he's going to miss Juno terribly. If you, by any chance, felt the need of another dog, it might be a good move for him to have a puppy of his own.'

Sarah considered this. 'I'll talk to Brad. One of our dogs is quite old now, so it might be very possible to get a puppy for Felix as a replacement for Bongo when he goes.'

Rawlings felt relieved she was so acceptive to everything and persevered. 'The other question I have to ask, is about a musical instrument for Felix. It turns out the boy is quite musical...' He proceeded to tell her about the Christmas concert and the solo performance. 'He has actually expressed a desire to learn the saxophone. I don't know whether that could be arranged? I'd be happy to pay for an instrument. We are trying to cut down on his luggage, so it would be better if you bought one when you get back.'

Sarah smiled. 'That would be just dandy. Shane plays the drums and we have a shed out the back where he can practice. Davey has just started clarinet lessons, so a saxophone would fit in very well. There are some great teachers at the school...' She broke off. 'There's a good local school where our boys go and Ellie will too, but if you thought it better that he went to somewhere more academic, there is a boarding school in Adelaide with a very good reputation.'

Rawlings shook his head vehemently. 'Definitely no boarding school. I think the same school as your children sounds like an ideal situation.' He looked at his watch. 'We'd better get back. Felix should be returned from his friend Sunil's by now.'

On the drive back he glanced at Sarah and could tell she was a bit daunted by this first meeting with her nephew. She had taken his advice and didn't hug the boy, but just smiled and said, 'Hello Felix, I'm very pleased to meet you at last.'

Isobel, tactful as ever, suggested that Felix took Sarah down to show her the boat, saying lunch would be ready in half an hour. As they walked down the garden, she looked questioningly at Rawlings who said, 'I need a drink.'

As she handed him the glass she said mildly, 'I do hope you are going to be on your best behaviour Rawlings. It is very important that the boy sees you getting on well with Sarah.'

'Naturally I will,' he said huffily. 'I've already been quite charming to her.'

Isobel looked amused. 'Well she seems a nice, motherly sort of person. I am sure she'll do her very best to see Felix is happy and welcomed into their family.' Rawlings was about to say something to this, but then thought the better of it.

'What did you think of the boat?' Isobel asked when they returned. Sarah replied in genuine admiration,

'She's a real beaut.' Isobel caught sight of Rawlings wincing, as she added, 'and it's such a great spot you have here on the river. We have a lake near us and if Felix brings those lovely binoculars with him, he can go bird-spotting there.'

Felix piped up, 'I've told Sarah I'm leaving the fishing rods and my bicycle here,' adding firmly, 'for when I come back next summer.'

Rawlings and Isobel exchanged glances at this intervention. Isobel said quickly. 'I've told Felix he will always be welcome to return here at any time Sarah, but it's a little soon to arrange anything yet.'

Felix looked as if he were about to argue about this, but Sarah quickly relieved the tension by saying it would be lovely for Felix to come back in the summer, especially as it would be their winter by then, and everyone relaxed.

The lunch passed happily. Felix was quiet at first, but with some prompting from Isobel, he told Sarah about how he had chosen Juno. He then added a description of the concert and singing his solo. After coffee, Sarah pleaded tiredness and Rawlings said he would drive her back to the station. Once again, she was careful not to hug the boy goodbye, but just said how lovely it had been to meet them all. She thanked Isobel and they agreed to have a discussion on the telephone about what Felix would need in the way of packing.

As soon as Sarah had departed, Felix left to say his goodbyes to Sunil and the Patel's.

'Well?' said Marnie later, when she and Rawlings were having supper in the boathouse. 'How did it all go? Isobel told me Sarah seemed to be a lovely person.'

Rawlings growled grudgingly, 'I suppose that is an accurate description. She was good with Felix and careful not to be over-affectionate with him.' He added grudgingly, 'I suppose you could say she didn't really put a foot wrong, except for calling my boat a "real beaut".' He made an effort at an Australian accent and Marnie burst out laughing. 'Honestly, Rawlings you are ridiculously prejudiced sometimes. Isobel told me she didn't sound at all Australian.' He refused to look repentant. 'I bet Brad and her children do,' he said gloomily.

Marnie looked cross at this but made no further comment.

After a moment she asked, 'Did Felix say what he thought of the visit?'

Rawlings shook his head. 'Not much. He made some remark to indicate he liked her. I think his exact words were "she's cool". He seemed more excited about being on the upper deck of the jumbo jet. My impression is that he appears to be looking on the whole thing as a sort of adventure holiday, rather than a completely new way of life.' He shrugged and added a little bitterly, 'Which is probably the best way for him to deal with it.'

★

By mutual agreement, it had been decided to keep the last evening as low-key as possible. Isobel had organised all the packing and into his bag went their presents to him. Apart from the CD Rawlings had made for Felix, which contained the pieces of music they had played together, he'd also given him a very beautiful copy of *The Wind in the Willows,* which he hoped he wouldn't consider too childish but would remind him of their time together on the boat. Instruction had been sent round to make sure the presents were small and light so they would fit into his case. Isobel's present was the most practical. Apart from the large canvas bag with wheels that she and Felix had chosen together, she had also bought a matching backpack for his needs for the journey. To her relief Sarah had said she would buy him appropriate summer clothes, so this had left room for other things. Felix had taken little interest in the packing and was happy to leave it all to Isobel, but had insisted on taking his binoculars and laptop, along with the camera and drawing materials he had been given for his birthday. Otherwise he was pleased to leave larger possessions, like his bike, his cricket set and the fishing rods, behind. It seemed to him to be a guarantee that he would be returning in the summer, and that was important. Marnie gave him a drawing she'd done of Rawlings, showing it to him first. He stared at it with mild distaste.

'Do I really look like that?'

She smiled. 'That is actually you in cheerful mode. I could have drawn a grumpy portrait, but I thought Felix would prefer this.'

Maria and Paul dropped in for tea and presented Felix with a book of photos taken at his birthday party. This delighted him and he declared again it had been the best day of his life. When it came to saying goodbye Isobel could see that Maria was getting tearful, but the boy gave her a hug and assured her he would see her soon, when he came over in the summer, and with that thought she brightened up.

Isobel, Marnie, Lydia and Rawlings had his favourite supper of chicken and chips and the boy talked happily throughout. At the end of the meal the goodbyes were kept to a minimum. Rawlings was surprised to see that Lydia was finding it hard to keep her emotions in check. She had obviously become very attached to the boy and told him firmly she would be looking forward to seeing him in the summer. After Marnie and Lydia had left, Rawlings, Isobel and Felix played a last game of Mah-jong, which he of course won.

Once he'd gone to bed Rawlings and Isobel sat together for a while.

'Well, that's that,' he said, adding, 'strange to think I was so daunted by having Felix here, and now I find it impossibly hard to see him go.'

Isobel was silent for a moment. 'You have been wonderful with the boy, Rawlings, helping him through so much. You should be proud of yourself.'

He gave a shrug, 'I don't know about that.' Looking at her he added, 'Darling Isobel, I couldn't have done any of it without you. I will always be grateful to you for that.'

'It's strange for me as well,' she said and there was sadness in her voice, 'I never imagined I could get attached to a child quite so quickly, especially one who is no relation to me. I have no family, only the one niece, who has that dreadful daughter for whom I feel no affection at all,' and she laughed. 'After the fiasco of Selena's visit in the summer, I doubt I will ever see her again and it doesn't worry me in the least. But with Felix... well, he is like the grandchild Peter and I never had.'

The two of them sat on, both with their sad and wistful thoughts about the boy, who had come into their lives so suddenly and who they were now having to let go.

★

The drive to Heathrow was quiet. Once or twice Rawlings glanced at Felix, who was staring straight ahead, his hands once more clenched on his lap. He imagined the parting with Isobel might be affecting him. It was obvious the boy really loved her. He'd also spent a lot of time

259

hugging Juno. He was going to miss that wretched puppy as well.

'Juno will be fully grown when you next see her and I expect you will have a lot to tell Isobel when you see her in the summer, and Sunil of course. I thought I might fly out to Australia to see you, around March, when my leg has recovered.'

Felix nodded and then suddenly said, 'Do you like flying E.G.? I've only flown once and then it was a very short flight.'

Rawlings now wondered whether it was the long journey that might be bothering him. Stupid of him not to have thought of it. In view of this he was careful with his answer.

'My work involved me in travelling on planes throughout my life, in all sizes of aircraft.' He thought grimly of some of the hairy flights he'd taken over the years, in very small planes, being tossed around the skies like cement in a cement mixer, with enemy fire threatening them as they tried to land. Making an effort he smiled encouragingly and added, 'The fact is, flying is the safest form of travel there is, and you are doing it the very best way. It'll be exciting. I envy you being on the top deck of the jumbo. There'll be plenty to keep you occupied, including lots of films to watch.'

Felix nodded and gave him a smile. After that they finished the rest of the journey in silence.

Sarah was waiting beside the check-in desk and waved as Rawlings and Felix walked towards her. 'Well done. You're exactly on time.' She looked at Felix and said cheerily, 'If you let me have your passport, I can check us in. Once we go through, you can explore the shops and we can have something to eat.'

Rawlings didn't want to prolong his farewell. He stooped down, took the boy in his arms for one last time and whispered in his ear, 'I am so proud of you Felix.' Then with an abrupt nod to Sarah, he turned and walked away as briskly as he could, without looking back.

Isobel and Marnie tactfully gave him space on his return and didn't contact him. Marnie watched as he walked past the boathouse, his head down, a fixed expression on his face. He sent them both brief messages to say the departure had gone smoothly and Sarah had promised to let him know the boy had arrived safely.

Once on the boat, Rawlings poured himself a drink and slumped into a chair. He felt completely drained, devoid of all emotion. Felix was gone and that particular episode in his life was over. Would everything now go back to the way it had been before Felix arrived on the scene? He doubted it.

He glanced at his desk and caught sight of the photo of Mia. It led him to wondering what she would have made of the boy. If he were perfectly honest, she'd probably have resented Felix, finding him an unwelcome intrusion. Whenever his personal life had interfered with theirs, she had shown her disapproval and been downright unpleasant when he'd returned to England for Hugo's wedding, refusing to understand he was doing it for Gillian's sake. It was the same when he left her to be with Gillian while she was dying. Mia had remarked coldly that he'd never lived with the woman so why rush to her bedside now. This had shaken him at the time, and he couldn't understand her lack of sympathy. Now, as he looked back, through less tinted glasses, he realised that Mia disliked anything that interfered with their life together, and she wasn't one to compromise. She would have made him make a choice, Felix or her. The boy could well have split them apart. She wouldn't have wanted him with them. After Luka, she'd never shown one jot of a maternal instinct.

He grabbed the bottle, filled up his glass and continued with his thoughts. Apart from Felix, how would Mia have coped with him, now that he was a cripple and forced to lead a static life? Not well, he was certain of that. She hadn't been the domestic or caring kind. Their life together only worked when they were equals. He gulped his wine. For the first time, he was facing up to the fact that had Mia lived, she would almost certainly have left him, in order to pursue her own career uninterrupted. It wasn't that she didn't love him, it was just that their situation had changed and this wasn't a life she could have lived with. She wasn't given to making personal sacrifices.

He gave a sigh and thought again about the boy. It struck him that when Sarah removed Felix, everything changed as well. Felix, who had so quickly become the centre of his life, was now gone. His relationship with the boy would never be quite the same. From this moment on he would just be the distant grandfather.

So, what now? He looked towards the window and caught sight of a casserole on the table, no doubt left by the faithful Marnie. With a sigh he reflected that these two women, Mia and Marnie, could not have been more different. Unlike the uncompromising Mia, Marnie was always patient, careful to give him space, indulging his moods and never judgmental. It would be easy to make a life with such a gentle and caring person, allowing him a passive and peaceful existence. After what he'd gleaned of her past life, he also felt protective towards her. In contrast he'd had no such feelings for Mia. They had been equals, there had been a shared passion – their work, their ideals, the excitements and the dangers. And there had been those long nights of love-making. That could never be replaced.

Exhausted he closed his eyes. Christmas was looming. Isobel had invited him to lunch. Somehow, he had to get through the festivities. After that he would make a decision about his future.

★

On the day before Christmas Eve, Isobel rang Rawlings and asked him over for a drink. She studied him carefully as he sat down, and decided that although he looked rough, he was at least making the effort to be sociable.

'I gather Felix arrived safely,' she said. 'Sarah sent me a message to say the journey had gone well and that he seemed to enjoy it.'

Rawlings nodded. 'I had a similar message. She is a woman of limited vocabulary. I also talked to Felix, who appeared happy with his new surroundings.' He added wryly, 'He said he was missing me. Very tactful of the boy.'

Isobel decided to ignore this. 'What are your plans now?' she asked.

He gave her a quizzical look. 'Do you mean in the next few days, or with my life?'

This produced a sigh. He was obviously in a difficult mood and she did her best to sound patient, 'I was referring to the week over Christmas...'

'Oh, Christmas,' he cut in scornfully. 'I've never indulged in celebrating that particular event...'

Isobel in spite of feeling annoyed, persevered. 'Well, I am pleased that you are coming to lunch on Christmas Day. Marnie and Lydia are joining me. In fact, Marnie has kindly offered to do the cooking. I believe we are having capon,' she paused, 'and, I should perhaps warn you, my actress friend, Fanny Markham, will be joining us as well. She is arriving tomorrow for a few days. I am led to believe she is going through something of a crisis, at least, that is what she tells me, but it is always a little difficult to tell with Fanny quite how serious it is.'

'You mean she's given to hyperbole,' Rawlings grunted.

Isobel laughed at this. 'Something like that. It does mean the lunch will be rather over-loaded with females, but if you think you could survive that, we'd love to see you.'

She was relieved to see this raised a smile.

'Thank you, I accept,' he said, adding graciously, 'I will not only survive it, I will enjoy your company.'

On Christmas morning, Isobel went into the kitchen and admitted to Marnie that she had many misgivings about the forthcoming lunch. Fanny was in an extremely volatile state; her latest partner having left her, and probably, more worrying for her, a leading role in a West End play she'd thought she was being offered, had fallen through.

'Quite frankly, the woman borders on the hysterical. We don't even have the calming influence of Lydia, who rather irritatingly, has taken up a late invitation to join a friend on a cruise.' She sighed. 'Added to this, I really have no idea how Rawlings will behave.'

Marnie agreed he might well be in a grumpy state but having not seen him since the departure of Felix, it was difficult to predict his mood. Privately she rather presumed he was drowning his sorrows and could easily arrive the worse for alcohol, but she kept this thought to herself, not wanting to increase Isobel's anxiety.

As it happened, they were both to be pleasantly surprised. Not only did Rawlings arrive totally sober, he was also smartly dressed, wearing the cashmere cardigan Isobel had given him for his birthday, a blazer and a necktie to finish off the dashing appearance. He was also laden with presents; a rose for Isobel, a potted bay tree for Marnie and a bunch of lilies for Fanny.

'The rose is from Felix and myself,' he explained to Isobel. 'He helped me choose it and we ordered it together. I talked to him this morning and he was in a highly excited state. I believe it was early evening there and it appears he'd had a very good day. He tactfully mentioned how much he loved all the presents we'd sent. His cousin Shane was standing beside him. Although the same age, he's totally unlike Felix, and appeared rather a short, stocky boy.'

'What a relief he's settled in so well,' Isobel said. 'Next time I talk to him I will thank him for the beautiful rose. Such a wonderful choice. Jake and I will choose a special spot for it.'

'Did he look well?' Marnie asked and Rawlings nodded. 'He already appears to have acquired a suntan. He tells me it is very hot, and he spends most of the day in the swimming pool. I'm relieved to report that so far he has no trace of an Australian accent,' he added, for Marnie's benefit.

Isobel laughed at this, 'Oh, really Rawlings, you are

absurd, the boy has only been out there five days.'

Fanny who had been silent during all this, now stepped in to take over the conversation. She kissed Rawlings on the cheek, 'I am so thrilled with these beautiful lilies darling. How did you know they were my favourite flowers?' Giving a throaty laugh she added, 'no "dame aux camelias" for me. I always liked my dressing rooms to be filled with lilies.' She turned to Isobel, 'I think they ought to be put in water, so they will survive until my departure tomorrow.' Rawlings noted with some amusement she made no move to do this herself but waited until Marnie took them from her and went out to the kitchen.

After this auspicious beginning, the occasion went quickly downhill. Fanny monopolised Rawlings throughout the meal, flirting with him outrageously. He could do little but respond, which he did with ease and charm. Marnie, hot and flustered from all the cooking, stared mutinously at the plate, her jealousy plain to see. Isobel did her best to introduce general topics into the conversation, but Fanny would immediately bring the subject back to herself, and eventually she gave up.

As the brandy was poured over the pudding and it was set alight, Fanny said in rather patronising tones, 'You are clever Marnie. I could never get mine to do that.' Rawlings responded to this by saying, 'What utter nonsense you do talk Fanny, you have never made a Christmas pudding in your entire life. The stage quite clearly is your domain, not the kitchen.' Although they both laughed, this had been meant as a slight reproof and Fanny recognised this. Sadly, it was lost on Marnie. She took it as a further comparison between the glamour of the actress and the drudgery of herself, the drab cook, and she sank further into her misery.

Isobel, annoyed with Fanny's behaviour, decided it was time to make a toast. 'To Marnie, thank you so much for the wonderful meal. Everything was perfect.' Glasses were raised and thanks murmured.

'Superbly done Marnie,' Rawlings put down his glass, took her hand and kissed it.

She flushed and the look she gave him was not lost on Isobel, nor for that matter on Fanny, who was not a stupid woman.

They repaired to the living room and Marnie brought in a tray of coffee. Rawlings had a cognac.

'It gets dark so terribly early in December,' Isobel remarked. 'I really ought to take Juno for a walk while there is still some light. Do you want to come, Marnie?'

Marnie shook her head saying she wanted to make a start on the clearing up. This sounded a trifle martyred and Isobel said sharply, 'You don't have to do anything Marnie. You have done quite enough today. Maria is coming in tomorrow morning, and will have it all cleared away in no time at all.'

Marnie nodded but stood up. 'I'll just put the pans into soak and make sure it's reasonably tidy.'

Fanny finished her coffee and said, 'I'll come for a walk with you darling. Just give me time to get my sensible shoes on. Back in a jiffy.' She left the room.

Rawlings, having drained his glass, judged this was the moment to leave as well, and pulled himself up, just as Marnie returned. 'Thank you for a delightful lunch Isobel and to you Marnie for cooking it. I think a postprandial nap is now called for.' He kissed Isobel on the cheek and then limped painfully back to the boat.

Marnie watched him go. She'd been hoping he would keep her company while she tidied the kitchen, and then they could have walked back together, maybe even have a drink. Her disappointment at his leaving was plainly visible. Isobel made a mental note to have a serious conversation with Marnie as soon as possible, before the situation got out of hand.

Rawlings lay on his sofa and stared out of the window. It may not have been a white Christmas, but by way of compensation there was now the most dramatic sunset, with red and orange streaks of sky reflected in the water. One of the things he'd most missed about England when he'd been abroad, was seeing the changes in the four seasons, each one having its own character. It had been even more noticeable since being on the boat. Marnie had described them through her artist's eyes, saying that each season had a particular colour scheme. Spring was all bright lime greens, whites and yellows, summer was lush with a more verdant green and the reds and pinks of the flowers, the autumnal colours were rich browns and oranges and then, there was winter, with the bare trees of grey and black branches, contrasting with flaming night skies and the occasional layer of white snow.

As he thought of Marnie's observations, he had a pang of guilt. He was well aware she was upset at lunch, but quite honestly it hadn't been his fault, the wretched Fanny had made it impossible for him to pay attention to anyone else. It was all the more annoying because he'd made a great effort for Isobel's sake. Bloody women, there was no pleasing them. Amends would have to be made. Marnie had over-reacted, but he really didn't like her being upset. A supper would have to wait until after London, a visit which would keep him away for the next few days and included extensive scans at the hospital. New Year's Eve could work, and it would be a good way to see out the year together. However, at the back of his mind, he had a nagging worry that she was becoming far too attached to him, and for the first time, almost possessive. Her behaviour at the lunch was evidence of that. It was a situation he would have to deal with, before it spun out of control.

He got up, shook his leg which had seized up, and turned his thoughts to Felix. Although he'd given Isobel an upbeat account of the boy, in reality, their conversation of the morning had left him thoroughly depressed. Gone was the intimacy between them that he'd so enjoyed. Now it seemed more like a boy who was doing his duty and making contact with some distant relative. This might be unfair to Felix, who had been excited to talk to him, but Rawlings knew instinctively things had radically changed. The boy had already moved on. He could go and visit Felix, but he would be just that, the visitor. From the moment he'd left the boy at the airport he'd lost something, something that had become the most important part of his present life and now it was gone. He wasn't sure where he went from here. Settling back on the sofa he wrestled with the problem. If they managed to patch up his leg, there was no reason why he shouldn't survive a few more years. It was therefore time to make a plan, if he wasn't to sink into a complacent old age. He needed a radical change, and fast. Another incident was needed, to send him off in a new direction. But what? They didn't arrive by order.

He closed his eyes. This was not a problem for today. He gently drifted off into a deep sleep.

Marnie was relieved to receive the invitation from Rawlings. In truth she'd been feeling rather ashamed of her behaviour at the Christmas lunch and could tell it had irritated Isobel as well. Had she allowed her feelings for Rawlings to become so transparent? She was doing her best not to let them show, but now Felix had gone, she'd hoped he would pay her more attention, not less...

Enough! She had to stop this. Deep down she knew it hadn't been his fault. He had merely tried to be polite, but even so... he'd been so damnably charming. From now on she would keep her feelings under control and stop behaving like a lovesick teenager. In any case, Fanny had gone back to London and on New Year's Eve she would have Rawlings all to herself.

Chapter Twenty

New Year's Eve 2017

The champagne cork popped as she walked through the door.

'Good heavens,' she exclaimed, 'isn't a bit early for the bubbly?'

'It's never too early for champagne,' he said as he handed her the glass.

She looked at the bottle. 'How extravagant, Rawlings, it's the real thing. Most people only give you Prosecco these days.'

'I am not most people,' he said smiling at her, 'but I have to be honest and admit I bought these bottles for Christmas Day, but then found I couldn't manage them, along with the plants and the flowers, which means that tonight we can really indulge ourselves. I also brought back other treats from London, potted shrimp and pate de foie gras, purchased in Fortnum's. We can use them to soak up the bubbly. I was tempted by the caviar, but that did seem like one extravagance too far.'

'How very sybaritic,' Marnie said almost reproachfully, but added 'a perfect way to see out the old year.'

They sipped in silence for a while until she commented,

'You've had a busy week in London. Was this to do with your work?'

'Partly,' he indicated the book on his desk. 'That, I am glad to say, is the final proof. I'll let you have it when I've finished one last check.'

She glanced at the cover. There was a black and white photo of Rawlings and above, the title in dark red lettering, *"Myriad Faces – The Memoir of a War Correspondent"* and underneath, still in red letters, was his name, E.G. Rawlings.

'The cover design is very striking,' she said. 'Why "Myriad Faces", where does that come from?'

'It's from a poem by Auden, from his "Sonnets from China" The quote seemed particularly apt...

"For we have seen a myriad faces,

Ecstatic from one lie

And maps can really point to places

Where life is evil now..." It's a poem you should read.' He gave her a strange look. 'I have some other news for you.' He paused for a moment before saying, 'I've bought a flat.'

This was totally unexpected, and she said in alarm, 'Does this mean you are giving up the boat?'

'No, but I felt it time I had a base in London again. It might also be useful for Felix later if he decides to return to England.' He gave a rueful smile. 'I bought the flat entirely on impulse, but I know I won't regret it. As you must have realised by now, I'm a great believer in the odd, unexpected event causing things to change. I call them turning points. This was exactly the case here. I happened to meet up with an old friend in The Frontline Club, and after a few drinks, he told me, in confidence, that he was in grave financial difficulties. It was the usual story, property rich but cash poor. This guy, like me, had spent most of his life abroad, as a correspondent...'

'Married?' Marnie broke in.

'No, officially single, although I think he's had an on/off girlfriend for a long time. Anyway, years ago he'd bought this house in Putney, with a garden going down to the river. It had been reasonably cheap to buy then, but now, as you can imagine, it's worth a vast amount. He's about to retire and the upkeep of the house and general expenses, added to his already large debts, have become unmanageable. I gather that over the years the situation which he'd ignored, had worsened, and now he finds himself in a crisis.'

He paused for another drink, this time draining his glass. 'Max, my friend, was distressed because there was now no alternative to his problems, other than selling this house, which he loves. There he sat, drowning his sorrows...'

'So, you offered to buy it?' Marnie intervened, wondering where the hell he would find the millions to purchase such an expensive property.

'Not all of it,' Rawlings said quickly. 'It so happens the house has a lower ground floor, with a separate entrance which could make a self-contained flat. The great glory of the place is a door in the main room opening onto the garden, which goes down to the river.' Here he smiled at her. 'I find I have become addicted to river life, so I was interested at once. Max has been using the flat for storage, and it will need some work to restore it into a living space, but once that's done, it will be perfect for my needs. I immediately made him an offer, and he immediately accepted. Easy as that. It's an all-round win. Max can pay off his debts and have enough to live on, while at the same time, still own the main part of the house. The more we talked about it, the more it seemed an ideal solution for us both…'

'Was this decision made after several hours at the bar?' Marnie asked drily.

Rawlings didn't take offence but laughed. 'I did make the initial suggestion over drinks, I admit, however, over the next three days, we talked it through soberly and seriously, whilst taking advice from others. I made no firm offer until after visiting my financial adviser.' Rawlings paused to refill their glasses. 'He had been urging me for years to do something with my capital. I'd inherited large sums from both Gerald and Gillian but never touched it. Money has never interested me. I've never been able to get used to having it. As a child, we never had any. I'd become used to living life frugally. So, when I was given these large sums, I let the financial man invest it for me, and by the look of it, he has done well. Therefore, happily, I can easily afford to buy the flat. The purchase and restoring it will take up a good chunk of my money, but I will have plenty left to live on, along with my pensions and freelance work. Who knows, the bloody book might make money, especially if they make a television programme out of it. So, there it is, the deed is done. I hold the freehold to a London flat. It must be the quickest property transaction ever made. I didn't quibble about the price, but having pointed out the work that needed doing, Max quite fairly reduced the price by a few thousand. He'd had a recent survey done, with a view to selling the whole house, so I could see the place was structurally sound. It seems another unexpected turning point in my life has been reached.'

Marnie sat in stunned silence, her mind whirring. The bottle was now empty, and Rawlings went out to the kitchen. At least, she thought with relief, he's keeping the boat, yet for some reason, the news had disturbed her. He soon returned with another bottle, along with a plate of the Fortnum's delicacies and she was invited to dig in.

After that, there were no more startling revelations. At some point, she apologised for her behaviour at the Christmas lunch and tried to explain.

'It wasn't just that you gave her all your attention, it was also the fact that Fanny hadn't offered to give one iota of help all morning but treated me like some sort of domestic help.' Rawlings couldn't stop himself from laughing at her indignant expression, but she blurted out, 'I also felt you would compare us unfavourably. Fanny looked so glamorous, and I felt so drab beside her.

'What a bloody stupid woman you are,' he broke in mildly cross. 'She doesn't compare with you, Marnie. Those layers of makeup have no effect on me at all. You have your own kind of beauty, and you don't need powder and paint. Why do you have so little confidence in yourself?'

She considered this and said sadly, 'I really don't know. The Fanny's of this world always make me feel like that.'

'Well in future,' Rawlings said firmly, 'don't let them. Trust in who you are, and for what it's worth you are attractive, with your lovely face and your beautiful red hair. I find you very attractive.'

She flushed and didn't feel able to speak. It was the first compliment he'd ever paid her. The second bottle was quickly finished, and he went off to the kitchen to collect the third. Marnie began to feel decidedly tipsy.

'Tell me about this project you're working on,' he said as he returned. It was a surprise to her that he even remembered her mentioning it. She began diffidently but then warmed to her subject.

'It's something I've been trying to get off the ground for some time, but I have an endless fight with the authorities getting funding for it. About a year ago, I started visiting a school for children with special needs and gave them a kind of art class. These children find it difficult to concentrate, but strangely when I gave them one specific thing to draw, they tended to become absorbed in their task. Their carers all remarked how good it was for them, so I have been trying to develop the idea.' She paused, worried she might be boring him, but he was looking interested, so she continued. 'For instance, I thought in the summer I could bring some of them down to the boathouse, so they could start drawing outside objects; the river, birds and boats. Naturally, this would need organising with transport and carers to go with them, and that all costs.'

Rawlings, at last, made a comment. 'I think it sounds a great idea, Marnie. You should certainly persevere with it. Your project is just the sort of thing this bloody government should be paying for if it wasn't so taken up with Brexit.'

Encouraged by this, she continued, 'I've also worked with people suffering from dementia. Drawing and painting seems to have the same beneficial effect. I've been visiting a home not far from here. Some are more responsive than others, but they do seem to enjoy the sessions. I knew that music is beneficial to them, and now it seems art is as well.'

Rawlings watched her face as she was talking, so passionately and earnestly. She was transformed, and he was surprised by a new feeling for her that hit him. Was it a kind of protectiveness, or deep affection, or even love? He wasn't sure.

The third bottle had been opened and nearly consumed. The candles were guttering, and the warmth given out by the fire added to the mellow atmosphere.

'I think I'm feeling rather drunk,' Marnie said, and Rawlings smiled. 'Nonsense, you can't get drunk on good champagne.'

Feeling emboldened, she said nervously, 'Rawlings, you know that piece of music that Mia played to you in Sarajevo…' he looked startled but gave an abrupt nod, 'well,' she said, 'I've forgotten what it's called and I've never been able to track it down.'

'It's called *"Lieberslied"*, he said abruptly, 'Schumann wrote it for his wife as a wedding present.' His voice had turned strangely cold, but she persevered.

'Do you have a recording? Would you be able to play it for me?'

There was a long pause while he made up his mind. She waited, wondering if this request had now ruined their evening. At last, without a word, he limped over to the bookcase and picked out a CD. He then put it on the player and returned to his seat. The music started to play. She didn't dare look at him. It sounded so breathtakingly beautiful she could scarcely breathe, as she remembered the whole scene that he'd described in such detail; the events at the orphanage, the bombed hotel, the rackety old piano and then Mia, sitting down and playing this beautiful piece.

It came to an end, and neither of them spoke. After a moment she turned to him and could see his head was bowed and his whole body was shaking, racked with silent sobbing. Horrified by what she'd done, she took him in her arms and stroked his hair, repeating over and over again, 'I'm so sorry, it was stupid of me, I should never have asked you to play it. Please, Rawlings, don't cry. I know It's brought back memories of Mia. I'm so sorry, so sorry.'

He eventually gasped out, 'No, no, it's not just that. It's about everything, all the terrible losses; Mia, Felix, those children at the orphanage...' His sobbing continued, and she wiped away his tears and started to kiss his face where the tears had fallen. Suddenly he kissed her back.

Afterwards, she could never quite remember exactly how it had happened. Maybe it was because they had both drunk so much champagne, or that both of them for different reasons, had feelings which for too long had been suppressed. But happen it did.

As she climbed, now naked, onto the bed, she said shyly, 'It's a long time since I have done this...'

He quickly stripped and fell in beside her. 'Don't worry; it's like riding a bike, once learned, never forgotten.'

He was right, except it was so much more wonderful than anything she remembered. He was gentle at first, stroking her body until Marnie responded to his touch and let herself go with a fierce abandonment. Finally, the moment came when he shouted out, and her body arched. Their bodies held together for a second, and then they drew apart, both falling back exhausted.

The moon was visible through the window and threw a light across the bed. As Marnie glanced at Rawlings, she could see he was smiling. He turned, gave her a quick kiss on her forehead, rolled over onto his side and fell asleep. Marnie, overwhelmed, and cocooned in this new happiness, remained awake for as long as she could, until she too, finally drifted off.

Hours later, she woke with a start. It was just light. Rawlings was not snoring, but from his heavy breathing, she could tell he was still in a deep sleep. Careful not to disturb him, she quietly gathered up her clothes, tiptoed into the bathroom to dress and then left the boat. The cold air hit her as she opened the door. Surprisingly she felt no adverse effect from all the champagne, only wonderfully alive. The winter sunrise had thrown a beautiful light on the water, and the world appeared to her a very beautiful place that morning. She walked slowly towards her boathouse, basking in a glow of contentment. What a glorious way to start the new year. Could life get any better?

Chapter Twenty One

January 2018

For Marnie the following days passed by in a happy haze. They had, at last, crossed the Rubicon, and nothing could change her mood of optimism. She didn't hear from Rawlings but was content to wait for him to contact her. She worked on her project and resisted the urge to call him. Isobel rang to say she had a bad cold and would Marnie kindly take Juno for a walk. This she willingly did and noticed that Rawlings' car was missing. It was, therefore, logical to assume he had gone up to London to deal with details concerning his new flat and this would explain his silence.

On January 5th, the day before her birthday, she walked over to the boat with a note, inviting him to supper. Jake was working in the garden, and she called out, inquiring if he had seen Rawlings. He seemed surprised by this question and told her enigmatically he thought Mr Rawlings had left, as he'd carried a lot of boxes out to his car. This still did not worry her. She presumed he was moving things up to his flat. She knocked, but there was no reply. Retrieving the key from under the mat, Marnie let herself in.

The boat was like the Marie Celeste, quite empty,

except for the furniture. His laptop, all the books, papers, and the collection of CD's and DVD's were gone. Only then did a feeling of panic rise within her. She went into the bedroom. The drawers and cupboards were empty, the bed was stripped, and a pile of sheets and towels were neatly piled on the bed with a note for Maria to kindly wash them and then give them to OXFAM. There was an envelope on the top which said, 'Payment for laundry and cleaning'.

Now in mounting distress, she went through to the kitchen and bathroom. They were the same, clean and stripped bare, all evidence of Rawlings completely gone. Returning to the living room, she looked around and noticed two envelopes placed on the top corner of the desk, one marked 'For Marnie', the other, 'For Isobel'. She snatched them up, leaving the boat, re-locking the door behind her and placing the key under the mat. Jake was still working, so she gave him the envelope for Isobel, instructing him to take it over to Lady Mallinson. She then returned to the boathouse and sat down, shaking and tearful. After a while, with trembling hand, she tore open the envelope, already dreading its contents and started to read.

Marnie my love, when you get this, I will have gone — for good. I know my departure will come as a shock, especially after our New Year's Eve together, and for this, I am deeply sorry. You are the last person I would ever wish to hurt, but in a perverse way, that night was the reason for my leaving now. We had reached the zenith you and I; there was nowhere further for us to go. If I had stayed, I would swiftly have become a disappointment to you. It may sound like a paradox, but you have to trust me on this. I find it hard enough to live with myself, let alone live with anyone else. It was a difficult decision to leave, and perhaps the first unselfish action I have ever made. I am too fond of you to risk ruining your life.

One of the war poets, Edmund Blunden, wrote some lines that sum up my present state better than I could;

"Tired with dull grief, grown old before my day,

I sit in solitude and only hear

Long silent laughter, murmurings of dismay,

The lost intensities of hope and fear..."

That's about it. My depressions can only get worse, and I would be an impossible person to live with. Now is the time to make a clean break. Please try to understand.

I have gone to London first, to undergo this wretched operation and then will spend some time recovering. Once I am fit – although I don't know how permanent or successful the outcome will be – I have a few plans. There are new places I want to visit and some old ones I need to revisit. The priority, of course, is to see Felix, which I shall do in the spring.

I am leaving you the boat and have written to Isobel to tell her of this. I will send you all the legal details in a separate letter, along with the document that states change of ownership. It is small recompense for all the kindness and patience you have shown me over the past year. The mooring fees will continue to be paid directly from my bank to Isobel so that you won't have any added expense. If either you or Isobel decides the boat is no longer wanted on the mooring, then sell it and keep the proceeds. It will go some way towards making up for your previous boat disaster. I have every confidence you will make the Esme Jane your own, in a way I never could. I even envisage you holding your art classes on it. My one request is that you should let Felix use the boat when he comes over in the summer. I will explain all this to him on my visit.

In this envelope you will find a cheque, please look on it as a birthday present. I hope you might put some of it towards your project, which is such a great idea. You mustn't give up on it.

Be happy Marnie. I know we will both cherish the memories of the year we have spent together. You are a lovely, kind and beautiful person and one who will always have a special place in my heart.

Rawlings.

Marnie looked in the envelope and found the cheque. It was for £50,000. She gave a gasp, then read the letter through twice more before bursting into loud racking sobs. At the same time, Isobel was reading her letter from Rawlings.

My dear Isobel,

I have decided to leave, which won't really come as a surprise, as you, more than anyone, know what a restless soul I am. As soon as my leg has sufficiently recovered from the operation, I will set off on my Byronic travels, visiting Felix first.

*What **may** surprise you is that the main reason for my leaving so abruptly is the realisation that Marnie's attachment to me is now so strong we have reached a point of no return. I, therefore, have to make a clean break. It would have been easy to settle down with her, but I am not a person who could sustain a relationship in a way she would want, so for once I am trying to be unselfish. I do not underestimate how much my departure will affect her, especially as it is so sudden. Could you possibly keep an eye on her and help her over the next few weeks? I have no right to call on you yet again, but I know how very fond of Marnie you are. You will be* the best person to get her through this. I promise I didn't intend for this to happen, but unfortunately, it has, and I apologise for leaving you with the aftermath. It will be particularly hard for Marnie, as it's her birthday on the 6th, exactly a year since I arrived, and I know she will have prepared a celebration.

I have made over the ownership of the boat to her and hope she will be pleased with this decision and maybe use it for her new art project. The mooring fees will continue to be paid directly to you from my bank. If, for any reason, one of you decides you don't want the boat to remain on the mooring any longer, let me know, and then Marnie can sell it and keep the proceeds.

With regard to Felix staying next summer, I hope this can still go ahead. He is so very fond of you, Isobel, and I know he'll want to spend time here with you, and probably for many years to come. You are the best surrogate grandmother the boy could have, and he is lucky to have found you. I will go out to see him as soon as I am recovered from the operation and explain the new situation to him. The fact that I am not on the boat shouldn't make any difference. It is you, this place, and Juno that he loves. I am sure Marnie will let him spend as much time on the boat as he wants.

I am not sure I understand why, but you have been very good to me, Isobel. I will be eternally grateful for your many kindnesses, not least in taking in my grandson and making him feel so welcome. Under separate cover I am sending you my contacts, should you need them, including my new mobile number, along with the address of my new London flat which I have recently purchased, and the details of my solicitor. I would be most grateful if you would keep these confidential. I think it best if Marnie doesn't try and get in touch with me. That old cliché of being brutal to be kind comes to mind.

What a strange year it has been. I would not have survived it without you.

My love and gratitude, always,
Rawlings

Isobel put down the letter and gave a deep sigh. While reading it through she'd been assailed with a mixture of emotions; first shock, then annoyance, and finally regret. Yes, she would certainly miss him, but obviously not as desperately as Marnie. How deep had their relationship really gone? Should she have stopped it sooner? Maybe she should carry some of the blame, after all, it had been her decision to let Rawlings stay in the first place. Now she had to try and pick up the pieces, and she thought sadly it might have all been so different had Peter been around.

Chapter Twenty Two

January 6th 2018

Marnie sat on her terrace, hunched and miserable, wrapped in an old quilt. It was early, and the watery sun was only just making an appearance. The night had been very cold, with a sharp frost. Truly it was ridiculous for her to be sitting outside, but she hadn't slept at all, and it seemed pointless to stay in bed, and anyway, she wanted to recall the events of his arrival one year ago, precisely as it had happened.

What a year it had been. Since that last birthday, she had been taken to the heights of happiness and now, to the depths of despair. She'd only read his letter yesterday, but with every minute since her devastation had increased. She missed Rawlings with every fibre of her being. It was a physical ache. Images of him filled her mind until she felt she was going mad. She glanced across to the boat he'd left her. There had been the cheque as well, both incredibly generous presents, but even that made her angry. Had he given them to her out of guilt?

She stood up and stamped her feet which gradually going numb. 'Bloody hell Rawlings, 'she murmured out loud and then flung herself back into the chair. It wasn't as if she had imagined their night together.

It had been special, amazing, wonderful. She wanted more and couldn't believe he didn't too. His explanation made no sense. 'They'd reached the zenith'… What did that bloody mean and anyway, how did he know? He hadn't given them a chance. She didn't care about his mood swings, drinking, nightmares and grumpiness. It wouldn't have worried her. For God's sake, she'd put up with them over the last year. No, the real reason had to be Mia. The nagging suspicion remained. Nothing and nobody could have replaced her, so damn him and damn Mia.

The swans made their morning procession down the river, but today she took no joy in their progress. How the hell was she going to get through this? She had tried ringing him, but he'd already changed his mobile, obviously not wanting her to find him. This started her crying again. Marnie, she told herself firmly, this won't do, you have to pull yourself together. A positive move is called for.

Getting to her feet, she gave up her morning vigil and shuffled indoors. Isobel had asked her over for a birthday drink and would be alarmed to see her in this hopeless state. A day of pampering was called for, a long bubble bath and scented candles. Maybe an old film? As long as it wasn't "Casablanca", and she allowed herself a smile. At least she would make a determined effort to arrive at Isobel's in a brave and cheerful mood.

In spite of these good intentions, Marnie's appearance gave Isobel serious alarm. She looked very pale, and her eyes were red rimmed from long bouts of crying. It didn't seem right to wish her a happy birthday when she'd obviously spent an utterly miserable day. Instead, Isobel poured out the wine, and they both sat down in silence, neither knowing where to begin.

After a while Marnie suddenly burst out, 'Do you think he'll ever come back?'

Isobel replied firmly, 'No Marnie. I really don't think he will. I am terribly sorry. I know how upset you are. In some ways, I blame myself for ever letting him have the mooring.'

'It wasn't your fault,' Marnie shook her head vehemently. 'You couldn't have known I'd fall in love with the stupid man. You really can't blame yourself for that.'

Isobel didn't like to say that she'd thought it highly likely from the moment Rawlings had arrived and indeed had tried to warn him against any involvement. To give the man his due, she presumed their relationship hadn't escalated until after Felix left, a combination of his needs and hers. It had been the perfect storm and the result? The human wreck that now sat in front of her. She gave a deep sigh.

'I suppose I could at least have warned you that Rawlings was not the settling kind. He'd never managed to sustain a long relationship.'

'He did with Mia,' Marnie retorted. 'How could I possibly compete with that paragon of perfection?'

She sounded bitter and angry. Isobel saw a difficult evening ahead of her, but said patiently, 'Well, yes, they did have a long and passionate love affair, but it wasn't of the settling variety. They were both strong, independent characters, who I am pretty certain, would have wanted their separate lives in the long run. But of course, that is something we will never know.' She paused, then added, 'I think Rawlings really did love you Marnie, but because of the character he is, he realised he could never make a relationship work.'

Marnie replied with a flash of anger, 'He didn't even give it a try.' She looked at Isobel, 'Has he told you where he is going?'

Not really,' she replied carefully, 'I think after his operation and recovery, he plans to go and see Felix.'

'I think he will go back to Sarajevo,' Marnie said suddenly, 'back to the orphanage and the people he knew. He may even invest his money in some cause or charity out there.'

'I really had no idea that Rawlings was quite so well off,' Isobel murmured and then added, 'I gather he has bought a flat in London. And he has given you the boat. That was generous of him.'

Marnie nodded. 'He also gave me a cheque for £50,000 towards my art project.' And she added, 'I think his wife's family left him large amounts of money and never bothered to touch it. He wasn't interested in money, or acquisitions. He was always making generous gestures. Nobody could fault him for that.' She paused. 'Are you happy for me to keep the *Esme Jane* on the mooring?'

'Of course.' Isobel was quick to reassure her, 'Rawlings is continuing to pay the mooring fees, so you can keep it there as long as you want. In fact, I'd like you to. Felix would miss it dreadfully in the summer if it weren't there.'

Marnie looked at her curiously, 'Do you think Felix will still come here if Rawlings isn't around?'

'Yes, I am certain of it.' Isobel spoke firmly. 'I hope he will regard this house as his home in England. Rawlings knows that I look on Felix as the grandson Peter and I never had.' She paused. 'In all likelihood, I will leave this house to him when I die. I have no other relations, apart from Selena, who would never be happy here and who, in any case, is well provided for. Felix talks to me endlessly about the house when he calls, and about Juno, of course. We have long conversations on Skype.'

Marnie was greatly surprised by these revelations. 'It sounds a bit like *"Howards End"*. Wasn't someone in that book unexpectedly given a house?'

Isobel laughed. 'I suppose it does sound a bit like that.' She was silent for a moment and then said gently, 'It will get better Marnie, I promise. When Peter died, I thought I would stay miserable and lost forever, but I haven't. It's boring to say it, but time really does help, and then'… she paused again, 'well things do happen, unexpectedly, that make you want to start living again. It has for me with Felix, and I know that it will for you.'

As she kissed her goodbye, Isobel said, 'Rawlings was right about one thing. It has been a strange year. When you look back Marnie, you will remember many wonderful things that happened during it, and gradually forget the grief you are now feeling. You will move on, I promise.'

Marnie nodded and started her walk back to the boathouse. It was a clear night sky, and the stars were out. In the far distance, an owl hooted, and the moon came up over the river. The sheer beauty of it gave her a feeling of calmness. She took a deep breath.

Right, Marnie, she said firmly to herself, there will be no more looking back. This is it. This is **my** turning point. To hell with Rawlings. My new life begins here.

A sequel to this book is due out in 2020.

Pre-order your copy direct from the publisher at
jjmoffs.co.uk/shop

Acknowledgements

There are various people who have helped me in the process of writing this book. Especial thanks are due to Dr Stephen Carver, who once again has given me detailed and excellent advice. I am also grateful for the great support of Rony Cambell of Breakaway Reviews, and to Bridget Armstrong for being the first to read the manuscript. I am particularly grateful to Gyles Brandreth for his continued support and his quote for the cover of this book.

While researching the life and work of the war correspondent, I found the writings of Janine di Giovanni, John Simpson and Frank Gardner, invaluable. There were many others too, rather too many to name, but thank you Marie Colvin for the inspiration you provided.

Thank you to my grand-daughter, Issy Robertson, who designed the back cover illustration and was so patient with my endless quibbles.

Great thanks go to my publisher Jane Moffett and her entire team at JJMoffs. They made the whole process of publishing an easy and delightful experience.

Finally, huge gratitude goes to my family and many friends for their interest, patience and continued encouragement.

Other novels from Jane McCulloch

Parallel Lines: Volume 1 (Three Lives Trilogy)

In the 1970s, beautiful but unhappy Celia Roxby Smith reaches a crisis in her life and seeks help from a famous psychiatrist. During her intense sessions, she reveals a painful past that includes a bleak childhood in the post war fifties, neglect from her parents at home in Oxford, and constant bullying received while at boarding school.

Now Celia is in her thirties and finds herself in a tragic and loveless marriage that resembles the same one her parents had. She sees frightening parallels between the past and present events of her life and is desperate to break away from her abusive and controlling husband. With the help of her psychiatrist and her new lover, she takes the first steps toward freedom and independence. But a shocking turn of events changes everything and leaves more questions than answers.

As intense as it is real, Parallel Lines is the first book in the Three Lives Trilogy. Author Jane McCulloch permeates this absorbing story with deeply relatable characters and situations that will appeal to fans of Daphne du Maurier, Elizabeth Jane Howard, and Nicholas Sparks, along with anyone struggling to find their way in life.

Triangles in Squares: Volume 2 (Three Lives Trilogy)

This is the second book in the Three Lives Trilogy and it is Euan's story. "To an outsider Garrick Square probably looked like any other London square, but it wasn't..." It is March 1989 and Lady Fay Stanhope, the undisputed monarch of Garrick Square, continues to organise it into an elite community of creative professionals and eccentrics. Euan, now a successful writer, is one of these. Natasha, Celia's daughter, turns up in his life and proceeds to turn it upside down. She is no longer the gawky teenager of 'Parallel Lines' but now an attractive and independent young woman. She moves into Euan's basement and she is not the only newcomer to the Square. Lady Fay has organised the Reverend Gerald Masterson to move into Number 39. He is the darling of religious broadcasting at the BBC but may not be as angelic as he seems. Thus begins a summer of passion, intrigue and betrayal, with allegiances forming and falling away against the backdrop of the Square's social calendar, until Natasha must make a choice that will change her life forever and which will lead us into the final book, 'Full Circle'.

Full Circle: Volume 3 (Three Lives Trilogy)
Life was back on an even keel; summer was on the way and Natasha decided nothing was ever going to depress her again. It was then that she opened the letter... It is 1994, seven years after Natasha's marriage to Gerry Masterson. Euan Mackay in self-imposed exile in LA receives a telephone call from England with the news that Natasha has now left Gerry and for a year has been living a reclusive life in a large house in Norfolk. Euan immediately returns to England and after learning as much as he can about the break-up of the marriage, he travels up to Norfolk to see her. Gradually Euan learns the full horror of Natasha's marriage. She is

bruised and broken. To add to his problems, Natasha now has Laura, her five year old daughter and Euan realises that her priorities are different now. Then Natasha receives news that shatters everything and changes both their lives forever. The dramatic and tragic events that follow finally lead to the story of the three lives in the Trilogy coming 'full circle'.

The Brini Boy

Trando is only thirteen years old, but he knows he is the one person who can save his best friend from the electric chair… It is 1919 in Plymouth, Massachusetts. Trando Brini, a promising violinist and the child of Italian immigrants, lives quietly with his parents and their lodger Bart Vanzetti. This is not a good time for Italian-Americans. Assassinations and bombings committed by a handful of Italian Anarchists on US soil has resulted in a tense climate of suspicion and paranoia. When known Anarchists Bart and Nick Sacco are arrested for their alleged roles in a fatal holdup, Trando knows for certain his friend is innocent. Thus begins seven years of trials and appeals, during which Trando, his community, and a growing number of political activists and intellectuals challenge a biased American Justice System. It is a struggle between David and Goliath, in which the 'Brini Boy' must risk everything – his musical career, his first love and the life of his dearest friend. In this true story of courage, bravery and determination, we can more fully understand the America of the present by revisiting its turbulent past.

Printed in Great Britain
by Amazon

36046704R00182